THE
DIARY
OF
LIES

ALSO BY THE AUTHOR

The Goldenacre
The Hollow Tree

THE DIARY OF LIES

PHILIP MILLER

SOHO
CRIME

Published by
Soho Press, Inc.
227 W 17th Street
New York, NY 10011

Library of Congress Cataloging-in-Publication Data

Names: Miller, Philip, 1973- author.
Title: The diary of lies / Philip Miller.
Description: New York, NY : Soho Crime, 2025. | Series: The Shona
Sandison Investigations ; 3
Identifiers: LCCN 2024059046

ISBN 978-1-64129-699-1
eISBN 978-1-64129-700-4

Subjects: LCSH: Journalists—Fiction. | Murder—Investigation—Fiction.
LCGFT: Detective and mystery fiction. | Novels.
Classification: LCC PR6113.I567 D53 2025 | DDC 823/.92—dc23/
eng/20230703
LC record available at https://lccn.loc.gov/2024059046

Interior design by Janine Agro

Printed in the United States of America

10 9 8 7 6 5 4 3 2 1

EU Responsible Person (for authorities only)
eucomply OÜ
Pärnu mnt 139b-14
11317 Tallinn, Estonia
hello@eucompliancepartner.com
www.eucompliancepartner.com

In memory of my father

Deep in their hearts, they remembered hell.
Beowulf

.

THE
DIARY
OF
LIES

It was a week before the killings at Stag Hall, and the world had been erased.

Edges had disappeared, and the true shape of things had been lost under a fall of heavy winter snow. Now, all was light and shadow. The fields were blank pages, and stark trees held the weight of a cold blossom. The pale hills had dissolved into the sky, which fell to the horizon like a soaked sheet. The landscape was a ghost of itself.

Fisher knew much about this transitory, irredeemable world. But on this morning, in the east of Scotland, at least, its bloody face had been wiped clean, and all was white, unsullied and silent. The snow had fallen and taken sound with it. Even the sea, down there, barely trembling in the harbour, seemed to be asleep. Fisher—just awake, tousle-haired—looked through the caravan window, saw the snow and remembered how as a child he had built a rough igloo in the grounds of the children's home and crawled inside, revelling in the strange glow of the snow light. Light that was not light. The memory appeared like breath in frosty air, then faded.

He turned from the window. Encased in its frozen new clothing, the caravan clung to the hillside above St. James. Nothing moved in the little fishing village in the East Neuk of Fife.

For the first time since his deployment, Fisher had managed to sleep. A deep, dreamless sleep. A green man under a sea of white. Now he was awake, and he made breakfast. The gas flame shuddered into a crown of blue life. Later, spooning porridge and honey into his mouth, he gazed down to the sea.

He could see the harbour, the high wall, the bristles of unused lobster creels poking through the drifts. The empty quayside was ringed with snow-capped orange buoys. The boats were out. Lights glimmered in the snaking rows of cottages, in the café, in the village pub, in the single store which stood at the foot of the steep, slippery, cobbled descent to the harbour. Ledges and roofs, submerged. The paths between, disappeared. The main road, gone.

Fisher looked closer. A solitary old man stood on the sea-wall, like a nail on a fence. A gull dove past him.

Somewhere out on that misty horizon was the north coast of East Lothian, the grey lump of the Bass Rock and, further along the coast, the capital city, Edinburgh. The city would be deep in snow too, Fisher thought. The roads impassable, the spires and towers and hills an absurd dream.

He knew he needed to scout again. To find the secret way to the hall. He could not approach it from the road or through its high gates. But a stream ran in a steep culvert through St. James, ending in an estuary west of the harbour. The path upstream led to a gradually deepening valley, which yard by hard yard delved deep into the kingdom's hills. That was where he needed to go.

Fisher left the caravan. He locked it behind him and tucked a service-issued knife into his back pocket. His boots sank with a clean, squeaking crunch into the fresh snow as he left the campsite.

Through the sleeping village, his breath in clouds about him, Fisher crept. The gabled roofs were uneven, mismatched, the guttering toothed with icicles. The air was sharp with frost and the salt of the sea.

He pulled up the deep hood of his waterproof. As he

walked on, he measured distance and time and the details of the village—its layout, its backroads, its lanes and dead ends. He heard children's voices, raised like bells against the hush of the muffled land. Somewhere in the village, an old, cruel man slept, oblivious. That was all to come. He moved on.

Rain began to fall in light sheets. The huge sky shifted, and the sun suddenly broke through. His boots were clogged with chunks of snow by the time he reached the river path. It was higher land here, and he looked back at St. James and the caravan site at its edge, perched on the low cliffs. He could see three tubby fishing boats returning to harbour and, further out, an oil platform like a fossil spider, spiked and black in the deeper waters.

He walked now on older paths. The Kingdom of Fife was ancient. The stream here had spent immemorial time cutting through rock to find its course. It ran down hard and clear, whitening with grinning teeth over boulders and pooling wide and deep where the valley evened. The snow was sparser in the woods—caught in gnarled branches, melted by the river, hanging in surreal globs from fern stands.

Fisher tramped on. He reached the falls. The trees here were tall, leaning inwards, draping their snow-lined branches over the rumble of the water as it fell five metres down over a rock face into a deep pool. The stone was weathered and smooth, shaped like an amphitheatre, its seats empty. He wondered if it had been mined or quarried in years past—it seemed too theatrical for it to be natural.

Crouching, he swung a bag from his shoulder and took out a flask and a bar of chocolate. He stopped for a while. Snow was hard going. He knew that well from the Brecon Beacons. From the Carpathians.

He found a slippery path up the side of the tumbling falls. With cold hands he grabbed and pulled himself up along a curl of iron root, then walked on, up the densely wooded valley, beneath the close-set conspiracy of trunks.

Up along the ridge, he could suddenly see the horizon he sought: a line of fencing that skimmed the border of the valley. He cut upwards to the fencing, which looked freshly cut, recently wired. He edged along its length. He could hear the river murmuring below.

He walked another mile until there, off to one side, deep in a bare fold of land, he saw the sharp burst of electric lights. This was the place. He knew it was not on any map; it was a new build on an old plot. A road to it had been laid, boundaries built, gates erected. He crouched in the trees.

Built in dark stone and slate, the building was elegant, modern, with high walls, arched windows and a vast lawn. There was a four-storey central chamber with a pitched roof. Several outbuildings stretched along a paved drive, flanked by lines of saplings.

He moved closer and brought out his binoculars, which he rested on a fence post. In the outbuildings, there was machinery. A garage housed several large black cars. Smoke drifted up from the chimney of a kitchen block. Through the glasses twitching in his hand, he saw, strewn around the courtyard, shrink-wrapped containers and piles of boxed supplies under weighted blue tarpaulins. The house itself was dark, apart from one window glittering with artificial light. A figure moved behind it.

This was Stag Hall. Here the dragon gathered its strength and flexed its cold metal scales. Here, the old warrior would come for his final battle.

PART I
THE GREEN MAN

1

Go to the CIVIC GALLERY LONDON. Ask for HONEYSUCKLE. There is a message from MORIAH.

Shona Sandison, freelance journalist, just wanted to win. She knew none of it really mattered; not now, not in a year's time, not in geological time. But she still wanted her name to be called.

The UK Media Awards ceremony was building to a noisy climax. All evening, praise had been given, awards handed out and free alcohol dispensed. Spotlights swooped around the ballroom of the New Headland Hotel, a refurbished town house which sat with recycled elegance in the thrumming heart of London. Most of the gathered herd of journalists, editors, sponsors and spongers were drunk or high, or hurtling towards a state beyond. There was a constant buzz of gossip and congratulation, of rumour and self-praise, of irony and flattery. The crowd was not only in the ballroom. It spilled out into the foyer bar, where editors held court amidst sozzled retainers and snickering juniors—young journalists leaning into the huddle, older hands looking for a way out.

Shona, far from her Edinburgh home, was neither drunk nor high. As she waited for her category to be announced, she sat in silence, ignoring her untouched "deluxe" chicken supreme, a slab of foul rubber under a paltry slime, and watched the loose-tied blaring men at the bar and the red-faced sportswriters stumbling to the toilets, again, to snort chalk-cut cocaine. She asked herself: After tonight, what next? She wondered what her next significant story might be. It could be contained in this message from Moriah. He or they had led her here, after all. But who or what was Honeysuckle?

The hubbub was grating. But at least she was among people she knew: the dead-eyed news editors, exhausted reporters, frazzled correspondents, clueless executives looking for sex, sponsors hoping for access and PR flacks angling for relevance. It was a rippling cacophonous sea of rented dinner jackets and iridescent gowns.

Shona was dressed in black, in a borrowed trouser suit that would have been perfect for a funeral. She did not have a posh frock and she did not want one. She had ironed her one white cotton shirt; her father would have been proud. And, of course, her walking stick was jet black. It was in keeping.

She closed the message on her phone. She had received it a week ago in the encrypted email account she used for tip-offs. And her question would be answered soon enough.

She looked around the room and gripped the handle of her stick. The flashing lights, the shouting, the sheer racket of it all—she wanted to leave. She wanted to run away, out into the dark, unreal streets of London, and head for home. But the huge blue screen above the stage read: UK MEDIA AWARDS SCOOP OF THE YEAR. It was the next, and last, category. Hers. After all, she reminded herself, scanning the room, she was the best—screw all these fraudsters and half-wits, all these chancers.

Then something caught her eye. A man in a smart tuxedo was waving at her from a table twenty feet away. He was saying something. She acknowledged him with a nod.

"Pal, I can't hear a word you're saying," she said, her voice dissolving into the wall of sound. She did not bother to shout. No one would hear her. But the shouting man was insistent. He pointed a finger, as if to say: *I need to speak to you.*

At Shona's table, Ranald Zawadzki, the editor of the free-lance investigations team to which she belonged, the Buried Lede, was holding court. A woman in a bespangled green dress was drooping at his shoulder, and several young men in various stages of drunkenness were hanging on his every word. Ranald—frenetic from his own surreptitious snorts of coke—was in his element. A drunken lord amongst his rapt retainers.

The shouting man had left his seat and was now pushing past people towards the empty seat beside Shona. A small attending cloud of antiperspirant came with him. He sat down, legs wide apart, and held out a slightly shaking hand. His shirt bulged. She could see hair and a soft belly.

"Good evening, Shona Sandison. I was just trying to tell you," he bellowed in a rich Home Counties accent, "that you must be favourite for the title. Scooper of the year. How lovely to meet you. Big fan of your work."

His face was deep pink and featureless, eyes the colour of belly button fluff. His hair was black, slicked back to his scalp. "Proctor, Reece Proctor," he said, smiling to display cosmetically perfected teeth, white like the keys of an electric keyboard.

"Hi," she said, shaking his wet hand briefly. She looked to the stage. The shortlist had been flashed up. There she was: *Shona Sandison—Brexit Act Revealed—BBC/Sunday Courier/Buried Lede*. The other candidates came from established print titles. One had a story on human trafficking in East Anglia; another, money laundering in London's property market. There was an investigation into the infiltration of local government by organised crime in the North of England and one on the pollution of England's rivers and beaches by privatised water companies. Frontline tales, she thought, from the disintegration of a failed state.

Beside her name was an old portrait, from around 2012, of Shona grimly smiling beneath savagely asymmetric hair. *The state of me*, she thought.

Proctor yelled again: "Tough shortlist, but I think you might have pipped the others. Yours was an interesting story. Very interesting."

Shona reached for her Jack Daniel's and took a hearty swig. The ice had melted; the liquor was diluted and warm. "Yep, so good they even printed it," she said.

"How did you get down to London from Scotland?" he said.

She noticed again that his accent was full English: pink, comfortable, fatty. Yet there was something in its plummy tone that was not quite right. Almost as if he was putting it on or at least mildly upgrading it. The way he pronounced "down" had a vein of the North running through it.

"I found a train going south and jumped on," she said quietly.

She found his advances confusing and uncomfortable. It was more than enough for her to be here, in this frantic and noisy place, with an appointment the next day with a contact she did not know.

She did not want to speak to this new man, with his assuredness and his direct intention, when she was feeling both more fragile than she had felt for a while, and more determined to carry on with the only life she knew, as a journalist. He wanted to give her something, but he also wanted something from her. That was usually the way. She was not sure she had the energy to undergo the transaction.

Also, she reminded herself, she had never found or been tipped good stories at these shindigs. There was usually a PR trying to press some lame exclusive on her, or a marketing account manager trying to mention his or her product. It was rarely interesting. Stories did not present themselves at media parties. They lay elsewhere, out in the darkness, out in the world of secrets.

But he was determined.

"Such a fascinating story you had there," he said, attempting to focus his eyes on hers. Shona looked away. "Brexit. Britain's future. The hunt afoot. The plans being planned—"

"The government's lawyers certainly thought so," she said, now irritated by his voice and his presence. "Who do you report for, Steve?"

He laughed, a silver tooth glittering in the back of his mouth. "It's Reece."

"Sorry," she said. "I can't hear a thing."

"Yes, it's terribly loud—shall we go outside?" he said, his eyebrows rising.

Shona flinched. She did not want to go outside.

He could tell. He held up a hand. "Absolutely no worries. So, no, I'm not a journalist, Shona. I was never clever enough. You won't ever find me in the public eye." He flipped back a rogue hair with one finger. "I'm with a . . . policy think tank."

"Oh?"

"Yes. We've been making some major inroads into government thinking, actually."

"Oh, aye. Which outfit, then?"

"Dovetail. Look, you've probably never heard of us—my people. Or me. The right people know who we are, though. And it is lovely to be here with such talented people, such *well-informed* people," he said, voice suddenly husky, looking at his fingers. Then, as if to change the subject, he looked over to a group of tables in a far corner of the hall. The News United Group—its portfolio led by the *Daily Despatch*, the UK's best-selling mid-market tabloid whose gothic font had remained unchanged since its hard-marching days in the 1930s—had bought up three tables. "Lord Baker's minions having quite the bash, I see," he said.

"Well, they've won all the gongs, haven't they?" Shona said, peering over at the tables. A champagne cork popped. Spume followed, briefly, and then fell. "As per usual," she added. "And it helps when you just parrot the party line and demonise those who don't."

"Too true." He grinned and leaned into her. "Didn't the government go for an injunction to try to stop your Brexit story?"

Shona shrugged in the direction of Ranald, who was still telling a tall tale to his audience. The woman in the green dress had her long fingers on his shoulder, her painted fingernails pressing into his black jacket. Shona knew Ranald's partner, Magdalena, was at home in Shetland, juggling three mad dogs, with a baby on the way.

"I think you'll have to speak to the bold Ranald there," Shona said, nodding in his direction. "I just get the stories and write them—he handles all that tedious shite. I would interrupt him, if I were you."

Proctor leaned closer, his cologne a toxic cape. "And you also did such an exemplary job on the story about Gary Watson MP," he said. "Such a tragic case. Terribly sad. We had a few meetings with him, you know."

Shona tried, and failed, not to wince. She looked Proctor in the eye. "Watson was a total cunt, actually," she said. "He tried to strangle me in his last interview. But, yes, another interesting story. 'Fascist thug drowns': it had a happy ending."

He shrugged. "Fair's fair, you won Reporter of the Year for it." His smile broadened. "You're a winner! And the world loves winners."

"Aye, but what does the world know? The world is screwed," she said and sipped her bourbon.

"No doubt. But you must have had a very good source for that Brexit story," Proctor carried on, regardless. "A very good source."

She shrugged. She knew she did. Or, at least, her source knew things only they could know. The story stood up; that was what mattered. Moriah had been right.

Behind Proctor, she could see the judges filing onto the stage and the host, a TV news reader, readying to return to the podium. She fished her mobile from her pocket. It was getting late. After the awards ceremony, she would have to trek halfway across London to her room for the night. Her eyes felt gritty.

"We need to speak in a quieter location, Shona," Proctor said. "Somewhere we can have a candid conversation. It might help you."

"Oh, aye?" She was looking past him to the stage. The ballroom's lights lowered. The music quietened with a swift diminuendo, and after a squeal of feedback, a voice cooed over the sound system, requesting that the audience return to their seats. Some people cheered and clapped. Men tucked in their shirts. Women smoothed their dresses as they sat down. Spotlights flashed on painted lips and damp foreheads, the rows of flushed faces staring at the stage.

"I have something for you," Proctor said to Shona. He reached into the folds of his suit and produced a business card, which he placed on the table between them. Shona peered at it; there was just a mobile number in a basic font. It was stiff card, smooth and edged with silver. "Are you in London for long?" His voice lowered with the sound in the room. There was a murmur now, a whispering shoal of anticipation.

Shona had been to many of these award ceremonies

before. Everyone pretended they didn't care whether they won or not. Silly nonsense, some would say. Buggins's turn, others said. But everyone shortlisted, she knew, wanted to win. Hacks were competitive. Exclusives drove them. She knew this because she felt the same. Especially now.

"How long are you down?" Proctor tried again.

"Just tomorrow," she said. She noticed he was chewing his lower lip. His thumb was rolling a ring around one finger over and over. "I'm busy in the morning but free in the afternoon. What do you want to talk about?" she said, reluctantly acknowledging his persistence.

"Great," he said, smiling, not answering. "Where are you staying?"

"A hotel in Victoria," she lied. She was staying in a friend's spare room in Notting Hill.

"Fabulous," he said. "As I say, I might have something for you. A follow-up. Is that what you call them? I can help you. You can help me. Yes, I suppose I have a commodity for you: a story."

"Why would you give me a story?" she asked.

"We have interests. Others have interests that clash with ours. I want to fill you in."

Shona was interested, but distracted. The host was now at the podium, smiling out over the room of expectant journalists. The audience had hushed.

"Look," Proctor said, suddenly earnest. He took a pen from his inside pocket and scribbled an address on his card. "Go here. After this. It's ten minutes away. Ask for bondage." His voice had changed to something harder, sharper.

Shona laughed. "What the actual? Bondage?"

His expression was serious.

"You taking the piss?" she said. "Like I'm going to stoat about asking for bondage in some rank hole in London!"

"You should," he said, his eyes flat as hammered nails.

"Look, pal, I'll maybe catch you later, over by the bar," she whispered, shaking her head. "Not sure when I'll be done here."

"It's worth it."

She glanced at the address—a number and street in Soho.

"Go here," Proctor said, tapping the card on the table. "*Bondage*—okay?"

Ranald suddenly swivelled around in his seat, his kilt dragging the hem of the tablecloth. "Good luck," he mouthed to Shona, his eyes glowing. He gave her a thumbs-up and grinned. The rest of the table, an assortment of freelancers, settled in their seats. Shona wondered if their clothes looked cheaper than those at the other tables or if it was her imagination. Their eyes seemed sharper, or maybe just hungrier.

The host, sleek in a shift of oyster-shell silver, announced the final category of Scoop of the Year. The shortlist whirred up again on the screen.

"It's my pleasure to welcome to the stage the CEO of Denholm Leisure Estates, recently crowned businesswoman of the year for the second time and twenty-third on *The Sunday Times* Rich List—Olivia Farquharson!"

Shona found herself laughing. "Well, bloody hell," she said to herself, as Olivia strode across the stage, clad in crimson, her towering hair a swirl of creamy waves.

Ranald raised a hairy eyebrow. Shona mouthed *later* at him, and he turned back to the stage, the fuchsia lights pulsing on his skin.

"One of our company directors," Proctor said, beaming. "Speak soon." He moved away, crouching a little, and vanished into the crowd.

Shona's mind was elsewhere. She knew, and remembered well, Olivia Farquharson—steely, brilliant, a laser-cut gem.

She looked the same as when Shona had last seen her at a society party at her family's castle in the Borders several years ago. Shona had been chasing a story about art fraud. She could never stand it up, but she'd found another story instead. An art expert had disappeared, and, not long after, Olivia's twin brother was found hanged in a Northumbrian wood, his body torn apart. Now, Olivia, blood bleached from her hands, stood on stage as a star, dispensing gongs to journalists, welcoming them further into her world.

"You are *too* kind," she purred at the row of male judges, who were all looking at her agape as if caught in a stunned dream of sudden and exquisitely painful erotic love. She read out a brief description of each shortlisted story and the stories' headlines, the journalists and the publications.

Shona found herself staring at Olivia, watching her animated, glowing face. She knew that Olivia was deeply corrupt in some way she could not fathom or make sense of, but there was no visible sign on her. Not a hint of malignancy. Here she was, standing before a ballroom of journalists, inviolate. Immaculate. Impermeable. Inhuman.

These were the people running the country, Shona considered, looking at the rapt faces of the judges, of the cow-stunned hacks in the audience. *These are the people we should be writing about. Not accepting awards from.* Shona flushed with a stab of sudden rage, which faded back into her marrow. She reached for her glass and downed the dregs in one sweet gulp.

"Without further ado . . ." Olivia Farquharson crooned into the microphone.

Shona slumped. Her head rested in her hand. She did not want to be in this room, with these people, another moment. She wanted to get up and walk out, take the lift down to the lobby, walk through the glass and steel of the vast hotel foyer, hail a taxi and disappear into the streets. She wanted to see her father.

"The winner of Scoop of the Year is . . ."

Shona's eyes were closed. She envisioned a scene of emptiness, of solitude. A place to be. She wanted to stand on a beach in the East of Scotland, be blasted by salt and wind and watch the mercury waves pound the empty miles of beach beneath crying white birds.

"Well, well . . . the winner is . . . Shona Sandison of the Buried Lede for her Brexit Act exclusive."

Hammering applause. A swirl of lights and a blast of music. Ranald shot to his feet, kilt swinging, and wrapped an arm around her shoulder. "Brilliant," he was shouting in her ear, his Shetland accent as thick as sand. "Ya beauty!"

"Well done, Shona," someone else was shouting above the applause.

Shona found herself standing up, gripping her stick, facing the wall of din and glare. Ranald held her elbow for a few moments and then fell back.

"Shona Sandison's dogged and meticulously sourced investigative reporting revealed the extreme steps being taken behind the scenes at the heart of UK government as it prepared a radical set of reforms that cut to the core of the British way of life . . ." a voice intoned.

Shona was moving forwards, drawn towards the light and the noise. She felt as if she was under water, drifting between tables and upturned faces to the steps to the stage. Her stick was clamped tight in her hand, its rubber pad banging against table chairs and feet. A man in a short-sleeved shirt, with a microphone set on his head, smiled and guided her up the steps—and suddenly she was on stage, above everyone in the room and keenly aware of her exposure, her tender body, before the gauzy mass below.

"Sandison's devastating story led the national news, was followed up by every media outlet and led to Parliamentary chaos as further details of the controversial bill, denied at the highest levels, were revealed to be on the mark. Representing the very best in public interest journalism and the old-fashioned values of . . ."

A warm hand grasped Shona's. "Congratulations," Olivia said in a low, smooth voice, with not a flicker of recognition, before stepping aside so a red-faced man could press the heavy plastic award into Shona's hand.

Shona leaned her stick on the podium. Her hands gripped its sides. The audience stopped clapping; the spotlights shifted. She raised her chin and looked out over the hazy sea of faces before her and found herself speaking. It was as if she knew she had a role to perform—the humble, grateful hack—and she was suddenly, as if in a dream, performing it. She thanked the judges (there was applause), she thanked Ranald and her colleagues at the Buried Lede (applause and some loud whoops), she said the story demonstrated the importance of independent and investigative reporting (more applause) and then, eyes closed, she said how important it was that independent investigative teams such as the Buried Lede had taken over from those on newspapers, which had been wiped out by decades of short-sighted cost-cutting (some scattered clapping). She said it was high time a female reporter stood onstage on this night, accepting an award (more whooping).

Then she took a breath. Small and alone beneath the hot lights, she realised she was shaking. She put the prize wonkily down on the podium and reached unthinkingly for her stick. She peered at the shimmering trophy, and her name printed in bold, white, etched letters.

"Finally, I would like to dedicate this award . . ." she said hoarsely. She took a deep breath. Her eyes tingled. "I would like to accept this in honour of my father, Hugh Sandison. He was a dedicated journalist like me—like us—or at least some of us," she said, to murmurs from the black sea of bodies. A smattering of laughter, like pebbles dropped into water.

"He is no longer here," she said, staring out into the darkness. It was easier to speak now. The maw of the universe opened up before her. The hall fell silent. She blinked hard. "Like thousands of others, thousands of vulnerable old sick people, my dad died from COVID. He died when there was no need for him to die." She was determined not to cry, for her voice not to break. She raised her voice. She leaned into its hard edges. They could bear the weight.

"He didn't really hold with awards for journalism," she said. "He thought a good story was the best reward. I didn't always agree with him, and I don't now. It feels really fucking good to win this. Mind, I also promised him that I would cut back on my fucking swearing." Someone whooped. There was light applause.

For an instant, there came a sliver of memory. A vast beach. She was sitting between her father's feet, digging a hole rapidly filling with seawater, the sun hot on her bare arms, her child's stomach, her skinny legs. And in the heat, he was singing her a song. The light glimmered on slick rocks, on the nestling boats in the harbour, on the waves rolling in from the Firth of Forth. They were at the place he loved the most, Elie Beach, his hand in her hair. He was murmuring to his daughter, whispering that he loved her, that she was loved. The seabirds wheeled, crying like the lost, crying like those that remain, wheeling higher and higher into the impossible blue sky.

This all flashed, real and deep, and then it was gone.

She was back in the hall, in the darkness, holding an award, heavy like a weapon in her hand.

"This is for you, Hugh Sandison," she said. "I miss you."

She somehow moved from the podium, from the lights, as music played and the audience clapped. She moved down the steps, ignoring the judges, ignoring the people trying to make eye contact, to say something to her, to grab her. Her stick felt and found the floor, the safety of the earth. She was impervious now, in a cocoon of grief. She reached her table. Ranald rose to greet her, but she avoided him and squeezed around the table to the other side. She shoved the trophy in her bag and left the table, the room, the noise, the crowd. As she reached the exit, a man opened the door with a nod, and suddenly she was out—into the cool foyer, into the hush of the hotel, then outside.

Car lights rolled past, and the great spreading darkness and oceanic noise of the city opened up before her. She was walking quickly, stick clattering, bag heavy. She thrust her other hand in her pocket, and in it felt the sharp edge of the business card. She waited at a crossing. The lights were green, and the traffic was flowing past in a blur of noise and gleam. She looked up at the Telecom Tower glittering in the night sky, a plane blinking on its journey into the deepening night, and took a breath. A tight knot of pain flared in her chest.

Shona looked at the card. Proctor's scribbled address.

She shook her head. The lights changed to red, and she crossed the road with the mass of late Londoners hurrying to their homes, or hurrying anywhere as far from home as they could get. A shoal of black coats and downturned eyes. She walked on, becoming part of the stream, gliding into the nocturnal city, into its sea of shadows and light, its beauty and poison.

As she walked on, her sorrow slowly sank back to where it

had been for months, to a deep and restless reservoir around her hidden heart.

She thought of her father—reading the morning papers, whistling at a great splash, shaking his head at a carelessly buried lede or smiling at a sneaky pun. He loved papers. He loved stories. She would write one more, for him.

She stopped, momentarily suspended, poised at a moment of dividing paths. Between anger and peace, between sorrow and consolation, between intention and accident, between action and inaction. And the small, quiet voice within her had decided, before she even realised.

Her eyes opened. She checked the address Proctor had given her on her phone. It was not far.

Shona Sandison turned on her heel and headed towards it. As she walked, in her tilting way, she heard a voice in her head—a paper-thin voice made hoarse by illness, but urgent, deeply meant.

"Take care, my darling," it said. "Take care."

She ignored it and pressed on, into the darkness.

2

Of course, he had packed his gun.
    After all, he was now just an old man with a gun. Without it, he was merely another old man in a world full of them.

It was his final weapon. He had decommissioned, sold, broken and spiked the rest. One was left: a shotgun. A shotgun for a man who was shot. If nothing else, he was still lethal. Somewhere, too, in his heaped belongings, was a bag of cartridges. Cartridges red as rust and wounds. But the ammunition was buried somewhere, lost in the three rooms littered with old leather suitcases strapped together, faded holdalls and cardboard boxes.

The removal vans had left, squeezing through the village streets, grinding like artillery on the cobblestones. He was alone now, and he held the gun for a while: heavy but evenly weighted, its stock smooth, the colour of deep brown eyes. He slid it back into its case, once his son's hockey stick case, he thought, or perhaps a cover for a cricket bat. He zipped it up and leaned it against the fireplace. A vague thought flitted through his mind—when had he last fired that gun? Did he have a license? Of course not, he reminded himself. He was not a man who had ever needed a license. He had other people to do that—or used to.

He walked slowly, achingly, through his new home. The low-ceilinged kitchen, its stove pulsing a comfort of reassuring warmth, was a scrambled clutter of more boxes, of open cardboard carriers of pots and pans, mixed cutlery and plates, bowls and cups inexpertly packed.

The winter light glinted on edges and lips, on blades and tines.

This is what was left. He had given much away. He had sold much, too. The house in London, the cottage in Wales: sold. His art and book collection: gone.

Now he was reduced, trimmed, tapering his life to a fine point. And the point? Death. Death had only ever been the point. He put a pot of coffee on the stove, and the damp base hissed on contact with the heat. Tiny bubbles fizzed and skated across the hot surface.

He remembered, long ago, pressing a captive face hard onto the red coils of an electric ring, the instant stink of singeing flesh, the evaporation of bubbling, sliding tears. Long ago. Many confessions ago.

The old man moved to the window and looked out at the village, the harbour, the boats and, distant, through a skein of cloud, the far grey shore where his son died, where a part of his life remained and where somewhere the truth lay. In earth, in stone or in water.

A new home and a new name. He was Mr. Wolf now. He looked to the table. On it was his empty diary and a pen.

The sky over the Firth of Forth was deep and dark and heavy. The world was about to change, and even he did not know it.

3

Hector Stricken was in his second week working as a media officer for a new government agency. He wondered if he wanted to see a third.

The thought rose and fell in his frayed mind as he tried to marshal the gathered press of Scotland around a robotics factory in South Queensferry. His mobile phone was repeatedly buzzing.

Hector knew that he lacked confidence. He had since he was a scared, red-haired child. He was prone to bowel-scrambling attacks of nerves. That all remained. But he also knew he was no idiot, and he could even, on his good days, be competent. His many years of work as a respected journalist meant he could, at least, speak to journalists in the language they understood. He knew most of the Scottish press pack already—he had worked with half of them before he had moved into this new role at Capacity and Resilience (Scotland)—but he knew he had left something of his self behind.

So it was with a sense of mild achievement that Hector had just, with cajoling, wheedling, jokes and false promises, herded a clutch of frustrated journalists into a small white room within the factory, which squatted massively in a muddy field beside the Firth of Forth. Outside, heavy clouds hung low and unmoving, as if loaded with snow. The far shore—the Kingdom of Fife—was obscured by high thorn bushes and the gritty, constant wind which dragged curtains of drizzle across the firth. In the distance, glinting cars slid over the Queensferry Crossing.

The bright windowless room smelled of sweat and deodorant, ink cartridges and capless felt tips. There was a white board upon which someone had scrawled ominous acronyms. The world was rendered ugly here: no colour, no weather, no shadows.

Hector was sweating now. A headache was spreading in taut tendrils across his temples. He pulled his phone from his pocket.

No one can leave, the text from his superior, Eric Kapp, read. *Wait for further instructions.*

Suited in various shades of blue and grey, the gathered press corps stood, impatient and bemused. They huffed and puffed, they stared at their phones and they muttered to each other. Sir Charles Dyce, the chief executive of Capacity and Resilience (Scotland), was touring the factory in his first major public appearance since the quango had been established, and he suddenly had no desire to answer questions from the Scottish media.

Hector did not know what to do next. He stood with his back to the closed door and wondered what would happen, or if it would matter, if he suddenly burst into flames or hammered a pencil into his eye.

"For fuck's sake," a veteran newspaperman said, looking at his watch. "This is amateur hour. We've not got all day."

"Hector, what is this Capacity and Resilience thing, anyway?" someone asked. "Do we get a brief on that?"

"It is, as I said, a new agency," Hector said, with a thin smile. "Think of it as an independent administrative office. Answerable to the government but separate from it."

"Just what Scotland needs," another voice said. "Another quango cluttering up the civic landscape. And the chief exec is a former minister?"

"Sir Charles Dyce," someone said.

"Charlie Kickback? I guess we won't be mentioning why he had to resign from his seat," someone said with a chuckle, and the gathered hacks murmured in assent.

"Well, whatever they're called, we all answer to the ministers," Hector said wearily. "In the end."

Someone moved a chair, which scraped along the floor like a knife blade on glass.

"We're being kettled in here," a woman said to Hector. The journalist, whose name he had forgotten, was furious but keeping her voice down. "Aren't we? Away from the chief exec. He doesn't want us to be here. It's a farce. Why invite us all and then cram us into a wee cupboard?"

"Kettled *is* the word," Nick from the BBC said, shaking his head, arms crossed over his pristine tweed jacket.

"Come now, Nick. Of course you're not being kettled," Hector said, shifting his mind away from violent suicide and holding up his hand. "Let's keep a wee bit of decorum here. This is just a temporary holding pattern until—"

"Holding pen, more like," another hack rumbled.

"Until what, Hector? How long will we get with him?" said another.

"Yeah, Hector, the email said we'd get ten minutes," said another.

"Fuck's sake, Hector"—this from a former colleague on the newspaper where Hector used to work—"I thought you'd know how to run a gig like this."

"I haven't even seen a bloody robot yet," said a grey-haired woman in the corner, holding a large microphone. "I'm only here for the robots."

"All will be revealed," Hector said, "I assure you. Let's keep our collective hair on."

But Hector had just been told, again by text from Kapp,

that there would now be no questions and no chance of press interaction with Dyce:

Press call is not happening. Wait for further.

Hector sighed. Why had the press been invited, then? Who had sent the press call notice, with its promises of face-to-face access? *He* hadn't. Someone in communications had made a promise they now could not keep. It was a fuck-up.

The day had begun less chaotically. After an anxious night in the spare room and a tense morning trying not to disturb Sandy as she fed the baby in a sleep-deprived fug, he had driven to the half-built factory from their flat in Leith, an hour and a half early, as requested. He had been stationed at the main door and told, on this dreich winter's day, to greet the press. He was to gather them together, cross their names from the list and stop them from wandering off, opening doors they shouldn't or falling over. He would then move them inside to a designated part of the expansive factory floor, where they would stand behind a conveniently painted red line and wait.

The fast-walking new chief executive would be toured around the shop floor by management, take a few questions from the media—three questions, one to camera—and depart. A simple plan.

Nervously but competently, Hector had welcomed the journalists, who had toed the red line and looked at their notes, whispering to each other, in the vast metal shed. Multi-jointed pneumatic limbs hung from the high ceiling like metal carcasses, looming over what looked like winding track for a moving floor, which had yet to be installed. New metal and fresh paint gleamed. The factory should have begun production, but there had been investment holdups and a lack of skilled workers, due to the shortage caused by Brexit. The factory owner had been a vocal supporter of the

UK government that had enabled this, so here they all were, in this cavernous, unlovely shed.

Kapp, with a slap of leather shoe on concrete, had appeared then, storming into the factory. His face was blotchily red. "Hector, a word," he said.

"Ladies and gentlemen," Hector murmured to the guests, "I shall be back in but a moment."

Kapp ushered Hector to one side. "Change of plan."

"Right."

"Move the hacks from the factory floor as soon as possible. Dyce doesn't want to even see them. He's five minutes away in the car with his private secretary. You need to get them all shifted."

"But—"

"He doesn't want to see them, okay?" Kapp said, his eyes wide.

"But—"

"He wants broadcast cameras only—I have them over there." Kapp motioned in the general direction of a large blue machine in the corner of the shop floor.

Hector stared at him, then back at the press pack. "Okay. They're not going to be happy."

"Not as unhappy as we'll be if the chief exec sees those wankers waiting for him." Kapp turned smartly and strode back across the empty factory.

Next, the factory's press officer had appeared, heels clacking. She said something Hector did not quite hear and pointed in the general direction of a grey door. Hector dutifully ushered the sighing journalists to a side corridor and opened the first door he saw. Now, tense and fractious, they all stood in the white room.

Someone knocked on the door behind him. He turned and opened it, to reveal a factory worker.

THE DIARY OF LIES • 29

"I'm sorry, sir, you'll have to move those people from here,"
the man said. His face was as pale and smooth as peeled
garlic. "The room's about to be used for staff training."

From another grey door, a bustling line of people holding
electronic tablets and bundles of papers began to enter the
corridor. They looked at Hector in confusion. The person
at the head of the queue, a heavyset man with smudged
blue tattoos on his hands, peered at Hector as if he were an
unexpected natural phenomenon.

"As you can see," the worker said.

"Right, right," Hector said. "Two ticks."

He turned to the room of journalists. A pool of exasperated faces looked back at him. One asked when they would
be set free from their incarceration.

"Robots?" the same woman said eagerly. "Is it time for
the cyborgs?"

Hector put his back to the door and texted Kapp: *I need
to move the hacks. Where?*

There was a rapping on the door behind him.

"Okay, everyone," Hector said, clearing his throat. "Time
to move on."

The journalists hoisted their bags on their shoulders again.

The corridor was now full of anxious trainees.

"You'll have to move," the worker said. "Now."

"I know, son, I know," Hector said. He was aware of the
press of bodies behind him. The bare white corridor was full
of people travelling in one direction. In the other, it ran for
fifty metres. There were two doors in the corridor, also painted
grey, and it ended in a green fire exit locked with a heavy bar.

Suddenly, from one of those doors, the press officer reappeared, waving at Hector. "In here," she said sharply, and then
with startling rapidity disappeared back behind the door, as
if she had been suddenly hooked.

Hector turned to the press pack and nodded. They trudged down the corridor, scrutinised by the waiting trainees, who looked vaguely hostile.

"Will it still be ten minutes with the chief exec, Mr. Stricken?" one journalist piped up.

"I'm not sure at the moment," Hector replied, his throat tightening. He headed towards the door from which he thought the PR had appeared and reached for the handle. His mind stalled. Was this the right door? Or should he be opening the other one? He came to a halt, and the journalists bumped into each other in a kerfuffle. He quickly checked his phone—no more messages from Kapp. No updates from the press officer.

The first grey door stood before him. He heard voices from behind it. Was that low rumble Kapp?

"Hector, do you know where the fuck you're going?" a voice said behind him.

"Total shit show," someone muttered.

"Robots?"

Hector took a step back and stood on someone's foot. A soft press under his hard shoe. He reached for the door handle and turned, his face hot but smiling, and ushered the journalists into the small, brightly lit room.

It contained Dyce, Kapp and a clutch of men in suits. A large internal window looked out over the empty shop floor. The men were murmuring to each other. Mouths full of words which were leaden with meaning. A kind of code.

"As you know, workforce is our biggest expense, so . . ."

"Exactly. Look, we have the next two years to get it all squared away."

"Music to my ears."

"That's why we're here. That's my job. It's all about the *sequencing*."

"Sequencing . . . yeah, the sequencing cannot be disrupted."

"The police . . ."

"Forget the polis, they don't know . . . Private security is the thing . . ."

"Mission critical phase will be the transition from subjects to objects."

"ECHR has been the block. Block no more."

"*Two hundred thousand*—and that's only the beginning . . ."

"Uh-oh. What's this?" A man in a blue suit looked directly at Hector with unblinking eyes. The chief executive turned, his mouth slightly open. His face moved in a flashing instant from shock to anger to a mask of vapid charm.

Then, suddenly, a chaos of noise: a howling, shattering klaxon splintered the air. One of the men moved towards them, his hands out, and said loudly, "Fire alarm! This is not a test, ladies and gentlemen! Everyone move outside!"

Kapp, his suit aflap and his face now puce, shouted, "Everybody out! Sir Charles, follow me, please!"

Hector watched the crowd move past him. He did not follow. He leaned against the office wall. As the alarm shrieked on, Dyce and his entourage exited in a blur, and the journalists removed themselves in a collective of angry faces and swearing frustration.

Through the window, out on the factory floor, nothing moved, but lights swam, red and blue, over the inert machinery, and through the skylight Hector could see the grey clouds darken to black.

January
St. James, Fife

T,

A new diary, a new page . . . and it is a fine diary. It has thick, creamy pages. It almost seems a shame to defile it with ink. The therapist said to keep a journal. He said it might help. He advised addressing it to someone, or something, and I thought of you. It could have been your mother. But we were simply not on these kind of intimate terms. I will write this as a diary. Journals, a doctor said, while I was sedated, are often kept by people these days.

You cannot be ashamed of me anymore. There is only me, and that is shame enough. Living is the shame. Shame is the cancer that grows into the shape of its host. I am all of it, now.

This empty page sits before me. It is reproving. It is as if it is shouting. I bought this notebook from a market in Siena several years ago. I was there for a conference, one of my last. We were discussing how to counter online terrorists and other "threats." It was perhaps the beginning of the end. I just checked out. I excused myself, no one demurred, and went walking. I stumbled across an antique market in a broken colonnade. I bought it not knowing I would need it. And here I am, defiling it.

Threats. Of course, after pandemic flu, man-made pathogens and what we breezily used to call "space weather"—the sun's electromagnetic bursts which disable electronics, and for which we really have no defence at all—it is the people, "the people," I should say, who are now regarded as the greatest threat. Thank God, they say, for sport, TV and shopping, or there would be scaffolds on Pall Mall. Tricoteuses on the Royal Mile. Mass graves in Surrey.

I have ink on my fingers. It has been a while since I used a fountain pen. And to what end? Are these words to be read? Or are they like the gold mask of Agamemnon: to be looked at, not through?

Oh, but what does it matter. After what happened, I had to be remade. I seem to have been remade with new working parts. With a seed of a conscience and a pen with which to express it. I have a new name—Benjamin Wolf. It was chosen for me. New passport, new NI number, all organised efficiently.

I am also alone. But how have I ended up here? It could have been London or Washington. Kuala Lumpur or Berlin. Cyprus. Hong Kong. Belfast. Baghdad. We used to relocate disgraced or blown agents to remote islands and far colonies. But, no, for me it ends here, in the Kingdom of Fife. The kingdom, they say! Can I be king? Not again. No. Not in Scotland. The problem with being king is the <u>inconvenience</u> of retainers. None here. I am my own retainer. I can order myself around.

Instead of a diary, I could have written memoirs. Others have. Of course, various legal restrictions would have forbidden me from publishing anything truly honest, useful or revelatory. There would have been a lot to say about 1989. About the wars. About certain wet work in the woods. The Miners' Strike. Greenpeace. Faslane. Bodies in ziplock bags. Brexit. And so on. Ad nauseam. Damning. Certainly damning.

You were not interested in any of that. You just simply wanted to see me more often. I felt, for many years, that our interactions were sufficient. But, mainly, I admit, I did not really consider them in depth. Your schooling was expensive and comprehensive, and your aunt took care of you. I did not worry about you or what was happening to you. I was purely concerned with the State. I had to be.

Yet you did appear in my thoughts and in my deliberations. 1989: you must have been 18 or so. A lot of changes were being made. We had to adjust the way we worked. I was reordering our men (predominantly men). I had the structure. The roles and responsibilities. But I was struggling with nomenclature. With categorisation. Your Aunt Zelda wrote to me. You had passed your driving test.

And thus I remember it clearly. It was a windy, wet day in Cheltenham. The three main cohorts I named (somewhat in your honour):

Red Men: for the wet and nasty work.

Amber Men: intelligence gathering, news gathering, readying, supply and logistics.

Green Men: provocateurs, influencers, infiltrators, liars, Fifth Columnists and turned traitors.

The Tallis Protocol, they called it. Still call it, I hear. Although the deskbound dullards called it the Tripartite Plan. I did that thinking of you and your driving test, you know. No one will ever know. How could they?

It is getting late. I shall return to this page. Despite all these words, it remains empty. I shall retire to my cot.

As the man wrote, all those years ago: "Alone with his longing / the old man lies down on his bed." I now know what that means.

4

The shambolic press event had riven Hector Stricken's nerves. He had a mandatory team meeting in five minutes, and his mind and body were jangling. The shrieking fire alarm and the shouts of the angry journalists echoed sharply in his mind.

Now, he was sitting in a toilet cubicle on the fourth floor of Alacrity House, deep within the heart of old Edinburgh. His chest was tight. He tried deep breaths. He remembered what sweet Sandy had said: *Breathe deeply, fill your lungs and mind. Concentrate on your breathing. Centre your mind on your lungs and your breath.* He wondered what she would think of him now, crying in the toilet, gasping like an animal. She could never see him like this.

A pool of water had gathered at his feet. He was relieved it wasn't his own piss; it was melted snow, dropped from his shoes. The fact of snow, its existence, steadied his mind. He wiped his eyes. There was wetness on the back of his hand, and the cuff of his new suit smelled of a well-hoovered department store.

Sandy had hugged him on his return from the debacle and gently kissed his forehead. He had been handed, and he cuddled, the baby, who was still nameless, small and pink. A relieving bundle of gorgeousness. Sandy had suggested the name Jessie. A native of Quebec, she could not quite grasp that a boy named Jessie in Scotland would be in a for a very tough childhood. Hector had laughed and suggested, once again, the simple names of John or Jack. Sandy—exhausted, flushed—had offered Richard. "Dick Stricken," he had said.

"I'm not so sure about that either." Sandy had thrown a cushion at his head.

Now breathing more evenly, Hector was aware of someone pissing nearby. Around them, Alacrity House hummed. On the top floor, past a thick security door, were the new offices of the chief executive of Capacity and Resilience (Scotland) and his deputies and, next door, those of the Special Advisors—the SpAds, as they were known. Down in the chilly basement, the admin staff toiled in vast, open-plan spaces that clacked with computer keyboards and pinged with email alerts. In virtual group meetings on myriad glowing screens, serious faces murmured into headsets and microphones.

Hector exhaled. Between his knees dangled his new security pass: on it, the beaming image of someone called Hector Donald Stricken. His russet hair was speckled with grey, his beard neatly trimmed. A new, tightly knotted tie, a clean ironed shirt. The photograph had been taken on the first day of his new job. He barely recognised the face swinging on the lanyard.

Why had he been smiling so broadly? He had been an uninformed optimist. The prospect of a new career, a new job at a government agency, had been exciting. There had been fresh certainties—a job for life (if he didn't fuck it up), a pension (if he lived that long), defined holidays (great), certain pay (his credit card might even be paid off) and the regularity of work (if that good be endured). A new, sober regularity to underpin his new, sober life as a father with a young family. He owed Sandy and the wee one that. But there were uncertainties, too. He was now an informed pessimist. The photo was a record of another man.

He twirled the security pass between two long fingers. The plastic oblong held within it a sliver of encoded information, which meant he could enter Alacrity House without security checks. It also worked on the magnetic doors of Westminster and Whitehall. But to do what? His mind reeled with new protocols, the alien IT systems, baffling scheduling applications and contradictory digital media advice. Stuffed inside the reverse of the lanyard was his personal employee number and his passcode, scribbled on a Post-it note. He had to remind himself of them every day.

His former life as a journalist had been erased, and with it, part of himself. His working day was no longer peopled by journalists, soundtracked by blaring sport desks and anxious news editors. Hector Stricken would never have a byline again. That world was gone. Behind him. His working life was now a permanent drinkless wake for a lost vocation.

Two minutes to the team meeting.

He gritted his teeth, found some kind of strength in his legs and stood up so he could button his new suit jacket, take a deep breath and step out of the cubicle.

How is wee Johnny doing? he texted to Sandy.

Asleep and that is not his name I'm napping bye x came back immediately.

He smiled. Not everything in this fallen world was chores and dread. A tinily breathing child slept beside his beautiful mother not two miles away, safe in their new beds, immaculate and tender.

He looked up from the screen, and his heart clenched again.

At the row of sinks stood his colleague Eric Kapp.

"Hector, my man," he said. "How goes it? Not too *stricken*, I hope? Ready for half an hour of excellent mandatory team chat with the fragrant Rhonda?"

"Of course, of course," Hector said, washing his hands unusually thoroughly, wondering vaguely if he was doing it correctly.

"That press shindig was quite the ordeal, wasn't it?" Kapp bellowed, wiping his wet hands on his suit trousers. "But it wasn't as bad as all that, Hector—don't you worry about it too much. We draw some, we lose some, right? Right." He moved to the door and ushered Hector through. "Rhonda will be expecting us, and she does *not* like to be kept waiting."

They returned to their desks. TVs were blaring. People in business attire were attacking their keyboards. Hector needed to pull himself together. He straightened his tie and glanced at the picture of their nameless baby on his phone.

It was time for the meeting. The team, five-strong, stood up and moved as one to a glass cubicle in the corner of the office. The window there offered an impressive view over the transfigured city. Beneath a sky as blue as a vein, the towers and serried roofs were all laden with two inches of white snow. Arthur's Seat looked as if it had been iced for a party. Gritters were moving slowly through the streets.

Hector sat beside Kapp, who flipped open his laptop and started typing. He was becoming familiar with the rest of the team. There was Clara Shift, who, behind thick glasses and a curtain of long hair, was still and slow-blinking and gave little away. Noiselessly competent, she seemed to know what she was doing. A junior member of the team, Jordan Grant, wore well-ironed shirts and dyed blond hair; he had a gym-toned body straining in a shiny suit. He lived with his mother. Rhonda gave Jordan menial tasks—printing, photocopying, organising diaries, updating the work schedule, sorting parking passes—but he did not seem to mind.

"So, the press call was a total disgrace," Rhonda said, clicking her pen incessantly. Her face looked like a soaked sandbag.

Hector flushed and looked intently at his hands. Kapp spoke up, his neck suddenly mottled pink. "A lot of things conspired against us. But I think we ultimately emerged with our dignity intact."

"The chief exec was off the reservation, I hear. A *lot* of anger," she said. "There have been questions—questions to his Private Office, poor them—and *furious* enquiries to the director of external affairs in London."

Kapp glanced briefly at Hector before saying, "We had a comms plan. It was signed off. Sir Charles decided to ignore it at the last second. Luckily, the fire alarm went off. To be honest, it was a godsend. He's not ready to answer questions from the media."

Rhonda snorted. "That's his job, Kapp."

"He's not up to it." Kapp shrugged. "Right now, he's fractious, snappy, totally unprepared. With the broadcast teams he just repeated his lines. He was especially rude to Channel 4."

Rhonda stared at Hector. She clicked her pen and sighed.

"I've heard worse," Clara said mildly.

"Yes, remember that train that didn't actually work—the one with the pretend windows?" Jordan said.

"We did a press call at a nursery and all the toddlers started projectile vomiting," Clara said. "One after the other. It was hard to stay upright."

"Pre-COVID, pre-election, ancient history," Kapp snapped.

"Look, we shouldn't have had to staff the event anyway," Rhonda conceded. "Not sure what his own team were doing. Slopey shoulders. The press notice was a mess. Let's badge it as a learning experience and move on. Private Office will, no doubt, be discussing *learnings*—or lessons, as we used to call them. We shall hear more of it; of that, I am sure. Dyce was raging."

"So you said," Kapp said impatiently.

Rhonda tapped the tabletop. "Okay—today's business. Let's move further down the funnel." Hector realised she enjoyed analysing spreadsheets, forward-look documents, portfolio planners and work plans. Her voice sluiced through a list of work to be done that day and the rest of the week.

She made mention of Hector being in his third week and mumbled something which he could not hear. Kapp was typing away on his laptop, as if ignoring her, although he put his thumb up every time his name was mentioned.

Hector stared out of the window at the spired city beyond. He wondered if Sandy had grabbed some sleep; he wanted to talk to her. He wondered if he would sleep tonight. Drink would help. The prospect of a warm, fire-lit pub rose in his mind.

". . . I have a diary clash. Hector, you can cover it for me. Thanks for that," Rhonda murmured. "Just listen in."

"Ah, that might be about the . . ." Kapp inclined his head. "Should Hector really be covering that?"

"Yes, yes," Rhonda said, visibly eager to move on. "Look, Hector, just log on, log in and say nothing, okay?" She peered at her online diary.

Kapp paused tapping away at his keyboard to look directly at Hector. "At that meeting—just don't move a muscle, Hector. Okay?"

"Fine, no problem. I'll dial in. I'm sure it'll be interesting," Hector said. "Whatever it is."

"It won't be interesting," Kapp said. "Actually, I should cover it."

"No, Hector can. There's no external affairs on the agenda," Rhonda said, "but—but!—someone in Private Office asked for us to be present. After the fiasco with the robots, I think they feel it would be wise to have external affairs cover."

"You know, I can pick it up. I'm already across it," Kapp said. "I think it's for senior—"

"Hector, you fine with that?" Rhonda said, ignoring Kapp, who had irked her. Now she was trying to make a point.

"Yes," Hector said, "sure. Can you send me the diary invite? I don't have it."

"Do you know where your diary is on the system?" Clara said. "I can show you."

"I'll do that, big man—don't you worry," Jordan said, winking.

A slab of snow slid down from the roof above, falling past the window like a suicide. Clara seemed to take it as a sign. "Right, I'm sorry. I need to go home early. Looks like the trains are being cancelled." She rose from her seat and peered out at the city of snow. The office window faced south, over the straggle and confusion of the Old Town that tumbled from the castle to the Parliament. "It's like a Brueghel out there," she said. "Tiny Northern people in the ice and snow. Minuscule lives in white oblivion . . . God, I think I need a new job. I wanted to travel after university. I should be doing that—not this."

"Sometimes in an online meeting, I use the cursor arrow to stab people in the eyes," Jordan said. "Do you ever do that?"

Rhonda ignored them.

"I wonder if they ever feel it," Jordan said.

"I'll fill you in after this," Kapp whispered to Hector.

The rest of the meeting went by in a haze of grey efficiency. Hector blinked and nodded, Kapp typed on, and Jordan smiled to himself.

They returned to their desks. Kapp, his eyebrows high, asked Hector if he wanted some fresh air, to which he reluctantly agreed.

The two men moved silently down the wide stairs to the ground floor, where there were pinging lifts and a glass-walled security entrance. Hector tapped his card on a black strip and a door opened. He followed Kapp outside. The sky was unbearably blue. It seemed to be the only colour in the world.

They moved slowly to the base of Calton Hill, a bunnet of rock topped with an unfinished pillared monument, and pecked their way uphill, office shoes slithering in the slush, their breath billowing. As the footpath circled and climbed the hill, the city fell beneath them. No people moved on the pavements. No buses moved on the roads. No planes flew on the approaches to the airport. Boats sat motionless in the firth. The far shores of Fife were dazzling. Hector heard only his feet and, up ahead, the huffing exertions of Kapp as he launched himself up the hill, one man against gravity.

At the summit, they both looked down over the silent city.

Kapp asked Hector how he was coping, and Hector said he was fine. He was lying. He wondered what he could do next. What he could escape to. He looked down and east to the flats where Sandy and the baby slept. He wished he could fly there.

Kapp, who had taken a packet of cigarettes from inside his bulky jacket, began speaking between pinched tokes.

"My dear man, you've joined at what I might call an interesting time," Kapp said. "You'd probably have been better off staying in journalism. You could have written about all that is to come . . ." He turned away, gently kicking at the smooth wall of snow at the cleared path's sudden end. Slivers of snow crumbled to the ground and melted. "Ah, Calton Hill. What a panorama. They used to hang people here, you know. What a final view from the noose this would have been."

Hector rubbed his cold hands together.

"Our new unit here: it's scaring the horses, you know,"

Kapp said, blowing out smoke. "Our very existence has upset people. Good, I say. If it sends shivers through the body of the Kirk, that's fine by me."

"Why was it set up anyway?" Hector said. He was sure it had been mentioned in his interview, but only in the vaguest of terms.

"To build *capacity*," Kapp said and held out a hand, as if he held capacity in his palm.

"And resilience." Hector nodded. "I understand the words. But not what they mean when put together."

Kapp spoke evenly. "Well, they don't have to mean anything. But, as it happens, it all began with Brexit."

Brexit: the British public's tumultuous decision, via a referendum, to turn its back on the continent. To leave the European Union—not only its laws and regulations, Hector thought, but its worldview, its social and political outlook.

To Hector's mind, the Brexit landscape was a sinking field of misbegotten confusion, rotten fruit sown by the deluded and the malevolent. Brexit had been a tantrum, yes, but also a disavowal. He knew his views were not shared by everyone. His parents had voted for Brexit; he had vowed to never mention it in their presence.

"A watershed. An earthquake. An historic departure," Kapp said.

"A calamity," Hector said. "A disgrace. A once-in-a-lifetime fuck-up."

"Now, now," Kapp said, smiling. "The people spoke. We have to listen."

"Racist pensioners spoke. And Scotland voted against it, of course."

"Yes—and so what?" Kapp said, lighting a second cigarette. "It was democracy, Hector. On the UK scale, it was a solid democratic vote. A beautiful thing. Are we not democrats?"

Hector opened his mouth to counter but lacked the will and the energy. He sensed the evil succulence of Kapp's cigarette. Its sweet rankness cut clear in the icy air. It smelled good.

"I was thinking of taking up fags again," Hector said, watching Kapp exhale. "To lose weight."

Kapp momentarily looked confused, but carried on. "I was saying . . . you'll remember that there was much talk of a 'bonfire of European regulations.' Getting rid of all the European health and safety restraints on private business. Seizing back the UK's sovereignty."

"Oh, yes, of course. Getting rid of all those irksome European insistences on safe food, clean water and non-lethal workplaces. Paid holidays. Maternity and paternity leave. All those socialist compulsions," Hector said, raising his eyebrows.

"Exactamundo! Although the *actualité* of stripping out the veins of EU law from the UK's body politic has proved to be a mite trickier than initially envisaged."

"How surprising," Hector said, "that reality is complicated."

"But that's all changing now," Kapp rolled on. "Capacity and Resilience has been set up. Look at us, with our lovely offices, a staff of two hundred and a budget of £45 million."

"Well, I am grateful for that," Hector said, doubtful if he was.

"And the UK government is bringing in the Great British Freedom Act. GBFA. It goes around and above the Scottish government. Or at least that's what the papers say, and the UKG hasn't denied it. And what we've seen of the Bill in the media, it looks pretty . . . dramatic."

Hector nodded. There had been a stir in the media about the GBFA, first printed in a national Sunday newspaper. It had revealed how the planned Bill proposed to taper down paid holidays, make sick pay optional, remove controls on food quality and privatise large parts of the health service.

The story had created a storm. The government had blamed a leak and said the information in the story was "premature and incomplete." Two Europe-friendly ministers resigned. The prime minister, wounded following a scandal involving one of his more fascism-adjacent MPs, had then been forced to deny much of the story. But the Act—technically now in Bill form—was about to be introduced to the Westminster Parliament. Some scattered and ill-tempered political forces were ranged against it, but the new coalition UK government had the majority to force it through. The original news story, broken by Hector's former colleague, Shona Sandison, had been largely true.

Brilliant, fierce, obnoxious, scintillating Shona. He still loved her, Hector knew. Even if it didn't matter anymore.

Kapp was staring at Hector, mistaking heartbreak for vacancy. "Let's get back to the office," he said.

At the side door of Alacrity House, Kapp said he needed to make a personal call and stepped away, his mobile pressed to his ear.

Hector, hunched and chilled, moved up three stone steps at the entrance. He stopped for a moment and looked down. The steps were worn and bowed in the middle of their span. For years, men and women of government, servants of the people, had trudged up these stairs—cheerfully, dolefully, in duty or in fear. Now the weight of his feet was adding to the erosion caused by their centuries-old devotion.

A sudden desire gripped him—to be back on the hill, under the vast sky, rendered small and anonymous in the manifest elegance of this silent city. But he needed to get back to his desk, to his computer, and listen in to that meeting.

Hector walked on through the unfamiliar corridors, over carpet and tile, and the pale stone of Alacrity House closed about him like an enveloping skull.

The walls are dry; the men did their work well. A clean barracks. It is better than the hospital. The bedroom is warm, nicely placed over the kitchen, and its window overlooks the neat little harbour. I shall watch the boats with interest.

Clouds this morning—heavy, grey, almost purple at the depths. Moving slowly from east to west, with almost imperceptible change in bulk and movement. The water was also grey and heavy, with hardly any breakers at the harbour, or along the cliffs.

After breakfast, I took a long walk along cliffs to the next village, Elie. Long, rather fine beach, with many rock pools. A handsome place. A small but working harbour, rather larger than St. James but with fewer actual fishing boats, from what I could see. I need to learn their daily rhythms: when they go out, when they return. The clouds were stretched and spread— rather like a fine paste—across the sky. A large sky at Elie reminds me of the sense of scale one encounters in Cornwall, in Dorset.

There was a secluded beach in North Cyprus, near Kyrenia, I used to go to, before it all went south. A shallow blue-green sea, with few breakers. With a snorkel, one could swim through the seagrass to where the ocean floor fell away—and down there, far below, was a field of sand littered with broken pots and ceramics. An earthquake had destroyed a port there many years ago. The ships were full of amphora. The debris is still there, a sub-sea field of shards, broken curves, eroded handles. Some still had their ingrained patterns. I used to bring pieces home, in my diplomatic baggage, on the large planes from Akrotiri. I wonder where they are now.

Tomorrow, I shall begin unboxing my little men. The blue regiments. I have a lot to get through. Most are assembled, although there is more to do, and I need a magnifying stand now to see the joins. My eyesight used to be 20/20, they told me. They told me all kinds of things, of course. How wonderful I was. How perceptive. How masterly. I agreed with them.

But now I am "out" and they do not tell me anything anymore. Now other things detain me. Violent moods. I eat one meal a day now, but have, in compensation, upped my sherry intake. I cannot say it is a bad equation. I know you liked sweet wine, too. I shall pour one for you.

I shall begin to bring some colour to the little soldiers tomorrow, I hope. The magazines say to always use a base layer and under-coat, but of course that is a bore. I have decided to begin with the riflemen. They look very sharp and neat and intent in their shakos.

I have been avoiding the news, so I have not been listening to Radio 3, which I am missing. I miss my Bach. I miss my Germans. I do not hear the news. But I know the news anyway—the long decline continues apace. A driverless car heading down a steep decline to a wall. It is probably a small blessing, son, that you will not see the collision.

It is dark now. Not a star to be seen. The sea is whispering. They say a snowfall is imminent. Midwinter weighs on me.

Later —

I woke early. A bad dream. Some old business in Africa. A man, alive, dumped into a septic tank. Why did we do that? Because we could. If there is one overriding rule I have learned, it is this: men can do anything.

5

Fisher was in the shower, practising voices.

"Robert," he said in a Northern accent. "Jamie," a Liverpudlian lilt. No. "Craig," a Geordie. No, too close to home. "Craig," he said, in a flat Yorkshire voice. Nope. Not right. "Angus," a soft Edinburgh tone. Maybe a little hint of Leith or fugitive Fife. "Angus," he said again. Yes, that seemed to work.

In the warm flow, he looked down at his lean body. The single winged tattoo on his upper thigh, fading now. The thick lines of a savage old wound near his belly button. He put his hand to it.

He wondered if any of the hundreds of tiny Napoleonic soldiers, painted and varnished, sitting in their rows in bubble wrap and polystyrene in a bag by the stove, had scars. Whether the makers had given them signs of war and wounding. Missing limbs or missing friends. He had not properly looked at them, the ranks and rows in their red-uniformed finery. White horses. Silver cannons. He knew he had to read up on the rules, the dice rolls.

Toys for boys, he thought. Yet men are undermined by such things. Tiny weaknesses. Minor fractures. Mr. Wolf loved these toys. In these wrinkles, wounds can be made.

After his shower, Fisher opened up his laptop. He entered a PIN, then a passcode, and placed his right middle finger on a sensitive pad on the upper right of the keyboard. The screen flashed into life. Green letters and numbers fell across the depthless black. Across the screen were faces and names: pen portraits, key facts.

He reread the briefing. He went over the section his manager, Gardner, had mentioned.

. . . Under RTT service realignment executed June 89—May 91.

- *Tripartite R/A/G model installed for Active Operations by 90, operation by 91.*

- *RTT extraordinary oversight over recalibrated training model re: tripartite AO.*

- *R/A/G ensured firewall cell activity of proactivity, intel and infil with system deniability* (see Annex re: AO Audit).

- *Offered K, 96, accepted.*

- *Daughter by mistress AH [disavowed]* (see Annex re: Personal) *b. 1997.*

- *RTT leave 99—2000* (MH see Annex re: Risk/ Vulnerabilities) *and 2019—22 (MH). Secondment to chair political action committee "Planchette"* (see Annex re: Watson/Bax).

- *2019—22 relocation to ROI. Cleaning operation required re: actions in County Clare, Paris, Sofia* (see Annex: Additional Actions [AA]).

- *Son Thomas b. 1973 d. 2022, subsequent AA activity by RTT* (See Annex:[AA]) . . .

There were images accompanying the text. He looked at the photographs again, of the father and the son, and tapped the laptop shut.

Beyond the boundary wall of the caravan site there was

little movement apart from the steady crash of waves against the harbour wall. Lights were on in the harbourmaster's office and the warehouse beside it. Two or three private boats were also in dock; their bright colours and clean decks gleamed under the metallic sky. A man in yellow waterproofs was shifting boxes about on one of the boats. He was tall, with straggly grey hair tucked inside a tattered cap. He stretched and went below deck, out of sight.

What drives a man to act? he asked himself. Lust. Greed. Anger. Rarely love, rarely selflessness. In this case, lust was out. Greed was also out—you cannot tempt a man who wants nothing. Anger? That was the calculation. Anger and its red-toothed, self-obsessed cousin—revenge. He was a green man—provocation was his job, after all.

6

London was a convocation of shadows and noise: grinding traffic, alarms, shouts, car horns, underground rumbles, the unending fall of feet on pavements. Shona hurried through the labyrinth of sound and surface, her stick rapping on flagstone and tarmac, her bag heavy, her mind fixed. She followed the directions on her phone, pausing at junctions, peering at street names. The buildings lowered, the streets became closer, darker, more medieval, as she reached the address Proctor had given her.

It was a brick building, with blacked-out windows. PRIVATE MATTERS, an electric sign said in blue. Shona checked the time—it was getting late. The street thronged with gaggles of revellers gathering outside pubs and spilling out of Chinese restaurants. She really did not want to go into a sex shop, but, she thought, no one would know. And, anyway, it was for a story. She could make her excuses and leave, if she needed to.

She ducked inside, pulling the door behind her and moving into dim light. Behind a till sat a skinny woman with long blue hair, engrossed in something on an iPad. The shop was divided into two rooms by a curtain of plastic strips. There were racks of magazines and DVDs lined on metal shelves.

Shona had never been in a place like this. There was skin on every cover displayed. Parted lips and open thighs and soft tissue. Her eyes tried not to see the shaved flesh, the pleading faces slick with cum, the bound manicured hands. So many pictures of women surrounded by headless men.

Shona began to feel sick. She moved through the display as fast as she could to the safety of the desk.

"What can I do you for?" the blue-haired woman said. She was watching an old 1970s police show. A man in a greasy trench coat was battering another man beside a canal. A distant factory poured belched steam into a porridge sky.

"Hiya," Shona found herself saying.

The woman barely flickered.

"I've been told to ask for . . . er . . . bondage," Shona said.

"Oh, you have, have you?" the woman said. On the screen, blood ran in a bright red stream down a man's face.

"Yeah," Shona said. "A man . . . he said to ask."

Now the woman scrutinised Shona. Her large eyes were ringed with iridescent makeup. A snub nose was pierced with rings.

"Where you from, then?" she said. "What's that accent?"

"Glasgow," Shona said quickly.

There was a large shelf behind the woman, displaying a range of restraining harnesses, fake mouths and anuses, rubber vaginas. Shona smiled. It all seemed absurd.

"Who sent you?" the woman said. On the screen, there had been a change of scene—a woman in a city café was reading a newspaper, her head covered in a patterned scarf. She ran a manicured finger down a list of personal adverts.

"Mr. Proctor," Shona said. "And he told me to ask for bondage."

"For what now?"

"Bondage," Shona repeated through her teeth.

On the TV, a man's body was dropped into oily industrial water. Sludgy ripples palpitated.

"Mr. Proctor, eh?" the woman said, as if hearing the name for the first time. "Could he not come himself? Or was he tied up?" She giggled.

"Look—just forget it," Shona said. This was clearly all a joke. Some kind of bizarre wind-up by Proctor or his people. How they must be laughing, she thought. She turned to go. She would head to the Underground and make her way west, to her bed for the night. She couldn't hang around this tawdry hole a moment longer.

"All right, love, all right. Hold your horses," the woman said. She reached for something under her desk, rummaged around and then pulled out a padded brown envelope. "What's your name?" she asked, and Shona told her. The woman smiled. "Yep, he dropped this off for you." She held out the package while still watching the screen.

Shona took the package. A weight slid within.

"Right. I'm closing up now," the woman said. Onscreen, a searchlight cut through a black sky. "I only stayed open for you."

Shona tore open the envelope. Inside was a mobile phone, boxy and old-fashioned. She fished it out. It felt heavy. Its screen was blank. It was dead. It did not seem to have a charger slot—it had a tiny pinhole instead. It was curious. Attached to it was a note: *7 Sheldrake Gardens, 11 a.m. We need to talk about monsters.*

"Did he pay you? To stay open?"

"What's it to you?"

"Just wondering."

"Yeah, course he did," the woman said, raising her arms and stretching. "Month's wages. He said if you didn't turn up to bin the parcel. But here you are. He said you'd come."

"Did he?"

"Yeah, girl." The woman was flicking off lights and gathering her belongings.

"Does he come here often?"

"Now and then. Now, I really am locking up, so off you go."

They moved outside, and both stood by the door as the woman locked up.

The woman quickly turned to Shona. "Is he a friend of yours?"

"Not really—why?"

"Watch out for him, love, I mean it," she said. She tilted her head and added: "You know, he likes the rough stuff. He's into choking. Violence. That's the stuff he orders."

"He could order it online—why come here?"

"No internet history, no pack drill," she said, as if it was obvious. "He uses another name when he does. He's lots of fellas, that one."

Shona frowned. "Most men are. What name does he use?"

The woman shook her head. "Nah. It's horses for courses, love," she said, shrugging and tramping off into the dark street. "Horses for fucking courses. You take care now."

Within forty minutes, Shona was pressing a button and entering a white apartment building in Notting Hill. Her host for the night, former colleague and old friend Ned Silver, appeared at the door, dishevelled.

"Congratulations, journalist of the year," he said, smiling broadly. He gave her a hug, which she briefly leaned into. He smelled of strong cologne and wine.

"Just let me in, will you," she said, pushing past him.

"Shona, Jesus. What's the matter?" he said, arms outstretched.

"I've just fallen into a midden," she said, tearing off her coat and bag. "I need to pull myself out."

"And here's me thinking you loved journalism," he said, chuckling, following her.

"A drink," she said, "that's what I'd love."

They were alone in the duplex apartment; Ned's wife and daughter were away. Unseasonal flowers in elegant vases were dotted around the clean surfaces. A black metal spiral staircase led from the spacious living room and kitchen to a roof terrace. After small talk, Shona had pointed upwards, and they had made themselves comfortable in metal chairs on the wooden decking.

On the roof, the stars were invisible. The light of London blocked out the universe. Ned brought her whisky and, when she said she was hungry, a burnt cheese toastie. She smiled at its charred crusts but ate it hungrily.

"Well, I needed some carbon in my diet," she said, brushing black crumbs from her lap and raising an eyebrow.

He shrugged. "Bee does the cooking. Did they not feed you at the shindig?"

"I'm glad some things haven't changed," she said, ignoring his question.

"Like what?"

"Like you being a lazy sod."

"I've never been truly lazy," he said, smiling. "I just closely audit my activity. I can't spread myself too thin."

"*Thin* is not a word I would ever really have associated with you, Ned."

He gasped. "Now, now, Shona—that's a low blow."

"My favourite kind," she said.

They grinned at each other. Below were quiet streets, and across from them, like another revealed land, the roofs of London stretched to a short horizon, slanted and flat, tilted and towered. Aeroplanes blinked in the electric sky. To the east, the far-off towers of the City flashed gilt and sparkle. Shona saw before her a city of cells, a walled garden of glittering enclosed electric spaces.

"Look, thanks for having me," she said. They talked for a while, somewhat stiffly, of how they were, how they had been, and about Shona's award. Ned had invited her to stay as soon as the shortlist for the media awards had been announced, offering her the spare room. He said it was the least he could do.

Now they talked and drank whisky. Ned said he was sorry about her father and how much he had liked Hugh Sandison. What a gentleman he was, what a great journalist he was, in his time. Shona peered at Ned as they talked. He did not seem quite real. She had not seen him for years. He had left journalism, left the *Edinburgh Post*, left Scotland—left her. He had married a London lawyer and entered the world of public relations and marketing. He was doing well, it seemed, in some kind of media consultancy, and was comfortable living here, in one of London's most expensive and least troubled quarters. He had jettisoned the past. There was no sign of it, here.

It seemed absurd now. Or a dream. But she had loved a version of this man once. But not enough. And that Ned had changed. He had been replaced by another. His hair was shaved very short, and he had a light but barbered beard, silvery around the chin. His eyes seemed larger, more watery. Deep lines were ingrained beneath his eyes, but he was wearing better clothes. He had once been sloppy, with a mushroom of shaggy hair that did not seem to know whether it was growing out or up. That person was long gone. His voice was the same—a light tenor, and a growly, mildly Northern bass when he was speaking direct from his heart. Which wasn't often.

"So . . . your dad," he said again.

"He's in a pot in my flat," she said as calmly as she could manage.

"Have you thought of a . . . a final resting place?"

She shrugged.

"On his blessed allotment?"

She took a gulp of whisky. "I don't know. And I can't decide whether to keep the allotment or let it go. I can't see myself gardening every week. I don't have a green thumb. I have a cursed thumb. Things die. I can barely keep a cactus alive."

He nodded and looked down into his glass. The reflection of the city's light was held there, in drifting lozenges.

"So where exactly is your daughter?" Shona asked, pulling a rug over her knees.

"Sleepover at her pal's. A lovely family. They live in a mansion in Barnes. Have a boat on the Thames. They're richer than you, or even I, can possibly imagine. London is not like anywhere else in this country, is it?"

"Aren't these the kind of people you work for?"

"It pays for the school fees. And provides a cushion for the future. Whatever that may bring."

"You like London now?" she said, teasing. "You used to hate the place."

He shrugged and gestured vaguely at the cityscape. "Every time I go somewhere else, for work, holidays, whatever, I think, we should live here instead. But London's pull is inescapable. Like a cosmic event. It sucks you back. And Bee has her work here, too. And, to be honest, I wouldn't go near the south coast. The future is in the north, somewhere. Yet to be decided."

"You have your work."

"Yeah. But the thing is, Shona, can I be honest?"

"There's always a first time," she said.

He whispered something inaudible.

"What?"

He shook his head, raised a hand and said he would fix more drinks. He suddenly smiled too brightly before reaching for her glass and disappearing downstairs.

"Right," Shona said softly. She felt herself relaxing. The city lights became gauzy and webbed, interlocking in flares and strobes.

Ned returned, and they drank their whisky in silence for a while.

"How's your new career?" she ventured.

"Oh, you know," he said. "It's transactional. There's no heart in it. But that's the world, isn't it? May as well be honest about it."

"Who do you work for?"

He shrugged. "Our client list is diverse. Look, they're a bunch of twats, really, to be honest, but—"

"But the money is good?"

"Very good. It has to be. What was it someone said? Marry for money, and you earn every penny. So it goes with me. Anyway, Shona multi-award-winning journalist Sandison, what are you going to do now? What's next for you?"

She shook her head. There were gears and wheels moving behind Ned's eyes that she could not identify or fathom.

"I was thinking about turning in," she said, swiping away the real question. "I'm knackered. The ceremony was such a farrago of bullshit. Then I had to . . . anyway, tomorrow I've got to go and meet someone about a story."

Ned did not seem to hear what she said. "You know what I mean. Your dad. That's a big thing. He was a big thing. For you. For anyone who knew you. How do you move on?"

She shook her head. She briefly remembered her father's desperate funeral. Masks on in the crematorium, and only her there, standing apart from the gloved registrar. A cold and lonely procedure. Observing rules and regulations, distancing. Everything atomised—everyone atomised.

And she remembered the end. His end. Her, his only child, smuggled into the silent ward by an exhausted nurse who bore the cruel red marks around her eyes from the days and weeks of masking, and her father lying there dead, no longer him, no longer her dad, but something else, as the machines whirred and the curtain swished as it was pulled on its track about her as if the world was no longer fit to see.

Shona had wept and shook at the inconsolable shock of it, and she had laid her head on his chest until she had been gently pulled away by kind hands. *"You need to go, love, you need to go . . ."*

And here she was, now, on a roof terrace in London. A siren shrieked somewhere in the depths of the city, and Ned stared, waited for her to speak.

"Yes," she said eventually. "It was a big thing. I don't really know what I'm going to do next. Apart from get more stories. Do my thing. Keep going. You know me: I need the dysfunction to function."

"Maybe, but that aside, you should cash in. You've just won an amazing award, well deserved, so I should bloody well think so," Ned said, surging on. "You should try and monetise—go on telly. Surely the BBC would have you on. Have you thought about doing some documentaries? You should do a podcast. People love those."

"Nah, sod that," she said. She could feel the alcohol seeping into her body, being absorbed, and she welcomed its fire and balm. "I'm too old for that malarkey."

"Shut up! You look younger to me," he said. "Maybe it's the hair . . ."

"It's the alcohol. It's pickling me."

"Maybe you should write a book? Get a big advance. TV serial rights."

"What—fiction? Fiction has its place, but the problem is non-fiction keeps happening to me. Then I have to write about it."

He opened his hands, as if temporarily defeated.

"Okay, well, just some ideas. Who you meeting tomorrow?"

She paused, then took a chance. "Actually, it's some political guy, from a think tank—you may know him. Reece Proctor?"

"Proctor?" Ned said. He seemed to think for moment. "No, not a dickie bird. I'll look him up. Is this who you're meeting tomorrow morning?"

"No. First, I have a lead on another story, a follow-up."

"Oh—now that's interesting. A follow-up to your big story? Who? Where?"

"Not telling," she said.

He leaned forward and smiled. "Come on, I'm intrigued. Who was the source for your big Brexit story? Surely only a few people in the country knew about that bill. I mean, did you get it from the bloody prime minister?"

She smiled. She would not tell. She could not; she did not know who or what Moriah was. Moriah was, perhaps, at the centre of government—conceivably a minister. Or a senior civil servant. Or a party worker. Maybe even a journalist—a compromised journalist who did not, or could not, run the story. Moriah could be a man or a woman, maybe even a group of people: an informal working party of concerned insiders operating under one name—a cell, a fifth column. Whoever Moriah was, it was certainly someone who was nervous about sending emails, dropping packages or printing hard copies. She had received the information from Moriah on a pen drive in a plain brown envelope with a typed address label.

"You know I can't say," she said. "Took me and Ranald six weeks to stand it up properly. I knew it was gold dust. And the source was accurate. Ranald wanted to know who it was, too, but I didn't even tell him. I couldn't risk it."

"Ranald doesn't know who the source is? Wow!"

"Nope. He trusted me. The lawyers wanted it, too, but I refused. It held up the publication of the story for a bit. The thing is, I knew it was all correct; I had the paperwork. Emails, WhatsApp messages, the whole thing, in a bundle. So when we went to the government press office for comment, they couldn't deny it. You know how it goes."

"How did they react?"

"A SpAd called me, shouting and swearing, but we had them. And it went to press the next day. The BBC were given a trail to run in the morning."

Ned shook his head. "So all that in one bundle straight from the source? They must have been sure they wouldn't get caught. That's breaking all kinds of rules, even the law, isn't it?"

Shona shrugged. Ned was beginning to annoy her. She did not want to talk any more about her source or discuss the minutiae of her job. Ned used to know how it all worked. Maybe he had forgotten—or wanted to forget.

In the morning, someone who knew the source would tell her more. Then she would go to the address in Holland Park and see what Proctor wanted to tell her. And ask why he had given her a mobile phone via a grim sex shop that stank of semen and shame.

Ned stood up and leaned against the metal rail. "I just hope you're being careful with all this stuff," he said quietly. "The government and their pals were nearly scuppered by your story. There are . . . will be a lot of nasty people set to profit in huge ways from all this deregulation. This loosening of bonds and boundaries. Lots of angry, greedy people. Powerful, well-connected and well-resourced people. Corporations with more assets than small countries . . ."

He was looking down into the street below, as if into deep water.

Shona frowned. "Yes. I know all about the Great British Freedom Act, Ned. I wrote the story. And are you actually warning me? Is that what this is?"

"No!" he said, raising a hand. He looked at her and then away. "Well, no and yes. I'm just worried, and I hope your boss is looking after you. Making sure you're being careful."

Shona drained her glass, and the last of the alcohol hit her in a tingling sliver of heat. "There's no need for you to worry about me."

Ned returned to his seat and spoke softly. "Remember, this is not new for me. I always used to worry about you."

"I know," she said. "I do remember some things. But your memories are not my memories."

Shona realised it was good to see Ned. Or if not actively good, then at least interesting. But there was always the rub—he had liked her too much. There was a hint of submission to his desire to be with her, back in the day. When they were both young, both careless and casual with everything—drink, drugs, clothes, people, truth, words—that submission could only be satisfied by one thing, the one thing that she had to give to him: herself. And she could never bring herself to do that.

"It's really good to see you," he said.

"Don't go all soppy on me," she said. This version of Ned was disappointing and predictable. He was in another world now. Something good had left him. Something else had replaced it.

"I'll take that in the opposite way of the spirit in which it was intended," he said.

She took out her phone for the first time since fleeing the awards ceremony. The blue screen glimmered. She had multiple messages and texts. She had missed several phone calls and a voicemail from Ranald. She would listen to them in the morning. Most of the texts were congratulations.

You're a superstar, her friend Viv said.

I knew that already sweetheart, Shona texted back.

She smiled, and Ned noticed and frowned slightly.

"Ach, let's get to bed," Ned said, rubbing his arms.

There was a joke to be made, but Shona did not make it.

7

"Hector, isn't that your call now?" Rhonda pointed accusingly to his laptop. "You can't ever, *ever* be late for a meeting with the chairman. He is a knight, you know."

"Of course. I'll just take it into a silence booth," Hector said, quickly disentangling the machine from its multiple ports and cables.

"Confidentiality cabin," Jordan piped up from behind his multiple screens.

"Cube of submission," Clara said.

"You're late," Kapp said.

Hector entered one of the three silence booths in the corner of the office. Its sealed door, thick walls and sound-proofed joints instantly muted the outside world. He felt as if he was inside foam packaging. He quickly connected his laptop and mouse and printed the attachment to the meeting invite. Time was ticking, and he was late to the call.

He clicked on the meeting request, and a series of windows flashed up. As he was late, he was automatically muted and his camera turned off. Hector was now a black box in the lower right of the screen, an anonymous silent square with *Ext. Aff.* as a title.

There were six other people in the meeting, only one of whom he knew. Some were visible onscreen, some were not. A bearded man in a wood-panelled office flashed up. His name was listed as Bruce Cowie. Hector guessed he was one of the new political advisors. His features were chiselled, all edges. He looked like he had hurt people—or wanted to. He was speaking into a phone, annoyed, as Hector's speakers came alive.

". . . the key thing is that the stakeholder group, Grendel, is squared away. Those who are not interested have now signed non-disclosure agreements. I'd like to thank everyone here for completing the essential stakeholder relations. Your work is done."

Sir Charles Dyce was also on the call. He was too close to his camera, his lips and nose bulging. It was unclear where he was; his background was blurred.

"Good," he said. "I like the list. Most of the big boys are there. Glad to see some of my personal recommendations have been taken forward. Happy to see the full memo when you're ready, Bruce."

Cowie cut in. "The main thing today is that Sir Charles and myself have had enough of sloppy risk management. We are not having the Rwanda scheme all over again. We're not having that here. Not on this matter. So Grendel is no longer Official Sensitive, it's Official Secret now. Okay? From this moment. And any addition or subtraction on Grendel comes through me. The full memo is with me and goes no further. Not even Cabinet Office can move a muscle on this without me knowing."

Hector noticed Cowie had a small tattoo on the left side of his neck. A blue diamond shape. It could have been a Kabbalah symbol. He leaned forward to see more clearly.

A colleague put up a virtual hand.

"Neil," Cowie said.

"Thanks, Bruce, thank you, chief exec," said Neil Mathers, a man with a gaunt face and a heavy thatch of grey hair. "Change in designation noted. Our list of stake—"

"Grendel," Cowie said.

"The final membership of Grendel," Mathers said, "I

don't think I've been forwarded that. If the Private Office could send that on, we can start to cascade that through the relevant teams and—"

"Stop there, Neil," Cowie rasped. "No more. Nope. I don't think you understand. Nothing is being forwarded to anyone. No *cascade*. Grendel is very much with me now. I hold the pen on the memo, and that'll be the case until the operational aspects are all in place."

Mathers nodded and put his silent mark on again. Then he turned off his video, and his face vanished.

"And given that designation, we all know the repercussions should this reach the open air," Cowie said, with emphasis on *open air*.

"On security matters . . . I have had assurances they are covered off," Dyce said. "With some diligence."

There was silence on the line.

"Now, on the matter of the legal aspects," Dyce began, "and how the Scottish government will react to—"

"The Scottish government will know their place," he said with relish. "This is not a devolved responsibility. The legalities are on the UK level. Brexit made this all possible. It was our green light. So we go around them," Cowie said. "St. Andrew's House will know nothing. This is why Capacity and Resilience exists, after all."

"We leave the European Convention—"

"That is the final step," Cowie said. "Everything hinges on leaving that. And that is a UK move. Then once A4 is out the way, we have Grendel ready, all good to go. On day one."

Silence.

Hector held a paused pen over his pad. Voices were speaking, but he was not listening. His mind had ceased to move, paused by stony boredom and calcifying fright.

"This is like building the damned Death Star," Dyce

barked. "It will appear fully formed, from deep space, all ready to go. I will be prepared to press fire. I cannot wait to make that phone call to the First Minister. Boom!"

Hector, broken from his reverie by the exclamation, squinted at the screen, perplexed. He thought someone had mentioned death. But no one seemed to be perturbed. Had someone just said *boom*?

A box on the screen came to life. A man, Doucet, with clipped red hair and clear-rimmed glasses. He had a fake background of a conifer-blanketed mountain range. He took more than a second to come off his mute setting, and Cowie muttered *for fuck's sake* under his breath.

"Sorry, stuck on mute," Doucet said. "Larry Doucet here. I'm here to represent the legal view. I note the secrecy designation. The new provisions we have prepared cover what is required for the trial in Scotland, in part but not in whole. The main issue, as we have previously said, is the denouncement of ECHR, the six-month departure period, and—"

"I've read your aide-mémoire, Harry."

"Larry," Doucet said quietly. "And then there are the regulations around security for—"

"Don't you worry about security," Dyce said. "I've said this before. We've got all the firms lined up. We're having a little get-together this weekend, actually."

"And the contracts—" Doucet murmured.

"There won't *be* contracts," Dyce said, distracted.

"Thanks, Larry," Cowie said. "Okay—I have another meeting. This time with real people. I mean, an in-person meeting. Also, this meeting is too big. I don't know why the roll call is this large. Who is on this call? We have myself, the Chief Executive, Mathers and Faucet—who else?"

Nothing stirred.

Still on camera, Cowie peered at his screen. "Ladies and gentlemen? Who is on this call?"

Larry Doucet and Neil Mathers unmuted themselves and repeated their names. Dyce said, "You know who I am."

"And I know who I am," Cowie said, "at least, most mornings. Who else is here?"

Hector did not dare to move. He was frozen. His finger hovered over his mouse button. His muted square stood unexplained on the screen, black like an open grave.

Cowie shook his head again, his eyes away from the camera, as if distracted by an email. "Look. Grendel is key to the agenda of the forward-facing activity of Capacity and Resilience," he said. "From now on I want in-person meetings only, on pain of death. No more virtual meets, okay?"

"Agreed," Dyce said, picking something from his teeth.

"Fine. This is the last time with this kind of theatre audience. And, for now, all the paperwork, submissions, notes, advice briefings—they stop. Okay? If anyone wants to discuss further, there are two guidelines: one—don't, and two—absolutely don't."

"Exactly," Dyce said. "So how long, in the full plan, are we waiting? Eighteen months?"

"A year, two years maximum," Cowie growled.

"Plenty of time for me to improve my golf game." Dyce laughed. "I'll be scratch by then."

Cowie continued: "Grendel is now signed and ready. Legally, we are waiting for the other shoe to drop. What cannot happen in the meantime is information indiscipline. Are we all agreed?"

There was, again, a bottomless digital silence.

Cowie nodded. "Right, I will take silence as assent. Thank you, everyone. Charlie, see you soon." Cowie's box disappeared.

THE DIARY OF LIES • 71

Everyone on the call followed suit.

Hector logged off as quickly as he could click his mouse. He sat back and breathed out heavily. He looked at the paper he had printed earlier—an agenda note. He folded it in two and slid it into his pocket.

As he left the booth, his mobile phone immediately buzzed with a text message. He smiled. It was from Adam Rokeby, asking if Hector fancied a pint after work.

Adam was a good friend. He was also a lawyer, an excellent one. Sandy would be sleeping; she wouldn't mind. Probably.

Absolutely, Hector replied.

Hector sloped back to his desk. Kapp was tapping at his computer, murmuring into a phone pinned between his raised shoulder and cheek. Rhonda was absent, her computer closed down. Clara had left to make her way home through the snow. Jordan was back at the photocopier, prodding buttons, sorting a jam and reloading paper into its wheezing innards. He looked up at Hector and smiled.

Hector checked his emails, a bold column of messages into which he had been copied. Carbon copied. Blind copied. Accidentally copied. Mysteriously copied. His eyes drifted over the unintelligible subject headings. In his former life, he had known how to chase, query, write and file a news story. This was a different beast. This constant, updating digital waterfall of information, anxious queries, orders, reactions and redirections fed his panic and chewed at his innards.

"You all right, my friend?" Kapp eyed Hector from across the desk. "How was the meeting?"

"To be honest, I'm not sure," Hector said. "They were talking about something called Grendel? I didn't follow all of it. And then there was some chat about security and accommodation and the ECHR?"

Kapp narrowed his eyes. "Sounds like it's nothing for us to get involved in. I would slope the shoulders, let it slide away."

"Hmm, I don't know . . ." Hector said. He was looking with a sudden blank horror at ten linked emails about mandatory online training. He had to complete it within the week. He thought of Shona's view of such training and suddenly, violently agreed: he would rather drill a hole into his head.

Grendel was bothering him. What was obligatory? What was secret? Why had they discussed security?

"This angry guy, Cowie, said it was now secret," he murmured, "this Grendel thing. Have you heard of it?"

Kapp shook his head, his ears suddenly as pink as ham. "No. Did the political advisor speak to you on the call?"

"No."

"Did he see you?"

"No."

"Well, I'm sure it will be fine. Look—if I were you, unless you have anything on the go for tomorrow, I would sign off and trundle on home through the winter wonderland."

Hector looked up at the clock on the wall. It was nearly five. He texted Sandy, told her he was going to meet Adam for a quick catch-up. He packed away his things, swung his bag over his shoulder and said goodbye to Kapp, who nodded slowly. Jordan waved cheerfully from his post at the photocopier, blue light flashing over his white face.

What you having? Adam texted him from the pub.

Every single drink they have, Hector texted back.

He tapped his security pass, and the doors opened like jaws. It was pitch-black outside. Alacrity House was ablaze with light, every window a rectangle of depthless yellow. The hulk of the building, with a new canopy of snow, looked like a beached ship stuck in an icy bay.

The city's streets and wynds had become treacherous underfoot. Hector cursed as he slithered along icy paths, avoiding the deep drifts. A walk that should have taken ten minutes took double that time, and he was breathing heavily by the time he reached the top of Broughton Street on the border of the New Town. From its height, he could see lights glimmering across the Firth of Forth, the distant hills white as paper. A tram's dinging bell sounded as it glided past him.

The tip of his nose was pink, his cheeks were frozen and his hands were beginning to redden by the time he reached the glowing gold of the pub, which sat at the foot of the street, opposite a lightless gothic church. Hector stumbled across the threshold as if falling into the warm arms of a lover. The pub was full of unwinding workers, chatting couples and old men staring into pints looking for any answers which did not involve more drinking. Adam Rokeby, a dark-haired and dapper man in a plum suit and gleaming white shirt, was sitting at a small table by the log fire.

"Hector," Adam said, gesturing to a pint and chaser which were standing ready for his friend on the wooden table. They hugged briefly, more of a shoulder bump, and settled by the blazing fire.

Hector swung his bag from his shoulders and, with a sigh, dropped it on the floor next to Adam's.

Adam's eyes narrowed as he regarded his friend's face.

"Bad day?" he said.

T,

I am snowed in. I shall carve a northwest passage through to the provision store. Sherry and port.

You won't remember. But there was a winter in Zermatt, and you rather enjoyed the snow. You were small, perhaps three or four. Your mother was ill. We had helpers. You went sledging. It was the oil crisis then, and I was busy. I should have stayed longer, of course. I used to ski well, you know. I saw these men in Finland, once, who could ski downhill and fire unerringly with their (excellent) sniper rifles as they descended. Remarkable people, the Finns. Drink too much, of course, but, then, I think we all drink too little.

I have organised the "living room" although I am unclear how much actual "living" will be done there. I have a very nice, beautifully framed picture of your son. He looks like you. Growing fast. He needs a haircut. He resembles Blondel. Prince Valiant. Or perhaps Childe Roland, who to the dark tower came.

This is new to me, writing in this way. I never went in for hobbies, as others did—gambling, or women, or boys, or sailing or cricket or whatever took their fancy. I do like my soldiers (undercoats currently drying in square formation, ready to receive a cavalry charge), but that is hardly a vice. And, of course, because of the limited readership of my writing, I do not have to lie. It could all be lies—and who would know?

Outside, I can hear people clearing the pathways. I am not sure why. It is a snow day; let us accept it. White and clear and, momentarily, frozen. There is nothing that can be done about it. It won't last forever.

They still haven't found you. I do ask. Often. Somehow, though, I do know that you are near. Which is why I am here, after all—to be closer to you.

Later—
The man in Suffolk came back to me. The double agent we found alone in his house, reading a book, his silly bint of a wife naked and drunk in the garage, raving. He was a quiet man, a reader, a scholar. Sold us out for money—money for his many addictions. A soft man, a shell. I observed only his first interrogation. After that, we reduced him. It was 1978—we did things in that way. He told us nothing. What was there to tell? I remember his mild face, his mild voice. He cried when I laid it out to him. Not for himself, I don't think. Just at the utter vacuum of it all. The meaninglessness.

I remember as I went through his house, looking out to the fens, the beauty of the light on the still water, the whispering trees, the screaming of his wife, the clunk of the car doors, I wondered where God was. The God of my youth: the quiet voice in the chancel. The falling light in the hushed cathedral. The murmurs in the quadrangle. Where was the sweet, elegant, calm Anglican God in all this, the petty, ugly, violent interactions of mankind? Nowhere. Gone.

He died in jail—he cut his own throat.

8

London was awake, and cars were purring on the streets outside as Shona ate breakfast. There was a hum and a bustle beyond the brick walls and windows of the apartment.

"So where are you meeting this contact?" Ned said. He was making Shona coffee.

"A place in Holland Park," she said. She cringed internally: she did not want to meet Proctor again. But, if he had smuggled a package to her and was prepared to meet her on a Saturday, he might have a story, and it might be a good one. He'd said he wanted to talk about monsters. Was he a monster?

"But, first, I have to meet someone at the Civic Gallery," she said, "so I'll go into town and come out again. After Holland Park, I catch my train north. What you up to today?"

Ned shrugged and mumbled his way through a list of domestic and professional chores as if recounting a dream which made less sense the more he proceeded.

Shona's phone had been bright with text messages, including ever more drunken texts from Ranald, who had clearly been partying well into the early hours. The journalism award was nestling heavily in her bag. She dimly wondered what she would do with it. In the past she had given them to her father, who used them as bookends on his bedroom shelves. His room in her small Lochend flat was still untouched. Dust gathering on his books. His clothes greying around the shoulders. She would need to empty his room sometime. Not for a while, though. He would be dead a long time.

"Look—before you go," Ned said, "I just wanted to say it's been good to see you again and can we not leave it so long next time?"

"Maybe," she said vaguely, responding to Ranald's texts. After noting his last two messages made no sense, she told him she might have found a new story. He didn't reply.

"Great. Magic," Ned said, with a bitter laugh. "Thanks for your attention. How about as friends on social media, then?"

"Nah, I'm not on it."

"Not even for your work?" Ned seemed to plead. Shona suspected he had probably searched for her online, to no avail. He wanted her back in his life, in some way, and she was not clear how that could happen.

"Honestly, I don't understand why I should, or would. I've no desire to have a following, to be public in that way," she said. "I've some logins for various platforms, but they're anonymous accounts. I just use them for lurking and sending messages."

"Is that how you got the source for your big story?"

"Come on, Ned," she said, plucking a tiny shred of bacon from her plate and standing up. "You were a hack once—you know fine well we don't tell anyone who our sources are."

"I know!" he said, smiling. "So—"

"So what?

"You're saying we can't be Facebook friends?"

"Ned, just give it up," she said.

"At least can I give you a lift to King's Cross? When you're done."

"Maybe, sure."

Shona got her things together quickly and shouted to Ned that she had to dash. He was waiting at the door, chewing his lower lip, seemingly on the brink of saying something profound—and she wanted to leave before he did. She rushed past him as he pondered, descending the tight stairs as best she could, she heard him call out, but she could not hear the words. She waved a wordless goodbye.

She stepped into the new day. The morning air was fresh on her face. The sky, icy and cloudless. There had been heavy snow in Scotland, but as she walked, her stick tapping its beat beside her, the way forward was clear.

Within an hour, she was crossing Trafalgar Square towards the Civic Gallery. The 1960s concrete block, located beside the columned elegance of the National Gallery, exhibited temporary shows, and its vast glass-ceilinged central hall—a former trading hall for wool, cotton and hemp merchants—held popular contemporary art shows.

The square was humming with tourists. Nearby, a man was bent over an acoustic guitar, playing a series of indie standards through a little speaker, on which he sat.

The rattling tube ride from Notting Hill had been straightforward. The deeper into the city she delved, the more she thought of her last tentative connection with the gallery. A few years previously, she had written a story about a painting which had been given to the people of Scotland by an aristocratic family—Olivia Farquharson's family. The painting was not what it seemed: instead of being a forgotten masterpiece by Charles Rennie Mackintosh, the noted Scottish architect and artist, it was discovered to have been painted by his wife, Margaret.

Shona had broken the story. Some noses were put out of joint. Most dramatically, the director of the Public Gallery in Edinburgh was found dead—a crime that remained unsolved—and the source for her story, Thomas Tallis, a rumpled man with the air of a tortured pilgrim, an art expert who used to work for the Civic, had vanished. The police had dredged Scottish lakes and searched the rivers. But nothing was found. He had left the Farquharsons' country house and walked out into the night. Shona had been the last person to speak to him.

Shona did not go up the forbidding black steps—which were already thronged with dithering tourists and excited children—to the main gallery entrance. Instead, she slipped down a side alley to an entrance for staff, caterers and cleaners. Her stick skidded on the cobbles, her balance thrown.

A tall man, wearing a black suit and striped T-shirt, passed her, then looked back as he approached the door. He turned to her. "Do you mind my asking—are you here for the symposium?" His eyes flicked to her walking stick.

"I am," she said, smiling. "Actually, I'm one of the speakers."

"Oh, fantastic! I'm not sure this is the right way in."

"Me, neither," she said. "I'm running late, too."

"Well, you mustn't be late. Shall we find out how to get in?" he said, with a nervous laugh.

"Oh, let's," Shona said. "Time's a-wasting."

Beside the staff entrance was a window from which a young man with a lanyard around his neck and a spray of freckles across his face peered. The door opened, and two men in blue overalls bustled out, their hands white with paint.

"Are you here for the Vali Grammaticus symposium?" the young man's voice said, filtered electronically.

"Yes, we are. Leeds City Council," the tall man said. Shona nodded, as if in agreement.

"Names?"

"Tim Small."

"Honeysuckle," Shona found herself saying. Tim Small peered at her for a moment.

The young man looked up from a document and looked

intently at her. He pressed something on his desk and the door opened, leaking noise and light into the alley.

As Tim Small ducked under the door frame and headed off, the young man came out of his office in a swish of dexterous efficiency. "Ms. Grammaticus said you would be here. Are you related? I can call her workroom, if you like?"

"Yes," Shona said, gripping her stick hard. "I'm the niece."

"Miss Honeysuckle?"

"Yes," Shona said, nodding. "If you could tell her I am here."

"I shall!" the young man said with a single raised finger. "Back shortly!"

Shona stood in the doorway and did a quick search on her phone for Vali Grammaticus. She found multiple entries, all relating to a now-elderly artist, a creator of large, complex sculptures. There were pictures of her in Venice, in Los Angeles. It appeared that Ms. Grammaticus held a formal position at the Civic Gallery. There was a press release:

We are delighted that one of the world's most esteemed living artists, Valerian "Vali" Grammaticus, will be the Civic Gallery's resident artist for the next two years. The Turner Prize–winning sculptor, 80, will be realising one of her most powerful, moving sculptures in collaboration with many bereaved families—as well as volunteers, family researchers, fellow artists, public health officials and social work experts—on The Names of the Lost, *a large-scale memorial to the dead of the COVID-19 pandemic. When completed, this epic work will fill the Trading Hall of the Civic Gallery . . .*

The young man reappeared.

"Please come through. Vali has been waiting for you," he said.

Shona followed him.

They entered a different space—white corridors with hard

lighting and stone floors. Pipes ran overhead, and bundles of electrical wires stretched along the walls. There were no windows, and the guts of the building hummed with climate control and air conditioning.

They turned a corner and entered a large space which stretched to a surprising distance. It had been divided into many offices and studios with glass partitions. Light came from high windows, which framed the blue London sky. At the far end of the room was a small central courtyard, with red bricks, adjacent to one side of the concrete cube of the Civic.

Several people were working on laptops; they looked up briefly when Shona entered, then returned to their work. The longest wall was lined with shelves, which were stacked with hundreds of bulging ring binders. A young woman was pulling one from the wall as Shona entered—it looked heavy.

At the centre of the room was a large metal-legged table. Placed on it was a maquette, a cardboard cube with one side removed and, inside, a multitude of wires strung with tiny glass globes.

A slim woman in dark, simple clothes, with a hawkish face and long steel-grey hair, was bent over the model, one hand on her hip, the other at her chin.

She looked up as Shona and the receptionist entered. "Ah, Martin, thank you," she said, nodding to the young man. "Please come back in twenty minutes." She turned to the rest of the room. "Would everyone else take a break? My niece and I have things to discuss."

In one slow-motion group shrug, the young assistants picked up their laptops and, murmuring, left the room with Martin.

"Honeysuckle?" Shona said, with half a smile. Vali tilted her head in acknowledgement.

"My middle name. My late mother was many things, but she was very fond of flowers," the woman said.

"Please call me Shona."

"I know who you are," Vali said. "You're quite well known, you know."

Shona shivered, shook her head, and moved to the model and peeked into it. She could see it was a replica of a large space, with the representation of a human at its base. The model figure seemed to be pointing up at the wires.

"That is our work," Vali said in a measured, deep voice.

"Can you tell me what it is?"

"That is the Trading Hall," said Vali, putting a hand on the model. Her hands were long and pale, spattered with liver spots, her nails short and bitten. Her scent was cool and expensive. "Every light hanging there represents a victim of the pandemic. More than two hundred thousand. At some point, we will have to draw a line because people are still dying. But we have two hundred thousand to begin with. So these wires—we hope they are unseen—will hold the majority of the lights. And then, between them, moving, will be these small drones, also holding lights. They will move between the stationary lights in successive, tidal, airborne waves. They will be powered for the day and recharged overnight."

"Quite an undertaking," Shona said. One of those lights was her father. She was that tiny cardboard figure pointing upwards, stunned, into the sea of loss.

"That is not the hard work," Vali said evenly. "Lights and fittings and drones, lattice and matrix, we can do. The hardest work—what we are really engaging with now—is the links between each light. The familial connections. The friendships. The work and play associations. The orbits and gravities. None of the lights shine in isolation. We are halfway through the deep research. The lights will be plotted into a constellation map so that you can find your loved ones. There will be a galaxy of the names of the lost. That is our aim.

"You see, information is one thing, but structure is another. For a long time, we were considering the example given to us of molecules, even of subatomic patterns. So we could gather the lights in that way: bound by unseen forces, clustered and combined. But it was a blind alley. It was confusing to look at in the computer models, and, also, we did not want the work to be medical. I did not want it to look like some DNA sculpture. So we looked to the stars instead. After all, that is where the dead go, some say, and from where we all certainly came."

They stood for a moment in contemplation. The sun glinted on steel edges and wood, on pencil tips and the curved rims of coffee cups.

"Let's have some tea in my studio," said Vali, showing Shona into an adjoining room. There were two leather-bound chairs, a desk, a computer and bookshelves stuffed with reference books and papers, magazines and cardboard tubes. Vali made tea in silence and handed a small green mug to Shona. It had no milk or sugar. Shona sipped it anyway and suppressed a wince.

"In the old days, I would have offered you a proper drink. But no more." Vali moved to the door and closed it. "So. Espionage . . ."

Shona noticed her deep green eyes, an air of surveillance. Vali's face was hardly marked by time. "You sent me a message," she said. "About Moriah."

"I am Moriah's interlocutor," Vali said, sitting back in her chair. "I cannot say I asked for the role, but we are . . . connected. He is a little younger than me, of course. He is a nervous and angry man, but, these days, a better man than he used to be."

"You know I don't know who Moriah is," Shona said. "I did not know he was even a man. What can you tell me?" She sipped the tea again, the taste of which she couldn't quite identify.

Vali blinked. "Do you always speak so quickly, Shona?" she said. "It is Glasgow, isn't it, where you are from? Maybe you are like the cockneys, here in London. They speak so fast because they want to make sure you don't wander off, I think. To catch people's attention."

"I'll slow down," Shona said. "Sorry."

Vali looked out of the window. "Forgive me. That was rude. I'm a little nervous. I am an artist, not a spy. You should know I sent you the pen drive from here. It went through the gallery's post system. We both thought it would be a good way of occluding the source."

"It was," Shona said. She was growing impatient now. Moriah had given her one of the biggest stories of her life—she wanted more. She wondered if Vali was lying: was Grammaticus Moriah? But how would she have access to information from the heart of government? Moriah could be a husband, a colleague, perhaps a son, a lover. "Can you tell me more about Moriah?"

"No," Vali said, "I can't. We knew you were in London to pick up your award. Well deserved, I must say. Moriah was anxious about sending any more packages after the press coverage. These things can be intercepted, and he distrusts electronic transmissions. So I have a message for you, from him, which you can take in any which way you want. And I should add: I don't want to see you again and you mustn't come back. Not to me. This will be our first and last meeting."

"What's the message?"

Vali opened a drawer in her desk and took out a torn piece of paper, which she passed to Shona. "Forgive the note. He was in a rush to get away and he said to wait for ten days, which I have. That is my handwriting, so there is no need to get a graphologist involved."

She reached into another drawer and picked out a packet of cigarettes. She slid one out and lit it. There was a brief crinkle of burning paper, then a small bite of tobacco and mint in the air.

"I have been told to put it in the shredder once you have read it," Vali said.

Shona looked at the paper. Two words, written in an elegant hand, in black ink: *Find Grendel.*

"Find Grendel?"

"That is the message," said Vali and exhaled a stream of smoke. She stood up and moved to the window, which she unlocked. Fresh air and the low hum of London entered the room.

"Anything more?" Shona said, staring at the paper in her hand, exasperated.

Vali shook her head. "No. And you better be going." She stubbed out the barely smoked cigarette on a silver dish and pointed to the office door.

"I'm not sure whether I should thank you or not," Shona said uncertainly.

"I'll have that back, please." Vali held out her hand.

Shona stared at the words and returned the paper to Vali. Vali took it gently, and then ripped it into small pieces. She dropped them in the ashtray.

As they left the room, Shona glanced at the artwork and said, "My father will be one of your lights. He will be one of your names."

Vali walked on through the cluttered office. "I am very sorry to hear that."

"He died in the first wave, before there were tests. Before the vaccine," Shona said.

Vali stopped at the office door, behind which Martin was waiting to take Shona back to the outside world.

"Well, then, he will be there. He will be a light," the artist said, her voice softer now.

"His name was Hugh—Hugh Sandison," Shona said.

Vali looked to the wall of files. There was a brief smile. "Well, his name will be in there somewhere. I will look. If it is not, I will make sure my team get onto it," she said. "I am sorry for your loss. There has been so much loss. You are part of it."

Shona moved closer to the artist, anxiety rising in her throat. "I need more. I need more than just two words," she whispered. "You said Moriah was going away—where has he gone?"

Vali looked at her impassively.

"Come on. Two words is almost no message at all," Shona said. "It's almost pointless coming here—a waste of my time and yours."

"He has gone north—to your country. To Scotland," Vali said quietly.

"Where?"

"No more," Vali said, resting her hand on Shona's shoulder. "It is part of my duties in life to . . . watch over Moriah . . . I will say that. But that is it." She turned away and strode back across the workroom. "Thank you for coming, Shona."

"Scotland," Shona said to herself.

She left the room, and Martin escorted her to the exit. The sky was still icy blue. The crowds of London jostled around her. She checked the time. She had another story to chase.

She thought of the word *Grendel* as she made her way to Holland Park. Grendel was the beast from the poem *Beowulf*, she knew that. A fiend in the shadows. A walker across boundaries. A mark-stepper. A descendant of Cain, the first killer of men.

Drifting in her daydream, she found a tube station and descended into it, as if pulled by unseen wires into a life not of her own making.

Not much sleep. When I dreamt, I saw teeth and blood. Great hills of flashing teeth. I saw a man with a sore on his chest. He pushed and pulled at it. I told him not to. He pressed the sore and out came a white head, then a white body, which dropped to the floor beside him. Then it sat up, an identical copy, all in white, like fat or lard. Then the other man ate him. I woke up.

The snow still lies, thick, but with a thin coating of ice now on top. Bad for driving.

I was pondering the concept of revenge. However, revenge without a target is a futile, neutered thing. A castrated urge. Rather like me, in this little cottage in the back of beyond. Reduced and diminished.

There is a new snowfall now, falling in slow spirals past the window. It looks like silver ash. I have a new bottle of sherry to open.

Have I ever mentioned my God? I must talk about my God.

I did not agree with much of the doctors' analysis. But one thing I did agree on: life is hard on all of us. And we're all doing quite badly.

9

Adam Rokeby and Hector Stricken were very drunk. The pub was now dark. They were the only drinkers left. It was past closing time, but the barman had not yet called time—he was drying glasses and appeared to be studiously ignoring the tall redheaded man and his well-dressed friend slumped in the corner.

The firelight flickered on the faces of Hector and Adam, who, having passed through beer, were now onto whisky.

Hector's vision, having spent a few fuzzy seconds birling out of his conscious control, was now fixed on the snow outside, the thick white fall which now glowed amber beneath Broughton Street's descending line of lights.

Their coats lay in a heap on a chair. They had been discussing mistakes. Mistakes others had made, and mistakes made in their own lives. Hector, encouraged by Adam's warm empathy—the hand clasps, shoulder taps and reassuring hums—had been outlining how, in leaving journalism for the civil service, he had made a gross error of judgement. How he was bewildered and confused by the new job and its demands. How disastrous the press event had been, and how ashamed he had felt after the press had finally left. How he had felt unable to cope, to keep a cool head.

Then, to change tack, he told Adam that he had attended a curious meeting.

"I had no real idea what they were talking about, why they were talking about it, what I was doing there, or whether I should even have been there," Hector said, eyeing the whisky, caramel and kind, in his hand.

"Grendel?" Adam said. "The monster?"

"Like in *Beowulf*," Hector said, picking up a final crisp from an opened packet. "There was some talk of security, of not informing the police. The political advisor was being a total dick, and the boss, Sir Charles Dyce, was chuntering on like he didn't know what the hell was going on."

"But what is it, this Grendel?"

"A new thing, a new policy, maybe? But they were talking about European law, about accommodations? I mean, I haven't a clue. What could it be?"

Adam rubbed his chin and drank some more. "Maybe an event? Look—Scotland hosts big multinational conferences—COP, NATO, the G7—doesn't it? All that stuff. Maybe there's some shindig in the Highlands being planned. Some big show-off international get-together? The US president, the leaders of Europe . . ."

Hector was unconvinced. "It didn't sound like that kind of thing. And it felt as if everyone was trying to avoid being precise."

"Who else was in the room?" Adam asked.

"It was virtual. There was no room," Hector said. "Various higher-ups who I didn't know. Lawyers. Senior staff. I was just hiding there like a wee boy in a cupboard. Ach, I'll probably find out more tomorrow—whenever that is." He frowned at his watch, as if it was lying to him.

"You should. Anything with a code name has to be interesting."

"Hold your horses. Even if I find out more, I'm not going to tell you about it, Mr. Rokeby." Hector smiled, leaning forward. "Forget it. There's a security code, you know . . . I've signed my life away. I can't tell anyone. Can't mention a word of it. More than my life's worth."

Adam burst out laughing. "But you've just told me about it."

"You got me drunk. You've put me at a disadvantage." Hector held his arms out and grinned. "Fucking *code*s," he said, suddenly serious. "What has my life become?"

Adam looked into the fire. His eyes flared. "Is the security tight at your place? Is it all top secret?"

"My first week, we were all turfed out onto the street," Hector said. "Some bampot had taped a speech of himself and sent it to the chief exec. An old VHS. Security thought it was a bomb. Everyone was out on the pavement while the cops worked out what it was. Think they blew it up anyway, just to make sure. Another waste of time. My life seems like wasted time now, you know?"

"Every job involves enormous wastes of time," Adam said. "That's why the Americans call their salaries *compensation*. To nominally compensate you for burning through the prime years of your life like a box of matches. But think about what you've signed up to: finally, you have some stability, better hours and, at the end of the day, the blessed pension."

"I won't bloody need a pension at this rate," Hector said. "I'll be long gone. Look at me now. Paralytic on a school night."

Adam sank his last dram. He was a handsome man, his face open and kind. He took his appearance seriously. As a lawyer, he had to. A trace of his Portuguese mother could be seen in his thick dark hair, his brown eyes.

"This Grendel . . . didn't the Viking fellow pull his arm off in the story?" he said, trying to recall the legend.

"Oh, wouldn't that be nice? I could get time off sick with an arm ripped off," Hector murmured. Adam snorted. "Probably get full sick pay, being armless. They'd definitely sign me off for that."

"Maybe that's what this Grendel is!" Adam said, with an air of triumph. "Maybe it's an arms sale?"

"Funny," Hector said.

There was silence for a time. Adam was swilling the dregs of his whisky as if they could be shaken back to life.

"I've made some too, you know," he said quietly. "Mistakes. Terrible mistakes."

Hector looked into the fire. His eyes were moist with the heat. "Oh yeah, Adam—what's the worst mistake you've ever made? Top lawyer, loaded, handsome devil."

"I should have done something else with my life," Adam said. "You know, a lot of my friends at law school became human rights lawyers, defence lawyers, or worked for the unions, Legal Aid."

"Yeah? Admirable."

"Yes, and look at me," Adam said, pulling at the lapels of his bespoke suit. "I just make money for idiots. Corporate deals for greedy arseholes. Private equity crap. People pay me a fortune, and I pocket the cash. Aren't I honourable?"

"Well, it's a service—"

"It's literally *nothing*, Hector. I add *nothing* to the world," Adam said, looking into the fire. "I just reinforce what's already there. Help people shift money about. I consent to the world as it is. And look at the world. It's falling apart. So what am I part of? Thank God my mother's not alive to see it. Or me. My complicity."

Adam had struggled to pronounce complicity; he grinned and wiped his mouth.

"You sound like me now." Hector smiled. "Self-pity. Come on, we're getting past the point of no return here. We're heading into the booze blues."

"We should all play the blues, Hector. Look at the shadows we cast. We're all living in the hard light of a burning world."

A charred log settled in the fire, sending a sudden shower of sparks fiercely into the chimney.

"Time, gentlemen," the barman said. "That's me closing up now."

"But it pays the bills, doesn't it?" Adam said eventually. "And we can forget about the rest. Forget about everyone else."

"Oh, Adam," Hector said with a smile.

"We are all different people at different times," Adam slurred. His voice sounded distorted. "From moment to moment, from hour to hour, from day to day. Our names mean nothing. We are nameless. From year to year, who are we? . . . All infinitely temporary, all contingent . . ."

Hector felt his eyes suddenly closing. He opened them with effort, then they closed again. He needed to go home, to sleep. He wanted to hold Sandy and kiss the baby. His head swilled like Adam's shaken whisky.

"You need to find out about that weird thing," the voice of Adam said, somewhere beyond the pleasant crimson darkness of Hector's eyelids.

"You're right! I need to find out about the *weirdness*," Hector exclaimed, opening his eyes, standing up and knocking back his chair, which clattered loudly on the stone floor. He reached across for his coat and picked up his bag, which somehow felt much heavier. "Better get back to the lady. Back to the baby. Who you seeing? You're not seeing anyone at the minute, are you?"

"I'm alone as the moon," Adam mumbled.

"What the hell happened?"

"As the man nearly said, *no woman delights not me—no, nor man either.*"

"What man said what?" Hector said, struggling to hoist the bag over his head without knocking off his glasses.

"The Earl of Oxford," Adam laughed. "If you believe the toffs."

The barman was now pointedly holding the door open. They stumbled outside. The door closed behind them, and suddenly all was hush. There was a cutting wind. Hector could see his breath. Adam stamped his feet. Coronas of silver and bronze circled the streetlamps. The two men slowly made their way through rutted snow to Picardy Place. As they climbed Broughton Street, the neoclassical ruin atop Calton Hill glimmered in blue light.

They reached the tram stop; a taxi appeared, its yellow sign glowing. Adam lived in Morningside, in the tree-lined, open spaces of the south side of the city—the opposite direction to Hector, who lived in the north, in the huddled tenements of Leith.

Hector urged Adam to take the taxi. He'd decided to walk home. He needed to sober up, to get some fresh air, at least. The trams had stopped for the night, but he did not have far to go. And it was all downhill.

Adam agreed. "You're going to be all right, my man," he said, his arms tight around his friend, his mouth close to Hector's ear. He felt warm and strong. He smelled strongly of drink and cigarettes. He then stood back and grinned. "It was so good to see you. And, look, sleep on all this. No mistake is the end of anything: things always change. I trust you. You are good enough," he said, his voice sonorous.

Hector nodded, not knowing what to say. He needed to get home. He raised a hand to say goodbye as Adam hollered something before disappearing into the black cab.

Hector was alone. The streets were empty. His last whisky was thick on his tongue and fiery still in his gullet.

Edinburgh was dead in the snow.

"Deadinburgh," he said to himself.

His bag was heavy on his shoulder. Definitely much heavier. He looked down at it. He touched soft black leather. Unlike his own, which was a cheap nylon laptop bag from the office.

"Oh, fuck," he moaned.

He'd picked up the wrong bag: he had Adam's, and Adam had his. Hector peered down the white road. The taxi had long gone. He fumbled for his phone in his coat pocket and called Adam. It rang out. Hector left a halting message. In his bag were his papers from work, his pass for the office and his laptop. He needed them back before work in the morning.

He swore again. He would call Adam first thing—they were both early risers, and he could nip into Adam's office on the way to work. He told himself that everything would be fine. He looked in Adam's bag. There were several blue paper folders, a yellow notepad and a nest of charging cables. There was a single apple and a collection of crumpled bus tickets.

His balance was off kilter. He stopped to hold a railing for a moment. When he reached his street—a canyon of high tenements off the Walk, its cars now all white-roofed, the hedges a confusion of line and form—the flats seemed to lean inwards. Blank windows stared, implacable, like a convinced jury.

As he neared home, his phone lit up. A message from Adam: *WTF? Grendel?*

Hector stared at the message and did not know how to respond.

He opened his apartment door and fell across the threshold, forlorn, incapable, as if tumbling into a grave.

10

Shona arrived at 7 Sheldrake Gardens, Holland Park.
The large white town house was just visible behind a
high wall, and she could see an ochre gravel drive snaking
through manicured bushes. She looked at her phone; she was
half an hour early.

She leaned on her stick and ran a finger under the strap
of her overnight bag. High above, a jet cut a slash of white
in blue. She looked at the drive; there were indentations of
car wheels. She followed them.

She thought suddenly of what the woman in the sex shop
had said of Proctor: *He's into violence.*

The two-storey house had a large portico and quartered
windows. A sports car was parked outside, a silver lozenge of
stilled liquid speed. Shona took a deep breath and walked to
the car. There was a half-drunk takeaway coffee in a holder,
and valet-cleaned surfaces. The registration number read
RCORP.

She turned away and walked up to the entrance. A flash
of red caught her eye—an estate agent's sign which had been
placed up against one of the fluted pillars. Soil still clung to
the point of its stake.

The glossy black door was ajar. She moved through it. Her
feet echoed in a spacious tiled white hall, empty of furniture,
devoid of decoration. The ghosts of pictures were traced in
squares. Brass light fittings had no bulbs.

There were open double doors ahead. She looked up the
stairs. Nothing moved. She could hear her own breathing
and the tap of her stick. She moved forward.

She entered a large, unfurnished room, with white carpet from wall to wall, French windows to the garden and, slumped against the far wall, a man's body.

His suit was torn. His right hand had smeared blood on the white wall. His head was down, hair matted with tacky blackness. One of his shoes was missing. A bare foot, horribly pale.

Her heart pulsed. She looked rapidly around the empty room, as if to find an answer, then approached the body and knelt down.

It was Reece Proctor. Or had been. His face had been smashed, and there was an awful hole in his forehead. One eye was a broken egg flooded with blood. His left hand was curled against his chest. There was a deep, rich iron stink. His wet mouth hung open, his silver tooth glittering.

He had wanted to talk to her about monsters.

There was a noise from above. Heavy, quick footsteps, moving with increasing speed from deep carpet to the creak of the landing's wooden floor and staircase.

She needed to hide. She remembered a slatted door in the hallway and moved to it as quickly as she could, then lurched inside. But the door did not lead anywhere—it was a small cupboard, rammed full with a bucket, mop, vacuum cleaner and shelves of cleaning products. She had no choice: she closed the door behind her.

She was gasping. She made herself stop, swallowed air quietly. Through the slats, she could see the room broken into lines.

The footsteps came closer, rising in number and volume, and, suddenly, a man entered the room. Small and wiry, he was wearing hooded black clothing and a medical mask that covered most of his face. He moved like an athlete. Slowly, crouching. In one hand was a hammer, its metal head wet and glistening.

Shona held her breath.

The man pulled back the hood and straightened up. His hair was long, tied back. He scanned the room, then turned round.

He looked straight at the cupboard door and paused. As still as a hawk above its prey.

Shona gripped her bag and closed her eyes. A series of things, people and places, moved rapidly across her mind.

Her father, a mask over his mouth, his lungs failing, the smell of bleach and the snap of hospital plastic . . .

A former lover, curled in bed, a deep yearning . . .

A man in a crumpled corduroy suit telling her about loss, about a fake painting, about how he himself was a fake, a bad copy . . .

The cupboard door opened with a snap.

Shona swung her bag as hard as she could. There was a momentary swirling sensation, and then the bag's momentum was halted by solid human head. There was a hard slap and a hissing of breath. The heavy plastic award for Scoop of the Year had connected.

The man fell back and to the side like a slipping dancer. He grunted. The hammer dropped from his hand.

Shona bolted from the cupboard as fast as she could, her stick left behind, through the door and across the hall, lurching sideways but keeping upright, to the front door, which was still open, and out, out into the world. Something hard slammed into the wall beside her.

She fell down the steps, onto the gravel, banging her hip and scraping her knees, moaning *fuck-fuck-fuck* between ragged breaths.

She ripped herself from the ground and hobbled down the drive. She looked back, frantically, and saw the man. But he was not chasing her. He was hanging onto the door, his mask dark with blood.

With a gasp, she reached the main road. A bus thundered past, its bulk and noise jolting her senses. She staggered onwards, into the city, into the enveloping forest of noise and people and stone.

11

The man had not followed her. She wondered if she had truly hurt him. Her arm was tingling: she had hit him hard.

Walking as quickly as she could, haphazardly, taking corners at random, moving deeper into the city, she swam through its onslaught of noise, of people, of light—such bright light. Past shuttered shops, whitewashed windows, men loading tools into a white van, people talking into their phones. The street was a moving river of voices, of car fumes, of desperation, of panic: it clanged and shrieked and rumbled in its trench of brick and concrete and glass. Jets moved across the sky. A helicopter thrummed high overhead. She moved through it all, as fast as she could, another unseen, unremarked face in the teeming city.

Suddenly exhausted and parched, she came to a halt in a crooked street of takeaway shops and newsagents. There was a café, and she pushed her way into it. A heavyset man was leaning on the counter, bright photographs of an Eastern European city on the wall behind him.

"All right? What can I do you for?"

She huskily ordered a glass of water and a coffee with two sugars, flinching as two fire engines howled past the café window, cars hurriedly pulling aside.

She leaned on the table with her head in her hands. Her right shoulder twinged. Her leg throbbed with ache. Her thoughts tumbled. That man had killed Proctor and would probably have killed her, too. Proctor had wanted to tell her something—something big. He never would.

She reached into her bag. The award was intact. It was evidently harder than a man's head. She pulled out her laptop—there was a new estuary of spreading cracks across its cover. She opened it, and it bloomed into life. That, at least, was something.

Then she remembered the mobile phone Proctor had left for her. She fished it from her pocket and pressed the button, but it was still dead. Her hands were shaking, her mouth was as dry as sacramental bread and her side ached. Her stick, abandoned in the villa.

She had to leave London. That man would be looking for her. And Moriah, the only real lead she had, was in Scotland. She felt hard the need to be home. She thought about her train, but she did not want to travel on public transport now. She did not want to be seen.

The café owner arrived with a glass of water and a large coffee. She drank the water quickly, adrenaline draining, and took a glug of coffee. The sugar entered her blood like a smile.

A sudden wracking sigh shook her, and she swore. She closed her eyes for a time. London moved outside her. Then she opened her eyes and took more coffee. She turned the lifeless mobile over and over in her hand. The day slowly darkened outside. Clouds moved across the sun. The footfall on the street lessened. Her heart, she realised, had stopped surging in her chest.

There was a piercing wail, and another fire engine tore past, lights pulsating.

"Big fire up the road," the man said. "Just heard it on the radio."

Shona turned to look at him.

"Big fire," he repeated.

"Where?" she said, her voice barely audible.

"Up Holland Park way," he said. "Sheldrake Gardens."

She turned around again and stared into her coffee. What could she do? She did not want to call the police; that would kill her story. She would be questioned, even arrested. And she just did not trust the police. She had one good contact in Scotland, an experienced detective, Benedict Reculver. But he had signed off for a year and was on a well-earned sabbatical somewhere in Europe. She had one other police contact in the West of Scotland, but he would not know or even care about a body in London. She could phone in her information and then run, but she knew nearly every call could be traced; even calls from public phone boxes could be pieced together with slices of CCTV and security camera footage to pin an identity on someone. Of course, she realised, she had probably been captured on multiple cameras, escaping from the house. Which was now, she knew, on fire. The crew would find the body—or bodies.

Shona looked out into the street. No police cars. No signs of surveillance here. Just mundane brick and concrete, cheap plastic signage, ugly fonts, snakes of wires clinging to walls, stained downpipes and ceaseless noise.

She decided to call her boss. As she dialled his number, she realised she had blood on her hand. She dabbed it with a napkin, but it smeared. She shoved the napkin in her pocket.

Her call was answered.

"World-renowned editor Ranald Zawadzki here, and, I am sorry, I only answer to award-winning journalists," Ranald said. His voice boomed. Then he laughed. "Oh, I know you, you *are* an award-winning journalist. Shona Sandison, my one true star. How are you? I'm at the bottom of a hungover pit of my own making. Threw up twice, had three bacon rolls and am currently in the bath. How can I help?"

"Hey," she said. She suddenly began to cry. She was

surprised. She brushed the tears away. Blood and tears on her palm. "Ah, Jesus," she said, eventually. "Jesus wept."

"Shona?" Ranald said.

"Look—I need some help."

"Of course, of course," he said. "Let me get out of this bath."

There was a sloshing sound and a loud thump.

"Oh, bloody hell," Ranald said, suddenly at a distance. "Hang on."

"Fuck's sake, Ranald."

Her irritation suddenly staunched her tears. She wiped them away.

There was more sloshing and slapping. The phone returned to his hand. "I needed to bathe, Shona!" he said. "My head feels like it's burst."

A police car slowly drove down the street. It passed from sight.

"Look," she said, whispering, "have you heard of something called Grendel? Or someone who goes by that name?"

"Well, now," he said, his voice rasping. "Are we onto a new story, then? What's this all about? Can't you take a day off?"

"Grendel—have you heard of it?"

"No. What are we talking about here? Beyond the monster in that poem, no, I haven't heard of it. You been reading Anglo-Saxon poetry?"

On the street, a couple of police motorcycles sped past. Shona's cheeks were still damp with tears. She swabbed them away.

"Shona? Hey, tell me, what's this to do with?"

"Well . . ." She wondered how much to reveal. "You know Moriah, the contact for my story?"

"I know the name, obviously. Such an odd cover name— the mountain where Abraham bound his son—"

"I know, I know. We've been through that already. But listen to this: Moriah is in Scotland," she said. "My contact told me. He's moved. And he's left a message for me: *Find Grendel.*"

"Hmm. How mysterious. Anything more?"

"Nothing. But I need to find him. And find out what this Grendel is. And then today—"

"What's happened? You sound a bit weird . . . I hope you're not as hungover as I am. I feel half dead."

Shona saw another police rider zip past, lights flashing. "It's nothing," she said. "But I think someone tried to tell me something. And they were stopped."

"What? Is this serious? Are you okay? Stopped in what way?"

A head smashed. A lifeless mouth gaping.

"Shona?"

"Look—if you can find out anything about this Grendel from your contacts or whoever you hang out with, let me know. I'm heading home. I need to find Moriah . . . I think it's another big story, Ranald. Maybe . . . the big one."

Ranald laughed. "Oh, man, Shona, isn't it always? But—"

"What?"

"Would you even know Moriah if you met him? How are you going to find him?"

"I don't know."

"Do you have his number, his email?"

"No."

"Well, if he's in Scotland, great. But Scotland is big enough to hide anyone, if they want to hide."

"I know. But I feel I have to head home. And he has left me this message. It might be the last I get."

Ranald seemed to sigh. Or perhaps he had turned the hot tap on again. "True. Okay, let's catch up when you're back in Edinburgh. And be careful."

"Another thing: I have a phone I need to bring back to life. Something . . . something Moriah sent me," she lied. "There might be something on it, but I don't know how to get into it. It's not like any phone I've seen before. It might be foreign."

"Oh, aye? Whose phone is it?"

"Come on. Don't ask. Do you have anyone you might know who . . ."

Ranald paused for a moment, as if debating with himself. "Yes, of course I do. I'll send you the details. Man called Loxley. Bit of a fruitcake, but he can basically get into anything and get information out of anything. Did some time for phone hacking back in the day."

"Where does he live?"

"Bath. Well, a place near Bath. Middle of nowhere. But we usually post him things to decrypt, or it's all done online—"

"Can you send me his details?"

"Of course."

"Now."

"What's the rush, Shona? Can I please—"

She hung up, feeling suddenly invigorated.

She rang Ned Silver.

"Hey, Shona!" he shouted. He sounded cheerful, somehow relieved.

"I need your help," she said, standing up, leaning on the table for support. She left some money, waved in the direction of the counter and moved outside. She could hear the distant wail of sirens.

"I need to get out of London as soon as possible," she said. "I need your help."

Another bad dream. A van on a moor, full of chopped-up bodies. I was trying to open the door. Their hands grabbed for the locks.

A memory. It was during the crisis in Cyprus. A poor fellow in Nicosia. We nabbed him, extracted some kind of information. I cannot remember now what it was. The information wasn't the point, of course. The point was something else entirely. ~~I gave him to two of my men to take him home. But they just left him in the boot of the car, out in the desert, and then went off to drink Keo in Larnaca and pick up hookers in the Russian hotel. The car was found weeks later, with him as soup inside. Very hot, Cyprus, in the summer.~~ I have dreamt of him often. It could have been anyone, any number of bodies, in Yemen, or Syria, or Berlin, or Londonderry. But, no, this poor Greek boy. He had dark eyes, like you. Like your mother. Like his mother.

I was very glad that you didn't follow me after your mother died . . . I lost focus. Then, with your passing, I felt focused again. There is something Greek as well, in there, isn't there? How Alexander wept for his lover, I wept for you.

Tomorrow I will paint my little scurrying voltigeurs. Rather handsome, they are, too. They will hide in the trees. Duck behind walls. Infiltrate buildings. Blend into the world. Strike from cover.

I know I will see you soon. Under the lake, under the walls of water. In the sunken trees, with the lost lord of this realm.

Good night.

12

Hector's mind swilled and spilled him out into the spiteful, inevitable day.

He was on the sofa, suit still on, trousers awry, jacket akimbo, tie lying over his face like an unwelcome cold tongue. He yanked the cushion from behind his head and sat up. Dim light slopped over the sad furniture. The contents of his head moved counter to the contents of his stomach.

Sandy entered the room, in her nightgown, the baby at her shoulder. "So?"

He pulled the cushion over his face.

"Hector," she said, not unkindly. "You'd better get going."

He groaned.

"You're going to be late. And we need to wash and sleep."

He groaned again, eyes still closed. He remonstrated with himself. One part of his mind—impatient, angry, conscientious—pleaded with the other—spent, despairing, exhausted. After gritting his teeth, he made it to his feet and moved unsteadily through to the bedroom.

Sandy followed him. "Look at this little sausage," she said softly, touching the squirming baby's tiny snub nose. Little rose fingers moved slowly in the air, tiny fingernails at their soft tips. Precious minuscule details on the soft, helpless, miniature body. "Daddy's hungover," Sandy said to the baby. "Daddy's in a whole heap of trouble. Daddy can't agree on a name for you. Our nameless baby boy."

Hector put a tremulous hand to Sandy's tousled caramel hair. She leaned gently into his fingers. Her head was warm and heavy.

"What about Adam?" he said.

"No chance," she said, chuckling. "Not a chance. But what about Elvis? I'd go with that."

"He was a hero to millions, but he never meant much to me . . ." Hector said woozily, trying to remember something that was eluding him.

"You sad drunkard. Get yourself a strong coffee and get going," she said. "I need you to go. This little man and I need to wash and sleep, and I can't with you glooming up the place."

"You need to wash and sleep."

"Did I mention that?" She yawned.

"You smell good to me," he said, putting his nose to her hair.

"You smell like a drain," she said. "Get away from me."

With the sleepy baby returned to his cot, Sandy showering for the first time in days, and an instant coffee in his hands, Hector leaned on the window frame. It was 7:45 A.M., and Edinburgh was waking to a steely sky and an orchestra of drips, meltings and slush.

Hector remembered: he needed to retrieve his bag. Not only did it contain his newly activated laptop—where all his work resided—but also his security pass to Alacrity House.

Hector called Adam. But the phone rang out. He sent a message. He tried to eat a slice of toast; it was like eating a shoe.

Hector sterilised a baby bottle and cleaned the breast pump, ironed a shirt and dialled Adam again: no answer. He needed that bag. He had to be at work, on the third floor of Alacrity House, by 8:30 A.M. Adam lived on the other side of town, but his office was in the city centre, off St. Andrew Square. Much closer. Hector would go there.

Once outside, the cold closed tight around his body. The

sky was grey; the streets were grey. As he walked between banked-up drifts and cars roofed with black-speckled snow, he called Kapp.

Kapp answered in a clear voice. He was already at work.

"Stricken, good morning," he said. "I take it you are at the doors? Just looking through the press cuttings and I have one or two tasks for you. We need some reactive lines prepared on a couple of items, there's a Freedom of Information response we need to gut and—"

"Eric, morning. Look—I have an urgent personal thing to attend to. I'll be in a little after nine . . ."

"And after the news conference, I think we should have a thorough look at your draft of the news release on the work-force regulations. It needs a lot of work. To be honest, you just haven't got the house style down yet. It's pretty messy, and . . ." Kapp proceeded to work his way through a series of tasks for Hector with an increasing urgency in his voice.

A tight pain in Hector's temple screamed and disappeared again. "As I said, I'll be in a little later today," Hector pressed on, his hangover smudging his usual nervousness. He was trudging past the Playhouse theatre to the confused junction where the road to Leith met the old city. He stopped for a moment to catch his breath. His socks were wet with splashes of melted snow, his black shoes already spattered with grime and salt.

"How late?" Kapp said brusquely. "Attendance at morning news conference is, not to put too fine a point on it, non-negotiable, Hector. It's the most important—"

"I don't have my laptop," Hector said, as breezily as he could. "I need to get it back from my dopey friend who picked it up last night by mistake."

"Someone else has your work laptop?" Kapp said. Hector said nothing. "Hector, everything we do is on that laptop. If someone works out your password, the whole of our agency is there to be read. They may even use it to access the government itself."

Hector watched a bus edge its way around the roundabout, a maroon slab of weight and electric light, the blurred occupants faceless, its wheels spattering a wave of slush over the pavement. Heavy heads leaned against wet windows, staring at blue-lit phones.

"I've explained all this to you several times," Kapp said.

Hector heard Kapp's hardened, insistent voice, but his attention had slid elsewhere. He felt, with a sudden plunge of emotion, an immense pity for everyone trapped inside that bus, being dragged to work, exhausted already by the daily routine, numbly moving through another day of enervating activity.

He suddenly felt close to tears. He hoped the bus would somehow not reach its destination. Or maybe it would change course and take its passengers to the beach. Or it would suddenly elevate and soar into the immense sky. They had to escape. They had to get out of there.

"Hector?" Kapp barked. "To repeat: Someone has your laptop?"

"Yeah, my friend has it. And my security pass. And documents I have printed off, like the stuff from the meeting yesterday."

The phone line was heavy with weighted silence.

"All the documents from yesterday's meeting?"

"Yeah," Hector said.

"This seems to be a situation," Kapp said.

"Well, it'll be fine," Hector said, watching the determined bus grind its way past a shopping mall and disappear from view, its prisoners reduced to fingerprint smears of shadow. "Look at them all—they've gone."

"What?" Kapp snapped. "How exactly will it be *fine*?"

"My friend—Adam Rokeby, look him up—is a respected man of the law. I've known him for years. There's nothing to worry about. I'm nearly at his office now."

He kept going, through the filthy, slush-lined streets, phone clamped to his ear.

"Right, well," Kapp said, with a heavy sigh, as if putting down an axe he was about to split a head with. "Get your bag and return. I'll have to file a report if you're not back here by half nine."

"Fine," Hector said. He passed the Catholic cathedral—warm, golden light glimmered inside. A man he vaguely recognised was walking quickly up the steps: bearded, intense, with a blue mark behind his ear. He shook his head—he could not place him.

"A report on your conduct," Kapp said and hung up.

Hector could see Adam's office now. Old bare trees, tall and dark, lining a series of private gardens, were slowly shedding their loads of snow. Birds drifted and fluttered.

Adam's firm took up two floors of a flat-faced building in an elegant eighteenth-century terrace. Lights were on. Tiny peaks of snow clung to pointed black iron railings which stood like racked spears in an antique armoury. Hector slipped as he moved up the stone steps. His hand touched the cold stone, then he righted himself and hurried inside.

At the desk, a woman was frowning at a screen. On the counter was a small bowl of sweets in twisted bright packaging. Hector took one, tried to unwind it, failed and put it in his pocket.

"Good morning," the woman said.

"Is Adam Rokeby—"

"Mr. Rokeby will not be in today."

"Ah," Hector said, his shoulders slumping. "Because I need

to see him—and I have his bag here. It has his belongings in it. You see, what's happened is—"

"Mr. Rokeby has a series of meetings in Glasgow," the woman said, "but you can pass me his bag and I can get it to him."

Hector laid it on the desk. Oh, how he wished that bag was his. "I don't suppose he left a bag for me—has he?"

The woman looked at him blankly. "And what's your name?"

"Hector Strick—"

"No, he's not left a bag for you," she said. She took Adam's bag from the desk, and it disappeared from view. She looked to him again, as if expecting something.

"Can I leave a message for him?"

"He won't be in today. As I said, he's in Glasgow. I would send him an email, if you have it."

"I do have it," he said, defeated. "Look—"

"I am looking."

"Can I ask where in Glasgow he is?"

"I'm afraid not," she said and turned away.

As Hector was leaving the office, his phone rang. It was an unknown number.

"Kapp here," Kapp said. "Did you get your bag? Have you got your laptop? Your papers? I'm going to have to raise this with HR and IT. This is a serious security breach, Hector. I'm bypassing Rhonda."

Hector sighed. The Portrait Gallery, decorated with carvings and posters, with the past and the present, stood in front of him. Poets and soldiers, statesmen and queens were carved in pink stone. He and Shona used to meet there. They'd swap journalist war stories, and she would sigh and smile, curse and laugh. He missed her, her intensity and rudeness, her constantly refreshed disgust for the world.

Hector closed the call without another word and walked aimlessly into the city centre. The jagged tower of the Scott Monument reared up ahead, a gothic spire at home in the winter murk. What if he lost his job? He could get another, he reasoned, with an electric charge of sudden anxiety. He could return to journalism. Maybe. Not that there were many jobs now. Or, more accurately, there were none that he wanted; he could not even pretend that he wanted to upcycle broadcast news for a website or rewrite someone else's story for a few internet hits on some crappy website clogged with ads and pop-ups.

He wondered when the pubs would open. He thought of Shona again. He decided to go to the hotel where, in its street-level café, he and Shona used to hide in a leather-cloistered corner and drink coffee and hot chocolate.

He walked in, and his glasses immediately steamed up. He ordered, and sat on green leather to clean his spectacles. The world outside receded. He was in a temporary sanctuary.

He quickly emailed Shona from his phone, his fingers shaking as he typed.

Hi Shona, hope you're fine. I don't know what it is, but you should probably look into this. One of our plans: Grendel. I can't tell you any more. Hector.

The email slipped into the ether and was gone.

13

Detective Inspector Benedict Reculver was on sabbatical. Thirty-five years in both secret and public service had exhausted his body and mind. His blood pressure was being kept down to merely high, but still dangerous, levels, only by a daily double dose of Doxazosin tablets and a half-hearted new regimen of walking and sleeping.

He had been given a year off. Three months had passed. He was now sipping a small glass of red wine in a quiet café overlooking the main square of Fontainebleau in northern France. It was winter, and the square was empty and drab. The carousel, its painted horses insane and suspended, was still. The cinema and the small shops were shut. But the lights in the cafés glowed amber, and down the road, the aggressively elegant palace would soon open to visitors. This was his mission for the day: to see Napoleon's greatcoat, his martial hat, his campaign bed, his throne and his army bath. Then he would walk in the spacious gardens, enjoy a lengthy five-course lunch and return to his gilded, velveteen hotel, where he would sleep through a long, soft afternoon, in order to keep his blood pressure within tolerable limits. He would then pack for his next journey to the south of France.

Reculver often wore makeup, and although no one had ever been brave or thoughtless enough to mention it at his current place of work, Scotland's national police force, he had not noticed any side-eyes or raised eyebrows in France, either. Maybe this was because Reculver was big, over six foot four, a heavy man with paws for hands and a face that was both battered and, from a certain angle, noble. His prominent nose had been broken years ago, and the lines around his deep eyes rendered them sorrowful. His skin was pockmarked and scarred, and the smooth remnants of a deep burn could be seen on his lower neck, disappearing down into his tailored clothes. With his cashmere coat, full beard and thick-brimmed hat he looked like a 1930s gangster who was slowly turning into a bear.

The edge of his fork was just breaking the icing on his cake when his phone rang. It was a work colleague—Detective Sergeant Menteith, calling from Glasgow.

He stared at it for a while. He reluctantly answered it. He did not feel eager to hear a Scottish voice. "I'm on holiday, you fool," he growled.

"A very good morning to you, too," Menteith said cheerfully. Menteith was not a very clever fellow, Reculver thought, but he was uncommonly handsome. In his uniform he looked like an actor playing the role of a policeman in a cheap TV series. His hair was a jet-black wave and his eyes were emeralds. There had been a footballer, Reculver dimly recalled, whom Menteith resembled. But he could no longer remember the name.

"Come on then, Menteith," Reculver said. "Spit it out. I have a date with an emperor, and I don't want to be late."

"With who?"

"Old Boney. The Little Corporal."

"What, Hitler?" Menteith gasped.

"Hitler? No, Napoleon Bonaparte, you nitwit."

"Ah. Right. Never been that up on my history. I'll cut to the race."

"Cut to the chase," Reculver corrected.

"Yes. Look—I was just looking through my emails this morning, and this report of an interview in HM Frankland has come across my desk."

"Oh, yes, in Durham. What of it?"

"It's with a criminal."

"I suspected it might be a criminal being interviewed, given that Frankland is a high-security prison."

"Exactly. This villain has been spilling his guts in an attempt to get his very long sentence down. He's a bad one, this guy."

"I remain unsurprised. He's in the Monster Mansion for a reason, son. Who is it and why does it have anything to do with this fat old man on a well-deserved holiday in France?"

"He's talking about his killings, his murders."

"I am waiting for a point to be made here."

"One of them . . . well, one of them is yours," Menteith said.

"Well, son, I've never killed anyone," Reculver lied. He popped a sliver of cake in his mouth.

"No," Menteith said. "It's about a case you handled. No body was ever found. Linked to the murder of a Mr. Love, a few years ago."

Reculver nodded to himself. Robert Love had been an artist in Edinburgh. He was found collapsed into his easel with his head punctured by something heavy. Days later, John Cullen, an Edinburgh councillor, had been killed in a squalid pub toilet in the same way. Nothing was ever revealed about either death. No arrests had been made. And, shortly after, an art expert from London, Thomas Tallis, had disappeared. Never found. Shona Sandison, his closest contact in the media, had assured him the cases were connected. But he and his colleagues in the force had not been able to find that connection. However, Reculver knew the murderer of Love and Cullen had been a professional, a gangland hitman—he had been convinced of that. No fingerprints had been left, and both had seen their lives ended with a fierce and efficient violence.

Eventually, he had been resigned to the incomplete, unsolved conclusion of the case. It was officially left open. Not every murder could be solved. Justice is fragile and rarely served. The world is too messy and unknowable. And so it went with the vanished art expert. Not every disappearance means a murder has been committed. Some people want to disappear. Some people tumble into rivers. Some people fall into the sea. Others find a locked room and wither within. And people simply slide unmourned into the sunless crevasse of uncaring time. Lost to history forever. After all, that is the fate of most people. Graveyards are full of the ignored dead.

Reculver's mind snapped back to the matter in hand. He could hear Menteith breathing on the other end of the line.

"Okay, I'm interested now. Who is this fellow?"

"Well," Menteith said with some exultation. "He's called Hurlock. He's had other names. They thought he was called Naylor for a while, then Burnhouse. He was arrested last year in that sweep of the Newcastle mob. You'll remember."

"I certainly do," Reculver said. Street drugs, a whole network of human trafficking, violent pornography, corruption, protection rackets—a nasty business.

"He was a big part of the case. He did their wet work. He was their prime housepainter. He admitted to three victims but that was probably just the tip of the ice pick."

"Berg. Tip of the iceberg," Reculver said.

"Yes. Anyway, I have the transcript here in front of me," Menteith said. "There's no remorse here—not a jot. But he is talking about a man he killed in the Scottish Borders, a few years ago. A guy he calls Trellis. Said this poor fellow got in the way. He killed him with a chisel to the head and then dumped him in a lake. But the owner of the lake got jumpy—"

"The owner of the lake? Who owns a lake?" Reculver rumbled.

"The owner of the lake," Menteith rolled on, "insisted the body get fished out. So he said he had to do a 'bad business,' recovering the rotten body from the lake and reburying it somewhere else. Messy. Said he wasn't paid for it."

"Right. Where?"

"Frankland, as I was saying."

"No, no. Where is this body?"

"Ah, got you. He said the remains can be found in a buried wheelie bin off the M6, near Shap. Cumbria. He knows exactly where it is. Can take us there."

Reculver took a sip of his coffee. The world blurred past the large windows of the café. "Tallis. Thomas Tallis," he said. "That's who he killed. That's who he's talking about."

The waiter drifted to his table and discreetly left the bill, folded in half on a silver plate.

"*Weak man, he was no bother*. That's what he says here," Menteith said.

"I don't believe Tallis was a weak man," Reculver said quietly.

"Anyway, he's in a bin buried off the motorway. This family that owns the lake, the Farquharsons, know about it. Maybe a little questioning is in order."

"The Farquharsons, eh?" Reculver said. "Was it their lake at Denholm House?"

"Yes, sir," Menteith said. Down the line, Reculver could hear the sound of a paper document being swiftly riffled. "Denholm House, yes, that's what it says right here."

"We had it dragged. Divers went down."

"Well, it was missed," Menteith said.

"It appears so. And now poor Tallis is in a bin beside

a motorway? How undignified. He was a dignified man, Menteith."

"Aren't we all, sir?"

"Tallis. There's a family there," Reculver said, standing up at his table and tipping some coins from his pocket onto the silver tray. "A family that has waited for his body to be found. His widow is a distinguished pianist. His father—well, his father was someone who could not be trifled with. A figure of substance. I believe he's retired now. So, Menteith, you have some work to do. Go to the Farquharsons, in the Borders. Present this to them. And you need to read up on the matter of a painting, *The Goldenacre*."

"I've not heard of it."

"Only a few wise people have, but it's worth reading about. You might even learn something. Now, what have you done with all this information?"

"I've printed it out and I'm reading it right now. Got my tea, got my biscuits."

"No," Reculver sighed. "I mean, where is it now, in the system? Who else knows about this?"

"I've sent it on to the Cumbria force already and let the higher-ups know, sir. It's very much in the system," Menteith said with some pride.

"Très bien. Now, I am on holiday. A vacation. I am not working. For the good of my health and the good of my colleagues' health, I am out of the game. So I cannot do this task—but, please, can someone sensible contact the family? There was an aunt in Portobello. There is the father—good luck finding him—but there is the widow I mentioned. They had a child. Can someone reasonably human please do that delicate and sensitive work? And when the body is found, can someone send me an email to the address I left in my handover note? That is all I require. And no more phone calls."

"I shall log your asks, sir," Menteith said. "I will make sure this is all done imminently."

"Immediately, I think, is the word you're looking for."

"Yes, sir."

Reculver was outside now, in the cool air. A wide parade ground and a château of startling size and elegance moved slowly into his view. It was as if a dream had suddenly risen from the ground.

"Adieu, Menteith," Reculver said, and he closed the call.

He adjusted his coat and took off his hat as if he were entering a church, and moved towards the royal palace of Fontainebleau, his mind already in another time.

T,

Today I appreciated how profoundly I had come to despise the Internet. That cursed Pandora's box. So much of my experience with it had been work: the dark web, secret tunnels, parallel worlds, entwining circles of content and intent. Vile pornography. Organised crime. Troll farms in St. Petersburg. All the sins. All viewable. All trackable. All there. The transition for us, in the Service, from pre-Internet to post-Internet was a huge adjustment. Our old ways—codes, drop boxes, blinds, miniaturisation—all rendered pointless, obsolete, almost overnight.

Today I found myself reluctant to connect my laptop. But, in the end, I did. I spent a day with a bottle of Jura and various entertaining war gaming websites. Scenarios and dioramas. A lot of sites where I can recruit more troops. And, also, forums of discussion where I can meet fellow victims of this toy soldier bug. I found one for Scotland. I have in recent days set up an online identity and I am arranging some battles. I suspect, like me, most of my partners will be men of a certain age and type. That is fine.

We never played soldiers, did we? I know that. We never played, full stop. I had neither the time nor energy for you. And now look at me—time and energy to spare, and no one to share it with.

A Mr. Angus Pettifer claims to have a complete British Army of the Peninsular War ready to face my Imperial French. We shall see. I might need to buy some more trees and buildings for cover. It is vital that the men have the ability to hide.

My son. I am glad, you know, that you did not follow me. From Malvern to Keble to Military Intelligence to . . . everything that then transpired. You may not appreciate that. You cannot appreciate that. I was glad to have left you behind. I wish you were with me now. I know I ignored you. I can lie to myself, say, well, I protected you. But that protection did not last, did it? I could not protect you. And, for a father, there is no greater failure than that.

0003

"*I will walk around the oak, with great ragged horns, and blast the tree, and kill the cattle, and make much kin yield blood, and shake the chains, all the wintertime, and at midnight.*"

14

"So where exactly are we going?"

Ned's car was speeding along the Westway, past high-rises and low roofs, heading deep into the green guts of soggy England.

Before she had been picked up, Shona had spent some time in the stinking café toilet, crying. The ruined face of Proctor in her mind. The long-haired killer loping towards her like a savage from a heathen past.

But, eventually, she had pulled herself together, laid out her next steps. She was determined to reach Ranald's phone-cracker, Loxley, and find out what was on Proctor's mobile. Then, she would take a cheap flight from Bristol back to Edinburgh. And there, at home, she would have time to assess, to review, to recalibrate. To breathe. Away from the noise and mess and violence of London.

Ned, his salmon-pink shirt open, wearing white leather driving gloves, had taken well over an hour to pick her up. His car was clean and empty. A rental, he said—his own car was in the garage.

The motorway widened. The traffic blurred and sped. Bare trees flashed past. The horizon became emptier, more rural. Plain fields were dotted with skeletal winter trees, their arms raised in warning. Ned's eyes were on the road, but he had asked her something, and she was not ready to answer.

Huddled in the passenger seat, her shoulder aching, Shona checked her phone for mentions of a fire in West London. There—under a picture of smoke rising—was a report of a fire in Sheldrake Gardens. The fire service would have found the body.

She shivered. Someone was after her. Someone who had smashed Proctor's face before he could speak to her. And who had sent him?

"Shona?" Ned said.

"Sorry," Shona said. "Miles away, there. Thanks for this."

She was suddenly aware that she had no stick to walk with. Nothing to take her listing weight. She wondered if Ned had a golf umbrella in the boot. But why would he?

"It's no bother at all," Ned said. "But I need to know where we're going, apart from 'west.' And I have to get back in a couple of hours—I'm meant to be at a reception. I've blocked out three hours for a private appointment. Which this is, of course." He smiled broadly. One of his molars was all black filling.

Ranald had just sent the details for Loxley. He mentioned that he'd never met the man, never been to his home or office. As Shona looked at her phone, she noticed she had multiple unread emails. She could not face reading them. What would they be? Notes from the bank, from the solicitor about her father's surprisingly complicated estate, spam about clothes, endless newsletters. It could all wait.

Something was looming—she felt it. As the car sped on, heavy clouds from the snow-choked north were gathering like ink swirling underwater.

"Where are we *going*, Shona?" Ned repeated. His index finger tapped the wheel.

"Hold your horses. I've got an address now. It seems to be in a village. If it's a town, I've never heard of it. But I don't know England very well," she conceded.

"Called? Called what?"

"Fleet Lanshome. 3 Carlbury Lane. Near the green. I

assume that's a village green, rather than some random colour out of space floating in the ether."

"Never heard of it either," Ned murmured. "Sounds like a typical Cotswolds village, though. Which would make sense."

"I've never been to the Cotswolds," Shona said. The word flung up an array of images in her mind. Rolling green hills. Cream teas. Little churches. Red corduroy trousers. Pretty gardens. Angry divorcees. English hymns. "'Jerusalem,'" she murmured.

"The green and pleasant land." Ned nodded. "It is that—if you can afford it."

"Pleasant, right. But with rivers choking on shit and sui- cidal farmers."

Ned programmed the name of the village into his dash- board map system. The screen flickered briefly, and a route was illuminated.

"So what did Proctor have to say for himself?" Ned glanced at Shona.

"He didn't say much."

"Nothing of great interest? No story?"

She felt a chill. She felt as if she was suddenly touching a cold wall of metal. She decided to lie. Ned would not know any different. And maybe it would be better for him if he didn't know.

"No. Not to me," she said. "But our meeting overran. So I missed my train. Then the day got complicated."

"I thought you said he had a story for you," Ned said, staring ahead. Trucks lined the slow lane, like a moving wall. The hawthorn hedges were black in the fading light.

"Nah. No story, no." Shona looked at her fingers. She had washed her hands well, as thoroughly as a surgeon, but around the nail of her index finger was a crescent of dried blood.

She had not painted her nails since her father died. In the past, Viv would sometimes do them for her, but she had not seen her friend for a while. Shona had been living in an isolated cave of bereavement. She had received a string of sweet and amusing emails from Terry, a photographer friend in the North of England, too. She wanted to reply to them, but she didn't know what to say.

"That's a shame. How disappointing for you."

"More for him than me."

"Why did he think he had something to interest you, then?"

Ned was buzzing with some kind of intense, focused energy, and Shona was not sure she liked it. Maybe it was just because he was driving, because he was impatient.

"So who lives in this village?"

"You know, we worked together for fifteen years, Ned," she said, "and I don't remember you ever being this interested in my work. Not a peep from you over the years, was there? It's just a contact, the next link in the chain, and he can only see me today. Tonight."

She waited for a response, watching the motorway glide by in a smear of speed and volume. Drivers—staring ahead, faces frozen, hands gripping steering wheels like penitents at the chancel rail.

Ned just shrugged. "I used to miss journalism. You may be surprised. I knew what I was doing, and I liked it—the simplicity of it. It's a black-and-white world: you want a story, you get the story—or not—and you write it. It's published, then it's done, and you move onto the next one."

"But it's not black-and-white, is it?" she said. He was vexing her. "I used to think it was. But it's not. There are oceans of grey."

"Yeah, that's what I've come to realise—especially now,

and with what's coming. For good or ill, I live in the real world now. In the complicated world of compromise, of practicalities, of necessary decisions—"

"And real stories do not just end," Shona interrupted. "You can't wrap up people's lives in five hundred words, or five thousand, or fifteen thousand. People's lives are not like that. The world's not like that."

"The world is cold and fucking remorseless," Ned said. "I wish it wasn't. I used to think it wasn't. But it is. What matters to me now is not what we used to hope matters."

"What do you mean?"

"Kindness. Respect. Striving to be on the right side of history," he said quietly. "These things don't matter. The only things that matter now are the things we don't want to matter—power, money, leverage. The ugliness has won, and we all have to negotiate with that reality."

"What are you on about, Ned?"

"The future," he said, flicking his eyes to her.

"Right," she said, annoyed by his preaching.

Ned put the radio on and told Shona that they would reach Fleet Lanshome in an hour. A burble of chirruping pop filled the car. Ned tapped a finger on the steering wheel in time. It distracted Shona from her thoughts. She wondered if she should call Reculver. She had interrupted a murder scene. She had struck a murderer. She was somehow liable for something . . . for someone.

Her conscience began to twitch into life. Even though she wanted the story for herself, there were other considerations, other risks. Other fears. To distract herself, she turned to Ned. "So how's your daughter getting on? How old is she now?"

He grinned. "She's doing fine. She's nine. She's into the world now. She has friends, parties, playdates. And opinions. All those things."

"Other people's opinions can be tricky things," Shona said, adding, "I always find."

"Thing is, Shona, she doesn't yet know what her future will entail. It's a hard time for us as parents."

Shona frowned. "What do you mean?"

He opened his gloved hands on the steering wheel and turned to her briefly as electric light flashed across his face. "The world. Our world, Shona, has gone. Dead. We're in another world now. Another era of history."

"What are you on about?"

"Do you watch the news, Shona, or just read your own stories?" He pressed his foot on the accelerator and stared ahead. "My task now—our task—is to prepare for what's to come. That involves some tough decisions. Far harder than our grandparents ever made."

"Isn't parenthood always hard?" Shona said, still not entirely sure what Ned was talking about. "Even before social media, the internet, AI . . ."

He shook his head. "Never mind," he said, his voice lowering. "If you don't know, you just don't know. But if you don't want to know, that's another thing."

Shona frowned. Then she used her phone to search for any information on Reece Proctor. She expected to find a log of his work on a recruitment site. But nothing appeared. She was flummoxed. She tried again. But no Reece Proctor matching the man she'd met came up in her searches. It was as if he had slid through the web entirely.

"Well, that's weird," she said, muffled, leaning against the passenger door as the beads of motorway lamps glowed against the winter evening. London was long behind them. Beyond the bounds of the expressway, the shadows were as deep as the sea.

"What's weird?"

"This Reece Proctor—I can't find anything on him online. Not a thing."

"That is weird. What about his company?"

"Dovetail."

"Never heard of it."

A website with elegant type slowly loaded on her screen. She checked the staff profiles—he was not there among the pictures of gimlet-eyed men and women looking efficient and purposeful.

Bold thinking for a challenging age, the website said. *Dovetail provides bespoke thinking for adventurous leadership in hinge positions . . .*

Shona rolled her eyes. She did a search on the website. No Reece Proctor came up. She scrolled down the list of the think tank's founders: R. Cotton, R. Hessenmuller and Y. Vardoger. Nothing.

"Nope," she said. Maybe Proctor had just lied. Who was he? "What is 'bespoke thinking'?" she said, almost to herself.

"Those policy units, those think tanks," Ned said, "they never give much away online. All their key work is influencing. Goading. Provocations. Papers for clients, offline advice to the government, that kind of thing. They do publish pamphlets—public policy ideas—but no one outside Westminster reads them. Anyway, that's not their real work."

"Deeply suspicious," she said.

"Do you never tire of all this, Shona?" he said. "The frustrations, the annoyances?"

"Of what?"

"Journalism. Banging your head against the walls? Driving constantly into darkness."

"No," she said. "That's the work, isn't it?"

"And there was me thinking I could tempt you into

leaving journalism for my side of the business," he said, staring straight ahead.

"You what?" Shona said. "You're joking, right?"

"Not really," he said. "This is our turnoff."

The car swerved at an exit, leaving the motorway behind. They descended into a road lined with hedgerows.

Shona's flight home to Edinburgh from Bristol was late in the night, well past ten o'clock, so she figured she had time enough to meet Loxley in this village and get to the airport. Night was here already; the daylight had surrendered. It was warm in the car, but she knew it was cold outside. A pair of eyes, glittering, were picked out by the headlights and then gone again, back into the nocturnal animal world.

The GPS indicated they were near their destination. Shona felt a surge of panic in her chest. She had decided to call Reculver, or the Met, anonymously. Leave as much information as she could and abandon this bloody trail. She would return to Edinburgh and try to find Moriah. Reculver would know what to do next. He always knew.

Ned, silent now for some time, slowed the car at a grassy junction. "We're really in the boondocks now," he murmured.

The car swerved right. A rutted landscape faded into darkness. After a collapsed row of corrugated iron barns, a village emerged. A white metal sign flashed in the car's beam—FLEET LANSHOME—then it disappeared in the starless night.

They entered the village. There was a central green, a pub and rows of small, silent cottages. Off the green was a row of pebble-dashed council houses: Carlbury Lane.

As the car came to a halt, Shona looked up at the winter moon in the night sky. It was a sickle in the dark, like a ripped fingernail suspended in blood.

0310

I have not told anyone of this before. For many years, I did not tell myself. And because it is a secret, it is true.

It was the early 1970s, and I was well established in the secret world. Not long after you were born, when your mother was still alive, I attended a conference of the great (who are not great) and the good (who are never good) in the Lake District. Not far from your school. A radio training station. The signals people used it, a mock castle overlooking the lake. Some fat Lancastrian merchant, high on coal and cotton, had built it, back in the day. But it was very useful for us. It was surrounded by trees and could be secured easily. The Americans were there, the French were there (for some reason) and the decisions made irrelevant and forgotten now.

I could not sleep. I was a station chief. Responsible. A lot of our people, and the people of our people, had died. A major situation in Bulgaria. (Again, irrelevant and long forgotten now—the bones long ploughed into the soil.) But because of this, I could not sleep. I was billeted in one of the towers. I looked over the lake. It was just a sheet of black, its length marked only by a few lights on the far shore. The mountains were jagged silhouettes.

I dressed and walked down to the cavernous door. The guards were jumpy, even though we were deep in the green country. I said I needed fresh air. That was enough to go outside. I lit up a cigarette and walked into the gardens. The sky was clear. I could see more stars than I had since Arizona, since South Africa. Every constellation, glittering. The great wheel of the galaxy, and all its many stars, were there before me. I felt like a conductor before his score.

I reached a gate, which led to a path along the lakeside, and walked along the track. Dark hills on one side, the deep lake on the other. I walked and walked, going over things, going over in my mind the profit and the loss, the damned and the saved. I lost track of time. After a while—I had not brought a torch—it became pitch-black. I could not smell the lake anymore, nor hear it lapping against the pebble shore. The trees were thicker and taller, older, and the canopy above seemed to be entwined. It had almost formed a roof.

I saw a light ahead and walked towards it, almost floating, as if in a dream of flying, that weightless drag, that curious combination of movement and inertia. I found myself moving towards the light.

I entered another space. A grove. A temple. A holy place. There was a kind of rocky, craggy ledge, deep moss-green, and stone steps leading to it, all covered in vines and dead leaves, roots as hard as iron. And through the walls of the high trees, there was water, but it seemed as if it was in the wrong place, the wrong direction, as if the water was somehow vertical, as if I was in *the lake. And I moved forwards in this sleep-awake state, as if partially paralysed. Or that curious sensation of rising from anaesthesia or sliding into it.*

I walked up the steps to the source of the remarkable light. It was not light as I had known it. Not a blaze of light from some electric source, or from gas or oil, or even wood fire. It was a glow, a pulse, an earthly, constant illumination. It was more like the illumination of the moon on water, of the morning sun on a wet field, of the stars on a rock pool. I thought I was asleep, then. That this was a dream. That I was tucked up under an army blanket at the castle, and this was all a subconscious hallucination. An ephemeral scenario conjured by my brilliant mind.

Then, as I rose to the height of the steps, he was there in the gloomy arbour, lying on a cracked rock, which was vast and curved like a huge anvil, a stone moon.

He was in the shape of a man. Of black skin and fur, with huge arms, a woven shift, a patterned coat, a writhing auric torque about his thick neck. His face in its rest was turned to me, even though he seemed dead. It was a face I cannot even fully summon again, a great shape, a visage I cannot describe: a king, a lord, a paladin, an emperor. Both real and unreal.

A huge soul, weighty from this earth, deep from the hot guts of the stone, with a weight and a gravity. It felt enough to unsettle the moon's orbit, an awful power outside and beyond anything I had seen or imagined or experienced.

He had deep eyes and a mouth set in such an extraordinary way. He was showing a kind of smile. And a hard, amoral, true cruelty. And yet there was something else—perhaps mischief, a playfulness. Some kind of robust humour set in that great grim grin. And, of course, there above his brow and temple were his horns. Antlers, they were, but different from a stag; they were multifarious, multi-pronged but growing, entangled. Vast. Almost like a tree, in themselves. Yggdrasil, or something deeper, back into space-time. Back to the earliest fires.

But this magnificent God was also lying in a scene of death. This giant lay there, dead, poisoned, forgotten in this temple of trees. I was in his grave. I reached for him, I motioned to touch this

*huge, inhuman form lying on the stone, and as I moved to touch
him, I noticed his head was resting on a garland of wildflowers,
of herb and grass, of beautiful flowers entwined and patterned,
which were fresh and bright, just picked, and as I moved to touch
his hard skin . . .*

*And then the dream was over. It was if I had been roused by
someone, splashed with cold water, as if I had been picked up
and turned about and put on my way, walking in the dawn
light, back along the path, to the castle rising from the tall trees,
in the morning mist.*

*I entered the world of reason once more. I must have walked and
slept in the woods beside the lake, I reasoned, I rationalised. In
those days, you see, my mind was one of gears and levers, of razor
blades and wires, of cast metal casings. There was no room for
lyricism. I read no Blake.*

*So I staggered along, drenched, wrung through, covered in
mud—no, not mud, but a kind of noxious black slime—and
I came to a boathouse. Those lakes have many. The big houses
have them there, down at the lakeside. I came to the boathouse.
There was a man there, a servant perhaps—a boat man, anyway.
He was leaning against the boathouse door. Big man. Beard but
no moustache. Six foot three, nineteen stone, maybe. Forearms
like hams. Smoking a pipe. Rough as a badger. He held an axe.
Enough to dismember me. "Seen the Lord, have ye?" he said. I
grunted. "Aye, seen the Lord," he said and opened the door to
the boathouse and walked inside.*

*I couldn't speak of it. I entered the castle through the kitchens,
the men barely up, scrambling eggs, frying huge slabs of bacon. I
washed myself up in a basement bathroom. My clothes had to be
destroyed. I never spoke of it. I pushed it away as a bad dream,
or the mental wanderings occasioned by bad food.*

But, but, but.

What was that, son? What had happened to me? What had I seen? I should have told you. You might have told me. But I know you are not like me. King and Country were nonsense to you. You didn't believe in it. I believed in it, I fought for it, I killed for it, I tried to maintain and protect it. But it was a dead allegiance, all along.

That great corpse, in the cave, the cave of trees under the dark water, was he the Lord? The soul of this island place. Whatever he was—and I know in some sense I know what he was—this giant is no more. He is dead and will not return. I think we feel it in us, in all of us, who once loved this country.

It has died. No, it has been killed. I saw it with my own eyes. It was a dream, but it was real. And now it is gone, for ever. What replaces it? Nothing. Oblivion.

0900

Oh, dear. I need coffee. I need breakfast. Not Herne. Not Karnonos. Not some avatar of Pan.

I sometimes think that I will leave the room, and when I come back in—when the kettle boils, when the toast pops—that you will be there. Looking crumpled. Slouching at the table. Reading a paper. Cocking your head to the radio. But you never are. You are never there. Where are you, my son?

15

The working day had begun.

Hector was now making way back to the office, snow clumped on his shoes, his hands cold, his breath dragoning before him: without his laptop, without his bag, and with no means of contacting Adam. Eric Kapp was bellowing in his ear. Again. He did briefly consider not going into work at all. But Sandy and the baby were asleep, and he did not want to wake them by phoning or returning home unannounced. He had so much on his mind, so much undecided.

Kapp was reiterating that Hector's mishap was a pressing security issue. Hector was repeating, with rising but unarticulated irritation, that his friend Adam was not a security risk. He was a solicitor, an honourable man of Scots law, and, most pertinently, did not have Hector's passwords. The laptop required three, including a seven-digit opening code which Hector could barely remember himself, and it was highly unlikely that Adam Rokeby had even considered breaking into his friend's computer. He was a serious, professional man, not a hacker.

"But your bag," Kapp had said, "has documents in it, does it not?"

"It does," Hector said. "But they weren't papers or submissions or . . . it was just a meeting schedule. An agenda. Just a few lines in a box."

"You need to come in tout de suite."

Hector was waiting at the pedestrian crossing outside the decorous pile of General Register House. Behind him, a bronze statue of the Duke of Wellington overlooked the office workers huddled in smart clothes and hats, who stood in silence waiting for the green man.

"Eric, Adam won't give a moment's thought as to the bag's contents," Hector said. "Losing his own bag will be more important to him. And he's in meetings in Glasgow all day—"

"It's just not acceptable behaviour," Kapp snapped. "It breaks the rules of the Code . . . maybe the Official Secrets Act . . . and it certainly breaks the guidance clearly outlined in your forty-page office manual. You will have to be disciplined."

"Surely there's no need for that. I get it. I understand your anxiety. But, actually, you're not even my line manager," Hector said.

Kapp fell silent. The lights changed, and the green man signalled that it was safe to cross, but Hector paused. "Come in right now," Kapp said. "And get that bag back before you get into real trouble—before you get *everyone* in real trouble."

Hector's mind was made up: he was going to quit. He would find another job—somewhere, anywhere. Maybe he would even go back to journalism, if anyone would have him. Maybe he could be a househusband. Maybe he would bring up his son—even if he was to be called Jessie, Elvis or Dick—and let Sandy earn the money. Why not?

He looked to the icy bulk of Arthur's Seat, the hazy blue horizon beyond. Its rugged sides were cast in rock and shadow. There was a sense of great distance in the view, and he felt a comfort in that distance. Not everything needed to be pinched and restrictive. Not everything needed to be stressed, pressed and harassed. The world, he thought, smiling, was much more than that. It was more than procedure, protocols, codes and operation manuals. There was the warm neck of his lover in the yearning night. There was the impossibly soft cheek of his new son. This world was deep green and breathing blue, still, despite its horrors and the foolishness of mankind.

Hector knew he was hungover, that alcohol was still firing in his blood and his brain. But surely it was forgivable to feel lightened, for a moment or two, amid the encircling carnival of pain.

He reached Alacrity House and made another call, turning his body away from the stream of workers jostling into the building.

"Hector," Jordan answered jauntily. "Where are you?"

"Can you speak?"

"I'm just at my usual place, man. Doing some printing for Kapp. He's acting up today."

"Tell me about it."

"No—Rhonda has literally just signed off sick, so Kapp's team leader for the day. So he's acting up. He's your boss now."

"Not for long," Hector said. "Listen, I just need some information. I have this problem with my laptop."

"Oh, right. Have you forgotten your login? I write mine down, to be honest. I keep my passwords in—"

"No, it's . . . it's not working. It's dead. Can I somehow work from a fixed station, a desktop or . . ."

"No," Jordan said, quieter. He seemed to have moved away from his station by the machines in the corner of the third floor. "But if yours is kaput, you can just call IT and get a temporary replacement. Just log into the server with another one. The server is there all the time. You just need to access it."

"Right, thanks. Oh, and I've left my security pass at home—do I just sign in?"

"Yeah, they'll ask you for your various ID codes. They'll ask someone to vouch for you."

"Ah, good to know."

"No bother. See you."

If the physical laptop wasn't the problem, why was Kapp so aerated? But he knew: it was the paper from the meeting. But others, surely, had access to those papers. And the information they contained was so spartan. They mentioned Grendel but nothing more. He remembered his hungover email to Shona and wondered why she hadn't replied. Maybe his emails were directed straight into her junk folder. He wouldn't be surprised.

An anonymous call buzzed on his phone. A Glasgow landline. He accepted it, relieved it wasn't going to be another fusillade from Kapp. It was Adam, his voice deep and reassuring, apologising for taking his bag and thanking Hector for returning his own.

"I can only say, in my defence, that I was rather generously overserved in a certain public hostelry last night," Adam said, in a theatrical voice.

Hector laughed. "Likewise. In my defence, m'lud, I was led astray by a man of the law who should know better."

"I plead 'unproven,'" Adam said. "I need to go, but I just wanted to let you know your bag is safe in the office. I left it there before I came through to Glasgow. Sylvia has it at the front desk, so you can reclaim your property."

Hector remembered Sylvia's irritation with him. She had taken her gatekeeping seriously.

"Thank God!" Hector said. "Thanks, mate. I'll pick it up at lunchtime. But I need to show my face in Castle Grayskull first. I'm thinking of handing in my resignation."

"Brave man," Adam said. "Have you told Sandy?"

"Ah . . . I should really consult my key stakeholders, shouldn't I?" Hector said, feeling suddenly lighthearted.

"Yes, I would. Courage, mon frère!" Adam hung up.

Hector walked up to the security desk in the marble lobby and explained his dilemma to the security guards. They rolled their eyes almost imperceptibly, and called his office. Kapp was not available. But Jordan was. He appeared in a glow of fluoride smiles and dry-cleaned efficiency, and signed Hector in. Hector was provided with a temporary pass. The security doors opened.

They made their way to the fourth floor, past the signs of warning appended to every cupboard and door—*Risk of Death Keep Out, Wash Your Hands After Use, Stay Two Metres Apart*—and entered the office.

Jordan handed him a new laptop and winked at Hector before slinking back to the photocopier.

"Where's Kapp?" Hector asked after him.

"In a directors' meeting," Jordan said. "Stamping his new authority."

In the next hour, Hector scrolled through his emails. There were none from Kapp. None from anyone in any position of authority. Jordan stood at his lonely post by the photocopier, pressing buttons and staring out of the windows. It crossed Hector's mind that maybe Jordan wasn't doing any real work at all.

Hector typed out his resignation email to Kapp and to Rhonda. He kept it short and to the point, deleting a few adjectives and overemotional observations. After all, they did not need to know how he felt about his job, about the place of work and the office politics. He was just another fungible asset on the move; he would be replaced and forgotten. He did not need to impart a further particle of his soul to them.

A woman suddenly appeared at his desk. She had heavy glasses and a halo of red hair.

"Hector!"

"Hello . . ." He smiled.

"I'm Debs. You were a journalist, weren't you? I need your writing skills!" She beamed. "I could do with another set of eyes on a news release. It's about this new drive to encourage healthy eating in the young—part of our capacity mission. Could you give me a hand?"

"Sure," Hector said, minimising the resignation email on his screen. "Send it over and I'll have a look."

Debs hovered in the winter sunlight, as if she had something else to say. "I heard you had a tough day out with the boss," she said finally.

"Yeah, not one of my finer moments," he said. "I panicked. Bit of a nightmare."

"It happens," she said. She leaned forward. "Between you and me, I've heard Sir Charles is a bit of a twat."

Hector laughed. Debs grinned and walked quickly back to her desk.

Kapp was back at his post when Hector's eyes returned to his screen. He looked to him and nodded. Kapp's face was impassive. Hector reviewed his resignation email but did not hit *send*. He added more: *I was also disappointed to be party to a meeting about a project or policy called "Grendel." At no stage was it explained to me what this meant, but it has been made fairly clear that I was not meant to know. How can I work properly if I am called to meetings where nothing is explained, and follow-ups are discouraged . . .*

A message appeared from Debs. It contained an explanation of the fitness and nutrition drive being launched. Hector opened the attachment.

The headline read: OBESE CHILDREN TO BE CUT IN HALF. Hector snorted.

"Something amusing, Hector?" Kapp said, pink eyes peering over his monitor.

"This news release. It looks like a bold and imaginative new policy," Hector said.

"What?" Kapp said, standing up.

"It needs a bit of work—Debs over there asked me to help."

"Well, get it done quickly. Deborah should know better— she should stay in her wee box," Kapp said. "I need to talk to you."

Hector took a deep breath. "Is it about Grendel?"

Kapp shook his head and quickly walked around the desk. "Don't mention that here, or anywhere else for that matter," he hissed. His eyes were wide. "We cannot speak of it." He was leaning over Hector now. His breath was as rank as a clogged drain. A shirt button was open, and Hector could see his paunch.

"You know what it is?" Hector said.

Kapp's tired eyes fluttered, deep pink like picked scabs.

"There are *protocols* to follow here," Kapp said. "It is designated as secret now. *Official. Secret.* Got it? Part of our job here is keeping things under wraps. As far as we're concerned, it never happened, okay? Silence on this matter is—and I mean this—mission critical."

"But, Eric, I was invited—"

"I know. That was Rhonda's error. And we won't be seeing her for a while. I'm acting chief now. Clara's working from home. Jordan is doing his thing. You and I are the only operational staff on the team. No more mention of it. Not in emails. Not in messages. Have I made myself clear?"

"Sure," Hector said, nodding. "But I think we need to ask about it."

"No more! No!" Kapp whispered furiously. "Believe me. You're just in the door. I know what's going on—you don't. Now, what about those documents? Your bag?"

"It's . . . in hand," Hector said.

"You don't have it?"

"No."

"Who has it?"

"As I said, they're safe in my friend's office."

"Has he looked inside your bag?"

Hector opened his hands in exasperation. He did not know what to say. Adam would not, he thought, have rifled through his belongings—why would he?

"So we have to assume they have been read," Kapp said, with an odd, constricted voice, as if he was choking on other words that could not be said.

"Do we?" Hector barely said, as Kapp strode back to his desk and began typing loudly. The desk trembled.

A few minutes later, Kapp left the office, trotting bizarrely like a show pony.

Hector's hands began to shake. Sweat prickled on his back. He looked around the office. People were working away, oblivious. He turned his attention to the news release on obese children, which he revised swiftly and sent back to Debs. He looked at his resignation email. His resolve wavered. His mind trembled. Sandy would not understand. She would probably support him in his decision to find a happier occupation, but he had agonised for years before leaving journalism. He had spent mere weeks in this new position, which offered certainty and stability. And there was their beloved child, who needed to be fed and clothed and cared for.

With a deep breath, he saved the resignation email in drafts and then grabbed his anorak. He needed to retrieve that bag as quickly as possible.

Hector turned and as he left, looked back. Debs waved cheerfully. Jordan's face briefly glowed blue as he scanned a document.

Hector jogged down the marble stairs, then stopped to buy a takeaway coffee in the office canteen before slipping through the doors of Alacrity House. The icy air was invigorating. Meltwater was dripping from roofs and running in twisting streams. Salt lay in gritty red stains. Flags hung limp.

Hector decided to take a shortcut. He turned off Princes Street and into West Register Street, a cobbled lane that led to St. Andrew Square. As he walked past the amber glow of the Café Royal, then alongside a hotel, he thought of Shona again. She used to like to drink there. He wondered if she would ever read his email: maybe she would be able to discover more about Grendel. The trail had been shut down for him—maybe it was for the best.

Lost in memory, intent on his journey, he did not see the black 4×4 bursting from a concealed lane to his left. He was only dimly aware of its hurtling bulk before it drove at speed onto the narrow pavement where he walked.

The vehicle hit Hector with a brutal full stop. His head snapped back against solid stone, and in an instant he was crushed. Wheels spinning on the wet cobbles, the car reversed and pulled away, then accelerated down the street, took a sudden right and disappeared across the square.

Hector lay in a bank of dirty snow. His eyes were open, his ruptured body bent beneath his dark winter coat. There was no time for final thoughts, or dreams of his partner, or their tender baby. His brain flickered and dimmed. And before a screaming woman could run to his side from the hotel lobby, Hector Stricken was dead.

PART II
THE RED MAN

16

The village of Fleet Lanshome was silent.
Beyond the streetlamps buzzing in the damp air, black trees plunged into an uncertain distance.

Shona bent down and looked into Ned's car. "I won't be long with this guy—and then we can go to the airport, right?"

Ned was looking at his gloved hands. Something had changed. He did not turn to her; he was looking straight ahead, into the distance, to the black road glittering with rainwater.

"No, Shona, I can't. I'm sorry. Actually, I need to go now," he said quietly.

Her heart clenched in her chest. "What? You said you'd take me to the air—"

"Listen to me. I just can't," he said. The engine was still running. "Something's come up. Change of plan."

"You can't . . . I'm in the middle of bloody nowhere."

The car began to move. The passenger door was still open. Ned looked at Shona, shook his head and unclipped his seat belt.

"Goodbye, Shona," he said. Even in the dim light, she could see that his eyes were watery. He suddenly looked distraught. Then he leaned across and pulled the passenger door shut.

Shona stood back, and the car pulled away. "Ned," she said, almost whispering. She knew he wasn't coming back—and that she would never see him again. The fingers of time and memory converged briefly into a pinch of pain. She pushed it away.

"Fuck!" she shouted.

"Oi! Language, young lady," a voice said.

Shona turned to the small two-storey house behind her. "Oh, hi," she managed as she limped up the path. She suddenly felt very weary.

An elderly woman in a grey tracksuit was standing in the lit doorway. Her long white hair was scraped back in a ponytail. A TV was chattering in the background.

"Well, hello," the woman said, her eyelids heavy, arms tightly crossed about her body.

"I'm here to see a Mr. Loxley," Shona said, breathing heavily. She felt suddenly sore. Like she had been kicked down a flight of stairs.

"Oh, really?" the woman said, unmoving. "In the heart of winter, a traveller. A cold coming you've had of it."

Shona looked behind her, into the darkness. Ned was gone. Her friend was gone. Not even the rear lights of his car could be seen. The darkness had fallen completely, black velvet over an unknown land. Where was she? Deepest England. To her, a mystery. Another country.

She turned to the woman. "I'm here . . ." She was struggling to speak. She put a shaking hand to the cold, pebble-dashed wall of the house.

". . . to see Loxley," the woman said. "So you said. Who told you this Loxley lives here?"

"Ranald Zawadzki. He's worked with Loxley. He sent me here. I need some information."

"Don't we all, darling?" the woman said. "Was that your lift gone, then?"

Shona sighed. She momentarily thought of calling Ned. Somehow she knew it would do no good. He had sickened of her. Again. At least he'd got her this far, she thought. Too far for him, though. Too far, again.

"Zawadzki," the woman said.

"Aye. He's my editor at the Buried Lede. An investig—"

"Yeah, I know, love. I know. Right, in you come." She cocked her head and ushered Shona through to the kitchen. Shona limped behind her.

"You crook?" the woman said.

"Old war wound," Shona said, not entirely inaccurately. "I had a stick . . . I lost it in London."

"Wait a tick," the woman said, bustling off into another room.

Shona blinked in the bright electric light of a small kitchen. The fridge was covered in magnets and pictures of children. Potted plants obscured the window, and dirty plates floated in white suds in the sink. She thought of her father, bent over their own sink, up to his elbows in soapy water. He loved to do the washing-up; it was work that had a beginning, a middle and an end, he always said. Unlike most things.

The woman reappeared with a walking stick: standard NHS design, with a black moulded plastic handle. "Will this do?" She handed it to Shona. "Can't have you carrying on like that."

"Oh. That's great, thanks," Shona said. She was grateful for the stick, for the weight it could bear.

"Follow me," the woman said.

They went through the kitchen to a living room dominated by a flat-screen television. On the screen was aerial footage of a forest fire. A red line of flames burning across a scorched hillside. Amid the swirling smoke, tiny helicopters were buzzing and skimming.

Beside the TV, propped against the wall, was a shotgun.

They continued through a hallway, where a washing machine rumbled and shook. Shona dodged rows of wet clothes hanging from a pulley. The woman opened the door and stepped out. The woman pulled out a pack of cigarettes. She paused to light up.

Through the pale corona emanating from the house, Shona could see a wooden fence. Beyond it, the deep, silent countryside.

"Over the stile and through the trees," the woman said. "Keep going straight ahead. There's a path. Keep the brook on your left. You'll come to a car which has been torched, and a ditch. Follow that and you'll come to a large house. The manor. The curtains will be drawn. You'll find Robin in there."

"Robin?"

"Loxley. You'll be entering the back of the house. Wait at the curtained window—you'll hear the radio. Don't go in, love—he's armed. Wait to be let in."

Shona looked at the woman, calmly exhaling smoke. She was warning of deadly violence, yet she seemed serene.

"Okay. This way?" Shona pointed to the fence.

"I'm not repeating myself, sunshine," the woman said.

"Right."

Shona walked across the grass, the chill descending about her, until she came to a gap in the fence and stepped through it. She turned on the torch on her phone and adjusted the bulky bag on her shoulder.

There was a beaten path through the grass, which her torch beam picked out. The trees were standing in a pattern—it was an orchard. Rows of squat bare apple trees. She looked back—the smoking woman had gone back inside.

Shona walked on, following the woman's directions. The torchlight shook in the dark, lurching from grass to trunk to bare branch to vanished horizon. She was cold, her jeans were sodden already, her socks, too. All she could hear was her own breathing. The moon seemed shrunken and sick, like a peeling scab.

A dense shadow lay ahead. It looked like a boat that had been pulled inland. As she moved closer, she could see it was the burnt-out car the woman had mentioned. The roof had collapsed, the tyres were melted, and the windscreen was reduced to jagged glass, like teeth. Shona wondered how the car had ended up here, sitting out of place in a country orchard.

The ditch opened up before her. Beyond it, bare grass stretched into the distance. She swore. She was running out of time. Even if Loxley was quick, even if he could access the data in minutes, she would still be pushed to get to Bristol in time for a flight home. It was not possible.

Standing in the cold, miles from home, in the middle of nowhere, she felt utterly alone. That morning, she had woken to Ned's uncertain friendship, warm food, a planned day. Then, there had been blood and violence. Her path had been disarranged. Now, she barely knew her way forward.

She had crossed a threshold into a cold, wet limbo. She could have slipped through time or passed into another world. She could have been in the deep past, before this was all here. She could have been in the future, when all this was gone. How had she got here, to this lost and barren place in a strange country's night?

Arid stars above, the trees fruitless, the earth inundated. She was alone. She was nowhere.

17

Shona heard music. A tendril of sound drifting through trees—hushed, but it was there. A fragile melody held by silvery strings.

Shivering, she turned her head to its source. There was light—a square window in the dark—and from it came the music. She tramped onwards, one hand holding her mobile light high like a miner's lantern, the other on her new stick, until the trees dwindled and the window became clear in its shape and dimensions. A radio was playing.

Underfoot, the wet grass was replaced by slabs of cut stone. Above her, an old manor house rose: parts of its roof were missing, and some windows gaped glassless, like sockets in a skull. Gargoyles, coiled and poised on the eaves, leered down at her. A face with fingers pulling back its lips. A dragon with cat eyes. There was a hulking tower, inky against the night sky, with a pitched roof and a weathervane of a hooded man with a sickle, motionless.

The orchestral music rose and fell—melancholy and forceful—then stopped. A small wooden door, at the top of a short flight of steps, opened.

A small white face appeared. A child.

"Hiya," the little girl said. She was wearing pink pajama bottoms, furry slippers and a white T-shirt decorated with an image of a unicorn.

"Well, hello," Shona said, leaning against the wall. She was exhausted. She needed to sit down and drink something hot.

"It's nighttime now," the girl said.

"It is. Shouldn't you be in bed?"

The girl shook her head. "Daddy says it's fine as long as I've done my homework. Which I have." Her mouth was smeared with chocolate. "Don't know why. I'm never going back to school."

"Me, neither. I'm done with school," Shona said. She peeked inside the house. There was a short corridor, flagstoned, with packed holdalls on the floor, and another wooden door. "Boring school," Shona said, surprised and suddenly happy to speak to a child.

"So boring," the girl agreed.

"Can I see Loxley, please?"

"Did you walk across the scary garden on your own?" the girl said, squinting at Shona.

"Yes, I did," Shona said. "And it was very scary."

"It's meant to be," the girl said and turned back inside. "I'll show you to Daddy. He's busy—*as usual.*"

Shona followed the girl into the house.

"Sorry about the mess, Shona Sandyman," the girl said. "We're moving to Greenland."

Shona twitched at the mention of her name.

"Oh, really?"

"What do you think?" the girl said, as they walked down a wood-panelled corridor. "Do you think it will happen quickly or slowly? Daddy thinks it will happen quickly."

"What will happen?" Shona asked, as kindly as she could muster.

"The *future*," the girl said, as it if was obvious.

"Oh, the future will happen quickly," Shona said. "Definitely."

They entered a wide medieval hall, half-timbered, lit by white pillar candles. The high ceiling sagged with black rot and swelling mushrooms of mold. A ratty stag's head hung upside down. An elaborately carved fireplace was filled with blackened timbers and debris.

"How do you know my name?" Shona asked as they crossed the hall, her wet trainers squelching on the stone floor.

"Daddy told me, *obv-i-ously*," the girl said.

"And what's your name?"

"Hecate."

"Hecate?"

"Hecate Beckety," the girl said, keying numbers into a pad beside a heavy steel door.

The door opened with a click, and they both moved into a deep room which fizzed and crackled with electricity, flickering screens and lamps and noise. It was strewn with cushions, blankets and beanbags. By a large log fire, which filled the room with warmth, was an L-shaped desk covered in laptops, blinking boxes, wires, cables, plugs and power bars.

A wiry man in combat trousers and a black T-shirt was at the desk, typing rapidly on a laptop. His hair was patchy— thick and spiky here, absent there. He had not noticed Shona and Hecate enter the room.

A monitor in a corner of the room was being used to play a computer game. Shona saw a small blond elf running through idyllic countryside. A teenage girl sitting in a trans- parent inflatable chair was playing.

There was a buzzing noise. Shona looked up. A tiny drone was flying back and forth, controlled by a shaggy-haired boy lying on a beanbag in another corner of the room. He wore glasses. A half-eaten meal lay on a paper plate beside him.

"Hi, Daddy! The angry woman says the end of the world is really *nigh*," Hecate announced and skipped off.

Shona grinned.

"Shona Sandison." The man turned to her.

"That's me," she said.

"You have money for me? Payment? Wonga?"

"No," she said, feeling her whole body deflate. "No money. No cash. I thought Ranald—"

The drone swooped low above her head before looping away again.

"Shut that bloody thing off, Mav!" the man shouted to the boy, then said, "I told that boss of yours no more wire transfers, no more banking, no more bitcoin shittery. Cash is what I need. Do you have cash?"

Shona couldn't place his accent. He was southern. He could be from Essex, Kent or Surrey for all she knew.

"I've got nothing on me," she said. "I came straight from London, I'm sorry."

"No cash."

"No," she said, firmly.

"For Pete's sake," he said. He smiled a crooked smile. "Hey, you sound like that woman off the telly. The Scotch one. Okay, just plonk yourself down there. I'll be right with you." He swivelled around again and resumed typing.

Shona thought of sitting—her bones ached, her brain ached—but she needed to keep going. She wanted the information from the phone, and she wanted to get to the airport. Through mullioned windows, she could see nothing outside but a black wall of dark. It could have been midnight. She walked across the room, leaning heavily on her new stick, avoiding the cushions, bags and mess, to stand beside the man.

"You are Loxley, aren't you?" she said.

"No one can call him that anymore," the teenage girl shouted. Her video game character was now flying with the aid of artificial wings through a Day-Glo sylvan glade. "We've all got covers now."

"Robin . . . of . . . Loxley," the boy said loudly. "Steals from anyone, keeps it all for himself."

The man pulled out another swivel chair and motioned for her to sit.

Shona pulled the bag off her shoulders and reached for the front zipped pocket. She took out Proctor's phone and placed it on the desktop. "This. I need to see inside this," she said.

Loxley picked up the phone. "What do we have here? Very old school. Hmm."

"Is it a problem?"

"Are you gonna be a problem?" he said, looking at her. His teeth were uneven, his face lopsided; it looked as if it had once been broken, and then remade.

"Not to you," she said, uncertain if this was true.

"All right, then," he said, and then turned in his chair. "Kids!" he yelled.

"What?" the three children yelled at once, in different registers.

"Time to hit the sack. Lights out. Busy day tomorrow. No whingeing either. Meg, no sleeping in the tower, okay?"

"But Dad—"

"It hasn't got a proper roof. Tarpaulin ain't a roof. Sleep in your room." He flipped open the phone and stabbed a finger at it. He frowned.

"But I've got the tent in there," his eldest daughter protested. "It's safe and warm and—"

"Don't give me it! Come on, guys! Meg, turn that shit off. Mav, land that bloody thing and go. Hecate, give your old man a hug."

Hecate sidled over to the workstation. Her face was sticky, and her eyes were half-open. Loxley hugged his daughter and gently ruffled her hair, and she smiled. She left the room with her brother and sister.

"I need to get to the airport to catch the last flight—" Shona said.

Loxley was now sitting with his knees up in his chair. "How did you get here?" he said, turning the phone over in his long-fingered hands. He was missing the tip of one of his fingers. There was a nub of smooth, pink skin and no nail.

"A friend dropped me off, but—"

"And they just left you?" he said, looking at her steadily.

Shona just nodded. She did not know what to say. She looked about the room, which rippled with firelight. The ceiling was arched and braced with ancient beams. Shona yawned. She suddenly felt a deep sinking sensation in her bones. There was another beanbag beside the open fire. She felt ready to crawl into it, curl up and sleep.

"Well, I don't think we're going to get much out of this phone. Not tonight." He reached for a small metal implement like an artist's palette knife.

"Why not?" Shona said.

"For starters, it's not a phone," he said, prising it open. He tapped the screen, then pinched his fingers together and peeled it off—a membrane came away and rolled up instantly in his hand. Underneath was plain black plastic. He threw it onto the desk.

"For fuck's sake," Shona said. "What is it, then?"

Loxley suddenly snapped off one half of the object. It came away with a click, and he threw it aside. He was left with an impermeable oblong. Sealed and discreet. "Someone has made it look like a phone. But it's actually a hard drive of some kind. A little arsenal of information. It's solid, watertight. There must be a way in—or out."

"Is that it?" Shona said, pointing to a tiny hole near one corner. As small as a pinhole.

"I was just getting to that," he said. From somewhere in

the depths of the house, music was playing—pop music, with an insistent beat, a wail of vocals. Loxley suddenly stood up. He looked down at her, eyes narrowed. "I'd rather just turf you out, to be honest, send you back to Mum, but you do look knackered."

"Right . . ."

He tipped his head to one side and stared into the fire. "But this is my last job for Ranald—my last job for anyone. I'm clearing out of here in a couple of days. Relocating. Migrating. Leaving this doomed shithole of an island for good."

Firelight cast deep shadows on his haggard face. He could have been in his fifties. He could have been found preserved in a bog. He could have been from beyond time.

Shona noticed a large crossbow, a long cruel dart in place, under his desk. "Who's that for?" she asked, pointing.

He flicked her a wary look. "Cunts," he said.

The pop music grew louder, and there was a squeal of laughter from somewhere in the ruined mansion.

"Fair enough," Shona said.

He grinned. "Listen, love, you sit here, make yourself comfortable," he said. "Can you stay overnight? I can't just get into this in a few minutes. First, I've got to access the thing, and then I've got to work out what the fuck is inside it. It may only be readable by bespoke technology. I've got to say: it looks proper. Military-industrial tech, this. The good stuff. Not seen anything like it for a while. So?"

"So what?"

"It ain't a quick job," Loxley said. "This is the Ark of the Covenant, believe you me. You can stay until I do it—but do you want to?"

Can I stay overnight? Shona wearily asked herself. Her entire body was aching. She desperately needed to sleep. She looked at Loxley. He was neither friend nor foe. But he had his children nearby and was a friend of Ranald. It was too late now, anyway. She'd missed the last flight home.

He didn't wait for an answer. He moved away through the shadows and disappeared through a large creaking door.

Shona moved closer to the fire. She bent down, picked up the largest log from the basket and laid it on the fire, which shifted slightly in its massive burn. The log was instantly filigreed with tongues of fire, and she felt the intense heat of its burning on her face. Warmth spread through her hungry, cold body. She collapsed on the beanbag and stared into the fiery cavern, the deep gold of its innermost recesses, the pulsating lines of orange and white.

In the distance, children's voices were raised in protest, and then there was a deep silence. Footsteps paced in a distant room. Wind shook the fragile panes in the high windows. *Where am I?* she thought. *What have I done and not done? Where am I going?* She lay back. *I'll just close my eyes for a wee while,* she told herself. *Just until Robin comes back.*

Ned appeared in her mind: his sudden coldness, his fear. She shook her head, and her conscious mind slipped away to another place.

The bees

"Have you told the bees?" Bernadette Comfort said.

She was dabbing her teary eyes with a scrunched-up ball of white tissue. It was late summer. A papery sunlight fell on the slumbering bungalows of Craigentinny in eastern Edinburgh. There were few cars. The retired and the aged lived quiet, respectable lives behind whispering net curtains.

"Have you told them?" she asked again. "The bees?"

Outside, an ice cream van glided past, its bells jingling forlornly.

"I have not," Shona said, "and I'm not quite sure what you mean, Bernie."

"The bees, Shona."

"Who are the Bs? Are they a family?"

She briefly wondered if Bernie meant the Boys' Brigade. But she was pretty sure her father's death meant nothing to them. They certainly meant less than nothing to her father. She had gratefully been freed from attending Brownies and Girl Guides as a youth—her father having, more than a few times, denounced them as paramilitary organisations.

"No, the bees, the bees," Bernie said. She smiled and gestured to the window. "The makers of honey."

It was late 2020, before the second lockdown, and Shona was visiting Bernie to see how she was and to tentatively talk to her about her father. She also wanted to apologise for not inviting Bernie to her father's abrupt funeral, even though he had loved her and Bernie had loved him. She also wanted to tell her that there would be no memorial, no service, and that she had her father's ashes and was not sure what would become of them.

"You must tell the bees your father is dead," Bernie said firmly as her son handed them both sugary brown tea before disappearing again. Bernadette, Hugh's companion, had once been a nun. She had never explained how she had produced this son, a tall, thin man with a shock of black hair and a stubbled face. One day, Shona decided, she would ask Bernie how she came to give birth despite living for years in a Cumbrian convent. But now was not the time.

"So you're saying I have to chat to insects—"

"Maybe you've not had the time, Shona, love," Bernie interrupted. "But they must know. If you don't tell the bees he has passed, they will not only be upset; they will continue to make honey for him. As if he was alive."

Bernie had survived COVID. But her lungs had been ruined. Her hands were shrivelled. Her eyes were milky. She seemed to look at Shona from elsewhere, a perspective far away.

"The bees," she said, "are blessed of God. They can move between the worlds. They may already know that dear Hugh has left us. I would not assume that they don't. And if they are not told, they will fly away. In the convent, we would cover the hives with black cloth. But we don't have hives."

The son was coughing in the kitchen. If this conversation continued much longer, Shona thought, she would break out in hives.

"And no memorial for my lovely Hugh?" Bernie said. "It's such a shame. I'm sad about that."

"I'm sorry, Bernie, but—"

"Oh, Shona, that is your right. You're his only child. But surely there would be folk who would wish to say a proper goodbye to the dear man. His friends from journalism, from the allotment. His pals down at the harbour. From church."

"From church?"

"Before the plague descended, he'd been accompanying me to chapel," Bernie said.

"No, he had not," Shona said. Her father, a lifelong socialist, an occasional self-proclaimed communist, did not hold with the church or religion in general.

"I know the truth of it," Bernie said, taking a sip of her tea. "But, latterly, he was interested. He was a learned man, Shona. We had been discussing the Gospel of Thomas. The Gospel of Judas. The scrolls."

"Aye, right," Shona said. Bernie's bungalow had an overgrown front garden. There were tall grasses, white and brittle in the sun. There were egg-yellow dandelions and an eruption of thistles. A single dark bee moved in the air, rising and falling like a note from one flower to another. On the staves of grass it moved like an errant minim.

"So . . . the bees," Shona said.

"I thought we were maybe moving off the bees," the son murmured from the kitchen.

"We abandon the bees and we are done for," Bernie said. "So you need to go out and tell them that Hugh is gone. Go to a wild place. Shout to them. Let them loudly know. And then all will be settled with them."

Bernadette had grown tired then, and she had said so, and her son, who had eventually introduced himself to Shona as Clement, took his mother gently to bed. Shona left Bernie a present—some mangled flowers from the garage—on the dining table and departed.

She walked through the overgrown garden, not spying any bees, and walked up a road lined with grimly identical houses. As she climbed the hill, rising above the horizon,

Arthur's Seat presented its mountainous bulk to her. Its sides were yellow with gorse and flowers. And so, even though she was tired, she took a bus to the foot of the extinct volcano.

As the summer sun laid a sheen of melting copper over the city, glinting on roofs and cars and glass, she made her way up the steep path to the peak. Walkers drifted past her, and dogs rooted around in the straggling yellow gorse.

She realised as she walked alone, her stick unsure on smooth rocks and stony tracks, that much of her energy, her psychic strength, was being spent on considering the passage of time. Of things lost and irretrievable. Her childhood, her younger years, the years living with her father, her old loves and friendships. So much of her time, now, when she was not working, was spent thinking of the past, of a past that only she could know. And how these memories would be lost with her, when her own light was extinguished. All this pondering, all this ruminating, exhausted her. And to what end? Who cared but her? Who remembered with such deep and plunging recollection a stolen, sweet, unrepeatable kiss in a lane behind a Glasgow nightclub? Dancing in her student flat with friends at five in the morning? The satin ripple of sand hissing over her bare feet on a childhood beach? A warm walk, a hand in hers, to the sodden hill above a hidden loch? Her father's sudden bursts of laughter? The distant, fragmentary memories of her beautiful mother, now long dead?

A bird rotated above her in the Edinburgh sky. It was looking for prey, or looking for a perch, or just enjoying the warm thermals as they buffered its splayed dark wings.

She moved off the well-trodden path to the summit and, after some time pulling through long grass, sat on a rock, with the old, spired city laid before her. The sun was slowly descending in the west. Light lay like liquid between each summer blade of grass, on every tilted rock face, on every fold and furrow of the earth.

A circulating bee, furry as an eyebrow, buzzing purposefully as if piloted by a miniature driver, nipped between yellow flowers on a nearby tangle of gorse.

Shona whispered to it, her uncertain voice husky. "Hey, bee."

The bee darted between flower and flower, unperturbed.

"Hey, bee," she said again.

A tiny yellow flower ducked and bobbed as the bee landed.

"My old dad is gone," she said. "Hugh is dead. The master is gone. But your mistress is here, and she is kind."

The bee rose in the air and seemed to hover for a moment, before vanishing into the thickening summer air.

Shona lay back on the rock as the summer heat rose to the void and cooled to darkness.

18

She was woken by the smell of lemongrass.

Dimly, through befuddled senses, she realised where she was—lying in her clothes, curled up on a beanbag. All that remained of the fire was silver ash and gently glowing embers. The room was still dark.

"Watch your elbow—there's some soup for you," Loxley's voice said.

She looked to one side, where there was a steaming bowl with a ceramic spoon in it. A broth of noodles, bobbing chunks of seared chicken, green vegetables and a sprig of some herb, bright and green. It smelled of citrus, of the earth and the sea, of goodness.

She thanked him. "Did you cook this? It smells amazing."

"Of course I did. I'm not a complete fucking barbarian," he said. He was tapping on a tiny laptop which seemed to have only half its keys. "Laura was the cook. I learnt from her. Couldn't rustle up beans on toast before that, believe you me. Glad we kept her recipes. Wrote 'em all down in pencil, she did."

Shona looked at her phone—it was 5:30 A.M. Hungry, she reached for the bowl and began to eat. The broth was warm and sharp and sweet. She hadn't tasted anything so delicious in a while.

"I don't mind admitting I'm finding this a hard nut to crack," Loxley said as he tapped away, an empty bowl of soup at his elbow.

Standing up, slurping from the bowl, she looked at his desk. He had connected wires to the black box, which fed through another box, silver with blinking lights, then through what looked like some kind of filter system and into the tiny laptop.

"Nicked this from a fella at the Shin Bet," he said, "back in the day. He was careless with his kit, especially when he was drunk on whisky and pomegranate juice. But I liked him. He got blown up somewhere—can't remember where. It's for fieldwork, it's bombproof. And it can find its way through the maze of fences, traps and sliding doors in our little friend over here."

"What is it?"

"The black box? It's what I said it was. Weren't you paying attention? Dear, oh, dear. Not good for a journalist. It's a memory drive of some kind."

He tapped on. The screen on the field laptop flashed and turned green. Type, in a language Shona did not recognise, began to dance on the tiny screen. It looked like a series of emerald-green squares with random horns, legs and tails.

Loxley dipped a finger in his bowl and sucked on the dregs. "Not enough lemon . . ."

"That language, what is it?"

"Hmm," he said, screwing up his face. "Jeez, not seen that in a while." He had large eyes, Shona noticed, which were bright and brown as gleaming chestnuts. "It's not language. It's a Norloch Cypher. It's an occlusion code. The old NLC. But I think I have something for that." He stood up and looked at Shona. "Eat that up before it gets cold. It kind of turns into slime after a while." He leaned across his desk, picked up a blue pen drive, like a tiny scarab beetle, and inserted it into a larger laptop, which came to life. "Half an hour, I reckon," he said.

"Who's Laura?" Shona asked.

He turned his head to one side and appeared to murmur

something to the computer, as if coaxing. As if praying. "My wife," he said quietly. "Laura was my wife."

"Oh," Shona said.

"She died," he said, watching the text on the screen scroll. "In the pandemic . . . Right, the data's running now. The languages are talking to each other. You know, I used to do this for Cheltenham, for GCHQ. Surveillance. As we used to say, the only part of government that listens. Haha. Now look at me. Patching shit together to winkle out the juicy stuff. Knocking about in the dark."

"I'm sorry for your loss," Shona said.

Loxley sat back in his chair and looked at her, fingers steepled beneath his chin. His hooded top had ridden up; the tawny hair on his lean stomach was revealed. "Laura was a nurse. I was doing this stuff on the side. Met the big fella, Ranald, when I was generating— shall we say "content" for the papers. Listening in to princes and footballers. Did a bit of double duty for the other side and all. Got a taste for it. Then 2020 came . . ."

"My dad got it in the first wave," Shona said. She scooped up more noodles and chewed.

"Ah, when the men in charge wanted to 'let it rip,' right? Herd immunity? A planned national catastrophe? Hoping the old would die and leave the young? But the young did die, didn't they? My Laura was young," he said, repeatedly tapping a single key on the laptop. "And she got it bad. Crap PPE in her gaff. She always had asthma. So does Hecate. Got it bad. Laura was sick straightaway." He pressed the heels of his hands over his eyes. "She did her last shift. I can see it now. I see it every day. An all-dayer. Watching the old folk dying. Night came, and she was really struggling. Had a fever, couldn't breathe. Then the boy went down with it, too. She knew she needed help—breathing apparatus. So we went to the hospital. Last I saw her was in the bloody car park. The godforsaken car park. She went in by herself, just waved at me and told me not to worry. To look after Mav. I was freaking about the boy. I saw her go through the doors, bent over double, coughing her guts up . . . and that was the last time I saw her alive. She died a few days later."

"I'm so sorry," Shona said.

"And that was me, a widower," he said, removing his hands from his face. He had not been crying, but his eyes were red. "Right, here we go." He moved his chair nearer to the screen and pressed a button with a small flourish. A light began to flash on the memory stick in the larger laptop. A loading bar appeared and began to slowly fill with blue.

"Is this good news?" Shona said, pointing at the screen.

"What's good news?" he said. "Well, yeah, it's downloading, but it'll take a moment or two. Have a seat. You'll get what you need. Then Ranald can pay me, and I can pack up."

The loading bar moved fractionally closer to being complete.

"What is this place, this pile? It's not yours, is it?" she said.

Loxley checked the time on his watch, a lump of retro black rubber and metal. "Too late to sleep now," he said. "Too late."

Shona looked at the data loading, the entwined wires, the blinking lights. This was not the journalism she had grown up with, in which she had made her way. This was about systems, codes, data and access. Arcane technologies. Words and numbers in another plane, not even existing in this world, somewhere between real and unreal: in wires, in rare metals, in hard plastics, in clouds that were not clouds. She felt uneasy. Aware of how afraid she might be.

Her phone sang a sad diminuendo and then, its battery

depleted, died. Maybe she would just chuck it away into the orchard outside. Be free of it.

"No, this gaff is certainly not mine," Loxley said at last. "Well deduced."

"Does it belong to your family?"

He laughed. It was an odd, high-pitched sound, like a wounded dog yelping. In his open mouth she could see molars capped with silver.

"No, sweetheart, no," he said. He righted himself. "No, this place is the product of a high window. We swooped in. Why the hell not? We'll be out of here, soon enough."

"A high window?"

"Yeah." After a deep breath, he said, "After Laura . . . I wanted out of London. Fucking London, sold off to all the fuckers, the crooks and the spivs. I wanted away. Mum— you've met her—lives here, has been living in Fleet Lanshome since my old man passed. She kept banging on about the big house. About how some fella had bought it. A big guy surrounded by even bigger guys in suits and dark glasses. A plastic wife. Place had gone to the dogs for years since the original family all keeled over or quit. So the old hall, this gaff, was bought by a certain Russian squire. Voroshilov was his name. Into aluminium, the usual. Just another oligarch looking for an English manor. But then, just after COVID began, Mr. Voroshilov decided to throw himself out of the twelfth floor of a hotel in Moscow, didn't he? Conveniently. His missus was found dead too: overdosed in a yacht in Venice. Needle in her neck. Both bumped off. And an only son somewhere in Argentina. Counting his days, I'm sure. Watching his back. Avoiding windows. Avoiding rooms with one door."

"So this place was empty?"

"Exactly. You're catching on," he said. "A manor with

no one to claim it. The Russki had done it up a bit, put in proper electrics here and there, a generator, some plumbing. It was in a state, still is, but it was perfect for us. I can run operations from here and no sod knows where we are. Mum can mind the kids. So we're in the ruins, hiding in the ends of the world, before it comes. Before it fully manifests."

Loxley got up from his chair and took both bowls. He asked Shona if she wanted tea, and she nodded. He left the room. Shona looked up to the ceiling. In the near dawn, she could see the full extent of the rot: the peeling paper, the great swelling blisters of damp and deterioration, an acne of mold.

Loxley returned with two steaming cups of tea. "Milk and two—that all right?" he said, checking his laptop.

"Exactly right."

"You look the type—no offence," he said, smiling.

"None taken. How long till this is done?"

"Ten minutes," he said. "And then you can get out of here. Again, no offence. I've got shit to do. Got to pack all this stuff up, get the kids' stuff ready. I've given Mum a bell and she can take you to the airport. There's a plane up to Scotchland late morning. You'll make it. Give me your email and I'll book your tickets, sunshine."

Shona wanted to go home. She wanted to sleep in her own bed. To contact Reculver. To call old friends and arrange a drink.

"That's kind of you," she said, and told him her details.

"Kind? It's nothing," he said quickly. "I need you out of here, out of my hair—what's left of it. But it's been a pleasure, darlin'," he said, pretending to bow.

Shona smiled and sipped her tea, the warm, sweet, brown liquid. It warmed her in an instant. Outside, through a filthy window, she could see the vertical shadows of trees.

Like people opening their arms, waiting. Like a row of crucifixions.

"Why are you moving?" she asked.

He coughed. "You're joking, right? Why are we leaving? You for real? This country is *fucked*," he said. He took a deep breath. "Do you not see it? I mean, where to even begin . . . The rivers are poisoned. Old trees felled. Hospitals collapsing. High-rises catching on fire, dozens of poor sods burning to death and no one brought to book. Towns with no future. Everyone defeated. Whole cities going bust. Beaches covered in crap. The infrastructure fucked . . ."

Shona thought she heard a door open and close somewhere deep in the ruined house.

". . . half the country surviving on food banks. A third of kids on the breadline. London, a nest of thieves. An extinction economy. Imploded biomes. Generational destitution. Credit card necrosis. And nothing will get better. We're past the point of no return. You know that, don't you? The world is burning. The fire is lit, and it isn't going to go out. It's not like that fire over there, Shona. It's done. We're done. We're all in the pot, and there's no one going to turn off the heat. And what will happen next? And I mean soon. Mass movements of people. Food running out. Water running out. And England—I dunno about your Scotland, you know better than me—is weak. It will break. Has it any resilience? No. You got kids?"

Shona said no. He was ranting. He sounded like another man she had met once, a starving stigmatic priest who lived up a condemned Glasgow high-rise. He had preached the end of times, too. But that mystic had stabbed her and rendered her lame. Robin Loxley was not dangerous, she did not think. He was angry. He was sorrowful and scared.

"Well, lucky you. It's all over, love. This is the boom of the wave before it breaks, and no one can fathom what's coming. When it comes, my kids can't be part of that. They can't be caught up in the fucking inferno. Laura's gone, but she lives in them. I have to save them. For my sins, for our sins." He shook his head. "If you can't protect your children, then what the hell are you good for?" He pointed to the window. "You think, right, the ones who want to survive, who have the resources to survive: They're planning? No, they've *planned*. Things are in place. Arrangements. In New Zealand. Norway. Alaska. Scotland. Believe you me, the cunts in charge, they think they'll survive, their families will survive and somehow they'll get by. Prolong and prosper. But what can *we* do? We just have to wait it out. Wait out another Dark Ages. Move to the north, the far south, try and get by. Survive."

"Are you sure, pal?" Shona said earnestly. "You think the world's going to end? You're talking about apocalypse? You sound like one of those online conspiracy theorists—"

"Conspiracy theorist—that's CIA terminology," he said. He turned to the door, as if he'd heard something. Then the window. "There's been a plague, right? Don't we know it. Next, there'll be mass movement. Whole continents. Droughts. Crop failure. Biblical floods. Starvation. It's coming, Shona. No doubt about it. Countries? Countries are bullshit. They'll disappear. Cantons and city-states, that's what we'll have. Armour and walls, moats and bridges." He rubbed a single finger in a circle on the desktop. Around and around. "This was a beautiful, rare and magnificent world," he said quietly. "And we fucked it."

"We might have," Shona whispered.

"Anyway . . . I've been doing all this phone-hacking work. All this geeky shit for Ranald and others. Saving up the cash. Getting my preparations in place. Moving into this ruin so we can leave with no trace. And this place, this England, this mean and unpleasant land? It's dead. England's not dreaming; it's deceased. Maybe you'll be sitting pretty up there in Scotland. In that Edinburgh Castle, right? Or maybe up in the Highlands. You'll be okay there—until the food runs out. Do you know how to farm? Thought not. Know how to hunt? No. Know how to process clean water? No."

"So you're going to Greenland?"

"I've told the kids we're going to Greenland, but that's so they don't worry. Taking the family. Not my old mum; she won't move," he said ruefully. "But not Greenland. It's more remote than that. You won't see or hear from me again. And the future . . . the boy will have to be a warrior. The girls will have to smart and strong. And be willing to do what's needed. You won't hear from Robin Loxley again, that's for sure."

"Fucking hell," she said.

"Past the point of no return, Shona," he said, softly. "Past the point of no return. There are two worlds now—the one we live in, where we carry on as if nothing is happening. Telly. Cars. Food in the shops. Hospitals. Heating. Law. Order. And there's the world to come. Like a wolf in the night. And everything will be turned upside down."

"It's not that bad, is it?" she said, almost to herself. "Have things got that bad?"

Loxley said nothing.

Shona moved to the windows. A feeble winter sun was rising. Through an arched stone window, now glimmering with lilac light, she could see the full outline of the rest of the building—there was another wing, black with ivy, curled around an overgrown central lawn. Beyond, the world was mist. A dream, a false horizon in a computer game.

She imagined the world transformed. The trees on fire, burning like kindling. The grass and weeds stripped and the earth exposed and parched. The horizon a brown blur. The sun angry, red and huge.

"Robin—is that your real name?" she said eventually.

"Yeah, I'm Robin," he said. "Not Doomscroll666 or any of my other mad concoctions. All gone now. Who cares? Oh, here we are! The motherlode."

He was staring at the laptop screen. He then swore and moved swiftly across the room. He pulled down a woollen blanket and revealed a printer. He pressed a button, a light blinked, and he returned to the laptop and pressed a key. The printer began to hum.

"Here you go," he said to Shona. "This is the info. But this process . . . it's a brutal one. I think that thing is dead now. To get this, we've broken it. I'll destroy it . . ."

There was a change in the air; ash puffed up from the fire as the main door to the room opened. Loxley's mother, wearing a neat blue tracksuit, stood, cool as marble, in the doorway.

"Mum," Loxley said. He was at the printer, scooping up the paper and tidying its edges, rapping it on the printer's lid. "So old-school, all this paper spooling. Shona, meet my old mum, Jennie. Off you go now, and tell Ranald I need the money by six today." He winked as he passed the pages to Shona.

She felt the uncommon heft of them.

"Come on, love," Jennie said. She twirled a key around her finger. "Time's a-wasting."

Shona looked down at the first page. In closely spaced text, there was a list of names, companies and organisations. The title of the paper was printed in a brutal sans serif: GRENDEL STAKEHOLDERS. She moved to the window to read the document in better light.

Her pulse suddenly stuttered.

Something dark and violent was moving across the lawn, towards the house. Something low and loping. A flick of hair, and hard bright eyes above a mask. She heard the faint crunch of boots on gravel.

"There's someone outside," she said, as loudly as she could manage. Her throat constricted. Her shoulders clenched.

"What do you mean?" Loxley said.

"There's a man outside," Shona said. She turned away from the window, her eyes wide.

"What man?"

"He . . . he's from London. A killer," Shona said, holding the papers tight to her chest.

"A *killer*?" Loxley moved quickly to his desk, crouching. "What do you mean a killer? A fucking *what*?"

He barked to his mother to get the children. Jennie nodded, unblinking, and moved to another door and vanished.

"In London . . ." Shona said. She felt an overwhelming urge to run and hide. Her body cringed. She saw Proctor's red blood pooling about her feet. His open, shattered mouth. Teeth washed in blood. "A killer," she repeated.

"Are you sure? You're not seeing things?" he said rapidly, leaning forward to look through the window.

She shook her head.

"Well, he's after you, sunshine," Loxley said, lifting his crossbow, a metal arrow in place. "No sod knows I'm here, and I've kept it that way. So you should scram." He pointed to a low wooden door next to the fireplace. "Get in there, into the chapel. Lock the door behind you."

She swallowed hard and made for the door, grabbing her bag—into which she shoved the fat stack of papers—and stick on the way, as Loxley disappeared behind a heavy tattered curtain, the crossbow at his side, then darted outside.

The chapel door was cracked and swollen, with black metal fastenings and a ring for a handle, which she turned. She pushed hard. It gave way with a groan, and she tumbled inside, down steep wooden steps to a stone floor.

The world jerked and slid. Her stick momentarily caught underfoot and then skittered away. She hit her head on something solid and unforgiving, and she opened her mouth to yell, but the world suddenly vanished.

19

Shona's eyes focused and unfocused, and light strobed in and out of her sight. A deep pain throbbed in her temple. The floor was tiled, empty of furniture. Dead leaves lay in piles, as if they had been brought in by the sea. They drifted with her breath. She lay for a while, fixed by pain.

Where was she?

She could not move.

There was suddenly a yelp. The cry of a child. And a scream, full-throated, then a sound like a blade slashing through canvas.

She could feel her toes, her fingers. Gritting her teeth, she pulled herself up and reached out for the stick. The floor righted itself, became horizontal again. She sat up.

She suddenly needed to vomit. Her chest spasmed. She swallowed. Then she tipped her head and spewed onto the chapel floor. "Sorry," she found herself saying. She wiped her nose and mouth.

Something nearby crashed—something heavy had been broken. There was shouting. A single gunshot sounded, cracking like a bone.

"Fucking hell," she said. She looked around. In an alcove over a bare altar was a statue of Christ, lying prostrate across the lap of his grieving mother. A faint morning light fell like consolation on the smooth marble, the open mouth of the man, the lowered eyes of Mary as she held her dead son. Shadows hung about her like robes.

There was a shriek somewhere in the building—a terri-fied scream and a kind of animal yelping cutting through the damp walls. Shona moved her hand up her stick and held it like a sword. Mary, the Mother, inconsolable, looked down at her with stone eyes.

There was a sudden eruption as the wooden door slammed open and a voice shouted, "Are you hurt?" Standing in the doorway was Jennie, holding a shotgun. "Let's go," she said.

Shona pulled herself up, wincing in pain. She put a hand to her head, but there was no blood. "What's happening?"

"We need to fucking go—now! The man's in the building," she said. "Robin's gone after him. We need to leave."

Shona tried to move, but she staggered a little and had to sit down beside the altar. Hard marble on her thighs. "I fell . . . I banged my head . . ." she mumbled. She felt nausea rising again, swirling up her throat like a backed-up drain.

Jennie moved forward, her free hand extended. "No, love. Get up. We need to get you out of here."

Jennie hustled Shona out of the house and dragged her through the orchard, both breathing heavily, running low. Wet branches slashed across them as they ran—past the wrecked car, past the sunken stream. Birds rose in squalls. Shona slipped in the mud, but Jennie's grip was strong.

The morning revealed the scale of the wreckage of Loxley's temporary home. The manor was a sprawling pile of red brick, broken slates, sunken walls and smashed windows. The guttering was choked with slime and windfall. A tower, broken at its peak, was engulfed in ivy. The roof collapsed. And somewhere in the ruin, two men were fighting for their lives.

Shona and Jennie tumbled into the back garden and then on through the house. A car was waiting by the gate. Sitting there, puttering away, the taxi looked absurd to Shona. Something from another, eventless, life.

"He's still in there," Jennie said, looking back.

Shona was bent double, her breath coming in ragged gasps. "I've seen him before," she said.

"What?"

"He attacked me in London."

Jennie looked at her, eyes wide, hands on her hips. "You brought him here?"

"I'm sorry," Shona said, close to tears. "I . . . Where are the children?"

"I rounded them up," Jennie said, moving her hand on the barrel of the gun. "They're fine. They're safe. You must have been out of it for a while."

"I heard a scream," Shona said.

Jennie shook her head, as if to silence any further questions.

Shona put a hand to her head again. It was tender, swollen, but the skin was not broken. Her mind was reeling. It was empty of all logic and sense. "How could he know I was here?" she said.

Jennie waved her hands in exasperation. "Who knew you were coming?"

Ranald had made the call, but Loxley was his contact. And Ned had driven her here. Ned Silver, her old friend. Now, suddenly, everything was too much. Shona covered her face with her hands and sobbed. Her fingers filled with tears. "I'm sorry," she said. "I'm so sorry."

Jennie shook her head. "Come on, love. No time for that."

Shona reached down far back inside herself, into the bedrock of strength and anger and tough love on which her chaotic life was rooted. She felt it, and she hardened. She wiped her eyes.

"Fuck this," she said. Not to Jennie, not to herself. But to the rest of the rotten world.

The taxi sounded its horn.

"You'll be all right," Jennie said. "You're a tough nut. But you need to go. Get as far away from here as possible. Here—take these. Good luck."

Jennie handed a packet of painkillers to Shona and moved away. She did not look back as she walked steadily back through the house to the orchard, the shotgun cocked.

Shona opened her mouth to say something but could not find the words. She stumbled to the taxi and collapsed on the back seat.

"Please go," she said. The car pulled away, the driver unperturbed. She checked her bag. At the bottom, under all the crumpled papers, was her press award, hard and heavy. It seemed like she had been given it in another age. Another lifetime.

She looked behind as the taxi began to pick up speed. There was no sign of the ruined manor house through the dense woodland. No sign of blood and murder. It all fell behind, into the distance. Into the past.

The driver played some pop music as they drove west, and its melancholy caught Shona by surprise. As they sped past fields shrouded in mist, trees huddling in their midst like ghosts, the winter sun glowed on the wet road. Shona felt tears prick her eyes again. She bit her lip. The driver glanced in his mirror, then glanced away. Shona swallowed two painkiller pills, then reached into her bag for the papers printed by Loxley.

The Grendel list. Its names were arranged in three columns: *Confirmed, Out, Unconfirmed.* Her heart picked up its beat. In the *Confirmed* column were the names of significant companies: PLCs, limited companies and some individuals whose names she did not recognise. Clothing companies. An oil firm. There were two major media organisations. There were weapons companies. Two large financial institutions.

Two banks. There were also several acronyms which she did not recognise. There was no Reece Proctor there, no Ned Silver.

Maybe Ned had been followed, she thought. Maybe he knew nothing about any of this.

At the foot of the page: *GRENDEL confirmed list pertains Scotland trial. See PEARL outline for full UK participation. MEMO with CARS.*

This was the information Proctor had been trying to get to her. This was a story. What was Grendel? What was being trialled in Scotland? Why did Moriah and Proctor want to tell her about it? Was Proctor, in fact, Moriah?

The taxi reached the airport at Bristol, and Shona realised her phone, which, if Loxley was true to his word, would have all her flight information on it, was now dead. She found an unmanned plug in the main concourse, plugged in her charger and sat on the floor beside it. Her legs hurt. Her clothes were still damp, her trainers black with mud. Her face was streaked with tears, and she could not even imagine her hair.

She closed her eyes, her back against a glass screen, and began to doze. After a time, the phone came back to life. A square of blue light lit up. Then it buzzed, twice.

Two messages, one an email from Hector.

I don't know what it is, but you should probably look into this. One of our plans. Grendel. I can't tell you any more.

What the hell? She looked around the airport to check her position in the world was real. To check she was not dreaming. But everything was normal.

She looked at Hector's message. One of "our" plans? That must mean the quango he was working for. She looked it up. It was something called Capacity and Resilience (Scotland). It had a neat but information-free website. Its chief executive was a former MP, Sir Charles Dyce. She knew his name. He had resigned from Westminster after allegations of corruption. These involved huge sums of public money being funnelled to one of his companies making personal protective equipment during COVID. He had fallen out of one warm bed and into another.

She closed the page. She would have to speak to Hector about his job, about the quango, about this Dyce.

Around her, the airport seemed artificial. Yet it was clean and efficient and functional, and eager travellers circulated like bottles trundling along the conveyor belt of a factory. The neon light was sharp. People's clothes were smart and new. Fresh faces gleamed like thermoplastic polymers. Nothing was wrong: there was no leakage, no mud, no darkness. Everything looked right. No blood, no violence. Children smiled. Men behaved normally. Women did not seem to mind them. The ordinary world clicked on like a smooth clock. No one knew about Grendel. No one cared about what Grendel might be, or its aims and purposes.

The second email was her air ticket. It came from an unknown multi-numbered email. The plane left in two hours. Loxley had been right: she would make it.

She wondered how Loxley was. His family. She thought, not for the first time, of how quickly these fugitive relationships could be forged and how quickly they evaporated. So many stories she had written depended on these intense but ephemeral relationships. And once the story was printed, the hinterland of complex ties and hard-earned confessions fell away, became redundant. Another hard-won, fleeting contact with a fellow human had been lived and gone.

As she made her way to Departures, she thought of Hector. She hadn't spoken to him for a while—for weeks. All she knew was that he'd left journalism and joined some PR team in government. He'd dropped out of view, submerged in his new, silent life. But Grendel, whatever it was, was a presence in Scotland. Hector had heard of it, even if, it was clear, he did not know what it meant.

After a tedious shuffle through airport security, she called Hector. But the number rang out. She swore and reminded herself to call him later. She answered the email: *Hector, good to hear from you. This is interesting—we need to speak. Call me. S*

Her phone buzzed again. It was a message from Ranald, a voicemail. She listened to it as she waited to buy a coffee. It was a cheery call, asking her if she had met up with Loxley and if she was any closer to finding Moriah.

She closed her phone and looked out of the departure lounge window to the bare fields. How far away was the sea? A lumbering plane crawled to the end of its runway, suddenly became weightless and glided into the grey sky as if pulled by a string.

"Take care, my darling," her father had said. When he had been so ill. When the virus had flooded his lungs. When he was being taken to hospital in that hideous wailing ambulance, carried by two masked men. "Take care, my darling," he had rasped. His last words to her.

Was she taking care? No. She did not want to. She had a new aim—beyond her grieving quiet life.

She had a story to find. Something to hunt.

20

The ranks were laid out. The files were in place. The troops were ready for inspection.

The old man leaned down so that his eyes were at the height of the table. He regretted having rushed the painting of his cuirassiers. Those noble men deserved more care and attention than splodges of silver enamel on their chests and blobs of metallic paint on their swords and elegant helmets.

He glanced at his watch—his foe, a Mr. Angus Pettifer, would be with him soon. According to the emails they had exchanged, he lived not far away. Maybe he was a professor at the University of St. Andrews. A retired major in the Black Watch. Or maybe he was just another old man, filling the time left to him with meaningless distractions and myopic amusements. He did not know much about Pettifer. But his days of checking people's backgrounds—their jobs, incomes, families, foibles, bank accounts, vices—were over.

Now, now, he thought. *Don't start that again.*

His living room—where the large table was spread with his French armies, a copse of autumn trees, an emerald river, a bridge and a scattering of historical buildings—was now clear of his packing.

He had a decanter on the side, newly filled with black port, the cut glass glinting in the clear winter light. On the white walls, he had hung some pictures: antique views of Hong Kong and Myanmar, and a faded print of a naval victory, all billowing cannon smoke and ragged sails.

The old man looked again with some pride at his expensively assembled model army. These war games detained him now. Movements of troops, dice rolls, precisely researched uniforms, the employment of rulers and rules. Impatient, he put on some music—his son's favourite symphony, Vaughan Williams's Fifth. The pain of heartbreak in surging melody.

He had put a framed portrait of his grandson on the window ledge. There he sat, on his mother's knee, a shock of white-blond hair, a gap-toothed smile. Face beaming, hands raised to clap. His son's large eyes, the widow's elfin nose. A beautiful boy. He had not seen him for some time. The boy's life was in France now, with his mother. Perhaps it was for the best that he never saw the child. How many young men could he ruin in his life? How much damage could he cause to others? No more.

He sat down heavily in a leather armchair as the music grew in volume and beauty. The snow was melting. Ice water dripped noisily from the eaves. It had all come to this—a small house in a small village in a small country. The old empires, lost. The powers, gone completely. The regiments and battalions, in the hands of others. The music wrenched at his thawed heart.

A shadow flitted past the front window: his guest had arrived. He moved to the door, the symphony swelling as if in sympathy, and opened it.

He looked the man up and down quickly. Mr. Angus Pettifer was younger than he had thought he would be—tousle-haired, white-faced, dark-browed, a nerveless look in his eye and dimples with a ready smile. Twelve stone, size ten feet. Black trousers, a pale blue shirt, a navy V-neck jumper, an expensive raincoat. And a holdall.

They said hello and shook hands. As Wolf ushered Pettifer

into the house, he smelled cheap shower gel and fresh new cotton.

Pettifer remarked on the cold weather and the state of the roads.

Wolf smiled. "Where are you parked?"

"Just near the caravan park," Pettifer said instantly.

As Wolf made coffee, they conversed in stilted bursts of forced bonhomie, quick laughs and incoherent *umm*s and *ahh*s—the wariness of men of similar interests meeting for the first time, assessing, testing, surveying.

How had the parking been? *Oh, fine.* Why on earth wasn't there a direct train from Edinburgh to the villages of the East Neuk? *Ridiculous*, they agreed. Isn't it pleasing to organise war games over the internet? *Yes, so convenient.* Isn't ordering miniatures from suppliers so much easier these days? *Oh, yes, compared to the 1990s!* No more lead, either. Such heaviness, and poison, a thing of the past . . .

Then, standing by the main table, with the music turned down, the heating on, hot drinks in hands and rulebooks produced, a scatter of dice ready, they agreed to play for two hours and see where the battle took them. A first tilt at each other—an exploratory skirmish.

As Pettifer carefully pulled his red-coated troops from the bespoke carrier—foam layered, couched padding and trays for the troops—Wolf returned to the kitchen. As he neatly sliced a lemon drizzle cake, he looked to the corner of the kitchen, where his gun stood, loaded.

"I've taken the liberty of roughly calculating the value of your troops as per your email and set mine out accordingly," Pettifer called. "I hope you don't mind, and of course you can always check that we are roughly balanced."

"Marvellous," Wolf replied.

"Your voltigeurs," Pettifer called again, "I have mirrored with my own irregulars."

"Oh, of course, of course. The Green Jackets. Armed with carbines?"

"Muskets," Pettifer said confidently.

"Well, indeed. Let's not worry about army points. They never did in real life, of course."

"Mr. Wolf, may I enquire as to your first name? Of course I can call you Mr. Wolf throughout, should you prefer."

"Please call me Ben."

"Ben Wolf," Pettifer said.

"Indeed."

Rejoined, plates of cake in hand, coffee steaming, they admired each other's legions. The British troops, immaculately painted, based cleanly, stood in line and file almost perfectly. At the front of their lines, in scattered patches, stalked the green-jacketed snipers. Flags glittered in frozen motion. Hundreds of pink faces, eyeless, glared towards the columns of the French. Ten millimetres tall, and ready to fight.

"Beautifully painted, your men," Wolf said, from across the table. "Absolutely. The buckles on the belts, my word! You must have had them painted professionally?"

He moved some of his own artillery around. He would pound the British lines until they broke, he thought, then advance the columns, his heavy cavalry sweeping from the sides. Slicing up the stragglers. Cutting down the broken formations. Routing the screaming survivors.

"Actually, no," Pettifer said mildly, peering at the rulebook, then snatching a look at the table. "I just don't have a lot of work to do these days. Sold my company and always wanted to take my little toy-soldier addiction seriously. So here I am. Shall we begin?"

He smiled, and the old man smiled back. He would put this diffident sort to the sword. Smash his immaculate army to pieces. His mind would scream the cries of the imaginary wounded, the groans of the dead, the smash and boom of the battle.

"It's Angus, isn't it?" Wolf said. An old habit. Checking the firmer details, to see if they held.

Fisher grinned. "Oh, yes, that's me," he lied. "Shall we cast lots for who goes first? I must thank you again for this marvellous games table, the conviviality of this place you have. It's a cut above, Ben. And such a pretty village. The East Neuk really is beautiful, isn't it?"

"I need to see more of it," Wolf said as he reached for the red dice, which clinked satisfactorily in his hands.

Fisher was poring over the rule book, a large black volume with a golden cannon on its cover. "Now, what is the range of those horse-drawn cannons?"

The battle game began with fusillades of cannon fire. Invisible artillery fire rent the air and ripped the earth. Dice rolled and men were pulverised. Small rips of cotton wool marked detonations. A metal tape, that snapped back into its holder like a trap, measured the hits and the misses.

Fisher and Wolf pondered and muttered to themselves. Martial music was now on the stereo, layered with a soundtrack of musket fire and cannon blasts. Horn signals and muffled shouting.

"Hard pounding, this," Wolf said.

Fisher remained impassive. He did not move his infantry, did not even to try to capture the mid-table village that may have afforded position, cover and favourable dice roll amendments.

"Let's see who pounds the hardest, as the great man said," Wolf said.

Again, Fisher stared at the table, unmoved. He moved his cavalry behind his own lines. And continued to pound the French columns. The dice rolled and tumbled. Hits were lodged and numerated. Casualties counted and mourned with smacked lips or low moans.

After an hour and a half of cautious movement and intense but frequently inaccurate cannonades, they decided to have a break. Wolf made some tea and Fisher looked about the room—neat, clean, recently decorated. A brass bellows beside the fireplace. Military paintings.

And down there, beneath the tumble of rooftops, the harbour.

"Your snipers, have you thought about moving them into the village?" Wolf said, appearing with two steaming cups.

His face, Fisher observed, was similar to the images he had on file: long, heavily lined, with sharp, sparkling eyes. A receding but still vigorous steely head of hair. Smart country clothes—a gilet and an aged, checked shirt ironed into submission. A sense of vitality and lithe motion in an old body.

"I should." Fisher nodded, raising his cup of tea as if in an alcoholic toast. "But I fear their movement will be curtailed by your cannon fire. They could be cut to pieces before they even reach cover."

"But once in cover, they would be almost immovable, Angus. And from there"—Wolf indicated the table—"they could enfilade my columns, in the event of an advance."

"You could set fire to the buildings and slaughter all inside."

"I could. We cannot simply pound each other from a distance all day. Like the early hours of Waterloo. No, something must break."

"Ben . . . if today works as well as I think it will, perhaps we could do this again? Have a campaign?"

Wolf flinched a little and then said, "That would be super."

Fisher pointed down to the harbour. "I've not been this way much. I should explore it more."

"Where are you from again? Not Edinburgh?" Wolf said over his steaming cup, eyes steady.

"Ah, no. London originally. Then a spell in the Royal Engineers. Then the City, and my little firm did quite well. I bought a place in the New Town."

"Ah, very good. What was your line?"

"Acquisition software." Fisher shrugged. "Broadly speaking. Bespoke solutions. And yours?"

"I'm a company man, too. Retired."

"Very good. London?"

"Mainly. Spells abroad. Here and there. Royal Engineers—whereabouts?"

"The usual places. A lot of sand. And, for you, retirement in Fife?"

"My son is here. I like to be close."

"Of course," Fisher said, looking through a square window at the harbour. The Firth of Forth was still, the waves a series of reverberating lines, tiny skeins of white, folding and enfolding. The southern shore was a long grey smear. Edinburgh could not be seen. The land looked depopulated from here. A distant, strange country.

Wolf looked down to the harbour. He had seen lights there in the early hours when he could not sleep and sat alone in his chair, with only whisky for company.

"Shall we resume?" Wolf said.

"I have all day," Fisher said, turning, with a grin.

"Oh, good—me, too."

"My turn," Fisher said.

They returned to their positions at the opposite ends of

the battle table. Stretching his fingers, Fisher reached gingerly for his snipers, his irregulars, neatly painted in green, and moved them towards the village. They would be safer in the buildings, where they could fire out at the looming, raggedly painted French Imperial columns, which Wolf was peering at, ready to sound the advance. Fisher placed the troops correctly, according to the strict rules. Screened by walls and trees, they would be an annoyance to Napoleon.

"Where did you say your son lived?" Fisher said.

"Near here," Wolf said, with a cock of the head, "or near enough."

"Lovely," Fisher said. He thought of the new house by the valley. This might take time. But there was movement.

"I order a general advance," Wolf said. He took off his gilet and rolled up his sleeves. He painstakingly moved his infantry columns forward—row after row of model Frenchmen, with their shakos neatly vertical, captains in bicorns waving curved swords. They advanced by inches upon their stationary enemy.

"A magnificent sight," Fisher said.

"La France, l'armée, la tête d'armée," Wolf said. He looked with some pleasure at his advanced army. And, still, the heavy cavalry in reserve. The Imperial Guard, the immortals, ready to strike beside the emperor himself. "Please excuse me," he said after a moment and left the room.

Fisher looked over the battlefield. There was colour and glitter. It was reminiscent of the real world: there were people, trees, green grass, hills, a river, buildings. But it was reduced, simplified and removed from the mud and slaughter of a real battlefield. Still, he had remembered the rules and remembered his brief. Somewhere in the cottage, he heard water flushing and pipes clanking. An old man, past his best, emptying his bladder.

He wandered over to the window. The harbour was quiet

now. No fishermen at work. Only a woman in a fur coat and a man in a dark jacket standing on the quayside, pointing out to sea. What was there to see? Nothing. Just the water and the gauzy, distant shoreline.

Suddenly, his body stiffened.

A double-barrelled shotgun was coldly nudging at his ear.

"So—a green man?" Wolf said. "A green man sent for an old man. Do not move. I'll happily pull this trigger."

"You wouldn't," Fisher said uncertainly, raising his hands. Not that he had anything in them. And only a penknife in his back pocket.

The gun nudged him again, and he turned around.

"Oh, I certainly would," Wolf said, his eyes fierce. "Sit down on the window seat and let us talk."

Fisher sat, staring into the loaded depths of barrels. The black eyes of certain death.

"Wellington's snipers used rifles, not muskets," Wolf said. "And you didn't paint all those beautiful soldiers."

"I don't know what you mean."

"You have no clue what you are doing on the battlefield. It's been a poor cover, Angus, or whatever your name is. You know I invented the green men, you stupid boy. Who sent you?"

Fisher said nothing.

"You know I could just end this here," Wolf said.

"Tell me more, grandad." Fisher shrugged.

"No," Sir Raymond Tallis, former deputy director of MI6, said. "You will talk, you utter incompetent. Tell me everything."

"I know where your son is," Fisher said.

The barrels did not waver. They levelled as smoothly as a machine.

Outside, in the melting world, a boat puttered into view on the far horizon. The village slept, like a child.

21

She dreamt of nothing until the sky suddenly opened.
As the plane bucked in turbulence on the short flight
north to Edinburgh, Shona had abruptly come to. Her eyes
had been filled by sky, and her mind took a second to adjust:
that this was real, this was the air, she was flying. With the
hum of the plane thrumming in her ears, the flood of angelic
light had cascaded about her, and her sleepy eyes were trans-
fixed, for a moment, by the sweet blue light. It had felt like
a gift.

After a slow descent, the plane landed with a staccato
series of bumps at Edinburgh Airport. There were still
streaks of snow around the airfield. Bare, scratty trees
trembled in the chill air. Beyond the terminal, the metal
fences and barbed wire, the grey smear of industrial
estates, she could see Arthur's Seat—a dusty diamond in
a field of ash.

Passengers began unfastening their seat belts and gathering
their belongings. Beside her, a heavyset man was fast asleep,
his weight touching on her shoulder.

Shona turned on her phone, and it blinked into life. As
the plane began to taxi to its berth, she searched for news in
London, a fire in Holland Park.

There were several stories, some from the day before
on online news sites and others in the morning papers.
The copy was roughly the same. It was clear that a news
agency had filed some basic copy, and the papers had run
it largely unchanged, all with a generic byline. She tapped
on one link:

BODY FOUND IN HOLLAND PARK FIRE
By Our News Reporter

A man has died following a fire at a house in West London. Firefighters were called to the blaze in Sheldrake Gardens, Holland Park, at 11:28 a.m., the London Fire Brigade said.

The £5.2m property, which had been on sale for several months, was destroyed by the fire. The man found on the ground floor was pronounced dead at the scene. The Metropolitan Police said the cause of the fire was under investigation and the man's cause of death was yet to be established.

A spokesman for Kemble Morris, estate agents, confirmed the house was owned by international banking firm Bjarki and had been used for corporate events.

A police cordon is still in place.

She read the other stories about the fire, but they provided no further details.

The body was Proctor's. Of whom there was no trace online. If he had been real, if that was his real name, the internet had had his presence wiped, cleaned, and removed. Ned had not known him. But did she even know Ned? She checked her email and messages, but there was nothing from him. Could he really have known of the assassin? Could he have led that long-haired killer to Loxley's home? Ned had been a gentle man. He rarely even raised his voice, even in his most drunken or passionate moments. She shook off the idea and made her way down the stairs to the tarmac.

After a long journey home in a crowded tram—with thoughts of a hot bath and painkillers—she turned the key in her front door and entered her flat. It had not been heated for days and was silent and cold. In the kitchen, a half-drunk coffee cup stood beside the kettle, where she had left it when rushing to catch the train south.

She looked into the living room. All was as she had left it. Then there was movement: MacDiarmid came into view, eyes narrowed, tail straight and quivering. Shona knelt and gently stroked the purring cat's soft fur. She felt vaguely guilty that she may have not left her enough food, but after a brief time reacquainting herself with the portly grey mog, they appeared to be on good terms.

Shona took the press award from her bag. It was cracked at one corner. She looked at it for a while, then put it on top of the television. She was glad to be free of it. In the past, she would have handed it over to her father, who would have placed it in his bedroom. Now there was no one to hand it to. She was aware the award had also become a weapon. She may hide it somewhere, she briefly thought, somewhere where she could not see it anymore.

After a long bath, she pulled on a soft hoodie and leggings—carefully avoiding the mottled purple bruise on her leg and the tender spot above her ear—and switched on her laptop. As she waited for it to limp into life, she found the number for Loxley that Ranald had sent her and called it. Dead. She texted him: *Are you OK? Shona.* It disappeared into the void.

The list Loxley had printed lay before her. On the list of confirmed firms, there were two from the news article about the fire—Kemble Morris and Bjarki. She immediately searched for more information. Kemble Morris had an anodyne estate agency website advertising page after page of properties for sale in London and South East England. She raised her eyebrows at the prices. They were absurd. She looked for the house in Holland Park: there it was, shot on an impossibly blue-skied day. It looked unreal. She flicked through the photos of its interior. There was the room where she had found Proctor—the white lounge, full of white furniture, shelves adorned with bland vases and bowls, fake books. She clicked on the Meet Our Team page—a row of grinning, tanned faces with perfect teeth.

She searched for Bjarki. It was an odd name. Was it Scandinavian? Indian? An ominous page came into view on the first click. *Bjarki: Business Challenge Management Change Solutions.* Shona rolled her eyes at the senseless jargon and scrolled through the menu. There was a mission statement which said nothing, at length. No real information on what the company did or didn't do. There was a link to senior management, which she clicked. MacDiarmid jumped onto her lap, unannounced, and curled into a weighty, silky, purring ball.

There, on the page, was a younger, tauter Reece Proctor. His face was pink and featureless, his hair a little longer, swept back from a widow's peak. But he was listed as Robert Cotton.

> *Click here to contact Robert, a noted expert in change management solutions, particularly in HR solutions for the post-EU landscape, whose extensive experience in politics, media and finance underpins our offer to Deep-Landscape, open-eyed business innovators . . .*

She opened a new tab and searched for "Robert Cotton." He was listed on a major recruitment website, for which she had her own password; she logged on. There he was. He had an impressive, steel-walled CV. For a certain kind of man, a man who wanted to suck the marrow out of business and life, he had followed an ideal route. He had been born in

Newcastle upon Tyne and educated at a private school in Sedbergh, amidst bleak hills and green Cumbrian beauty. A first in political, philosophy and economics—of course—from Cambridge. There had been various stints working at big banks in Germany, Hong Kong and the US, then, a year before the Brexit referendum, he had moved to Bjarki as a partner. A move to Dovetail, which he helped found, had followed.

Robert Cotton? She said his name out loud. She pulled on the thread and looked for him elsewhere. There was only a scattering of articles about him, mainly in business journals, brief mentions of his various career moves.

Then, she found a short social diary piece in the *Edinburgh Post*, her former employer, from more than a decade ago. She expanded the picture that accompanied the story. There was Cotton, in a sharp dinner suit, grinning with a champagne flute in his hand, alongside similarly attired men and a familiar tall woman in a shimmering dress. Shona expanded the caption:

SOCIAL WHIRL: Elegant heiress Olivia "Liv" Farquharson and her well-heeled friends at the fundraiser for Denholm House, her father's ancestral pile in the Scottish Borders, at the Assembly Rooms in Edinburgh last night. The house needs a new roof, and at the £2,000-a-table bash, Liv and her old Cambridge chums popped some corks. Guests included top investment banker Rob Cotton, who, the Diary understands, has recently hooked up with the fragrant Olivia. But her lips were sealed . . .

Shona stared at the photograph for a while. A link between Cotton or Proctor—whoever he was—and the Farquharsons.

Of course, Proctor had said she was a director of his think tank. Perhaps once they had been lovers. She was not surprised. They lived in the same rarefied world. Of course they'd know each other. She wondered if she knew he was dead.

She saved the diary article and moved on, looking back to the Grendel list to double-check Cotton's connections. They were all there in black and white: Bjarki. Kemble Morris. Denholm Estates . . . and Dovetail.

"Bloody hell," she whispered.

Cotton had wanted her to have this information. He had led her to it. What had he wanted her to do with it? And what on earth was Grendel? She scanned the list for Ned's company, Pushback Public Relations. It was not there.

An image slipped into her mind: Hecate standing at the door of the mansion in the orchard. Where was that little girl now? Shona looked into her father's room. His books were still on their shelves. Beside his bed lay his blue asthma inhaler. On his desk stood a simple urn containing his ashes—waiting to be scattered. On the bed, neat piles of ironed clothes to be given to charity. The rest would be sent into a landfill. What would Hugh Sandison think of this story? she wondered. What would he advise her to do? What would he want her to do, after finding a dead man and being hunted by an assassin? What would he do with the information for which some would kill? *Find the real story*, he would have said.

Get the story, she told herself.

She made herself a fresh coffee, and the caffeine began to tingle in her blood. The cat repeatedly brushed her legs. She felt stronger. She had survived. She was home. And she had a story.

She really needed to call Hector, she scolded herself. He

knew something about Grendel, and he wanted to share it with her. Comparing notes, if he was willing, would be helpful. Then she'd call Ranald and run through what had happened.

Then an unfamiliar noise sounded: a plaintive ringing.

At first, she thought it came from outside—a bin lorry or a delivery van. Then she realised it was the landline; the red plastic phone was trilling in her father's room. He had never wanted to be disconnected from the wires.

No one knew the number apart from Bernie and the doctor's surgery. It must be a scam call. Shona swore, and as she suddenly moved, the cat burst away from her as if a bomb had just detonated.

She stepped quickly across her father's room and reached for the receiver. She put it to her ear.

"Yeah?" she said.

"Shona? Is that Shona Sandison?" a deep male voice said. He sounded breathless.

"Yes?"

"You don't know me . . . I'm sorry to have to—"

"What? Go on—what is it?"

"It's about Hector. Hector Stricken. He's dead. He's died. I am so sorry."

There was a silence. Her mind was a sudden blank. She put a hand to her father's curtain. The fabric was soft and thick.

"Hector's gone. I'm his friend—I need to speak to you."

"How? What? What the . . ." she said. She sat down heavily on her father's soft bed. The frame creaked. It had always creaked.

"It's awful news. He was killed. Car accident. Can we meet? We need to meet."

Shona shut her eyes. The world fell from its moorings. The room shook—trembling scenery on an amateur stage.

"How do you have this number?" she said haltingly. "Can you tell me again? Hector has died?"

"Your dad's name was in the phone book," Adam said gently.

"There's still a phone book?"

"I know. Look—can we meet? I really think we should meet up."

"What? Why?" she said. "Sorry, who are you?"

"A friend," Adam Rokeby said.

22

Night had fallen, and the sea had become one with the sky.

The harbour was quiet, water slopping against its sheer stone walls. Across the firth, distant towns glittered.

On the long table, the warring armies were stalled. The French, in their massed columns, paused, trembling, in their advance. The British, stuck in their ragged red lines, were disordered. In the tiny village, stands of green snipers were upended and on their sides. Dice lay, their choices unread. There would be no more fake killings.

In the kitchen, Fisher was sitting in a chair by the Aga. Its warmth flushed his cheeks. Warmer still was the whisky he had been given. A swirl of amber in a crystal tumbler. He gulped it. It smelled of bladderwrack and tasted of fire and moss.

He told the old man what he needed to. As a green man, his job was only half done. He had scouted. He had made contact. He had secured face time. He had planted seeds. It was not a perfect job, far from it. But he had done his utmost on a restricted budget and with little time.

Raymond Tallis sat in the window seat, the gun still trained on the younger man. Apart from the lights above the oven, the room was growing dark, and his features were indistinct in the shadows. He spoke up.

"I fully understand you are here to prompt me to action. To provoke. If I were a woman, or even inclined to sleep with men, you may have even enticed me into bed. You know we trained the first green men to form intimate relationships, to become ardent lovers? I expect you've done that?"

Fisher nodded. He had done that before.

Tallis continued. "There is no doubt your information is interesting."

Fisher had not mentioned his son again. They had not discussed him. Instead, he had told Tallis of Stag Hall and who would be gathering there. The gun had been trained on him throughout. There was not a quiver or a tremor. The old man's nerves were fine. He was still fit, still capable.

"Stag Hall. Two miles up the river," Tallis said.

"Old, but newly renovated."

"I think I heard of this in the village. I heard the workers in the shop one day. They were in overalls, covered in paint. A lot of work going on, I understood."

"Bought by a company to use for conferences, corporate events, parties. Expanded. Upgraded. Revamped."

"And?"

"There will be some bad business this weekend. Right there."

"Then call the police," Tallis snapped. "Why this ridiculous subterfuge?"

"You were here."

Tallis sighed. "To think I used to work for these people. And you know all this from your amateur surveillance?"

"No, not just mine . . . You know, it's the blind men and the elephant."

Tallis smiled faintly. He knew the old legend from India: a group of blind men, all standing around a fallen elephant. One man holding the trunk. Another, the wispy tail. Another, the feet. None of them feeling the true picture. None of them being able to fathom the descriptions of all the others.

"All we know is—"

"You have made for a poor green man," Tallis said. "You are not focused enough, not controlled enough. No subtlety.

Green men take weeks, months, even years, for their work to bear fruit. This is why I called them *green* men: they are growers. They sow seeds. They inveigle and suggest. They lay trails for others to follow, create false stories of misdirection and misremembrance. They must write a diary of lies for the targets to read and digest and believe and thus act upon. And yet here you are, blundering in like an amateur, although I accept the war games are a weakness of mine—a good access point."

"Thanks."

"But you are too young, and you really don't know what you're doing. We used to lace our targets for years. Decades. Green men in Greenpeace, in the unions, in the media, in the IRA, MPs, MSPs, subterranean, hidden . . . You didn't even do your research properly. I'd have had you sent to the marshes, little man. How long have you been in the service?"

"Seven years," Fisher said.

Tallis laughed. It was a dry sound, like gravel sliding down a chute. "I am genuinely at a loss as to how to explain how disappointed I am that you are here," he said. "They should have kept you as a red man. Anyone can do that."

Outside, heavy rain began to fall. It pattered against the window, like nervous fingers.

"I was sent in a hurry." Fisher shrugged and drank more whisky.

"And still, time is not on your side," Tallis said. "I am considering what to do with you. I am minded to send you back to your masters with a simple report card. A fail."

Fisher looked at the old man, his eyes sharper, harder. "They said you were weak. Easy to influence. You lost your focus. Lost your mind. After your son was killed. You disappeared. They said you had a breakdown."

"I did not bloody disappear," Tallis spat. "Who sent you?

Who's your line manager?" He stood up and moved closer to Fisher, who leaned back in his chair, instinctively. Tallis pulled up a chair and sat close, aiming the hard gun at Fisher's soft face. "Go on."

"Don't know what you mean," Fisher said. He knew the weapon was loaded. One pull of an arthritic finger and his brains would be pulverised.

"Stop trembling," Tallis said. "I'm not going to kill you. This is my home. I want to live here. I don't want your brains all over my kitchen floor. I just want you to go, to be honest."

"Go?" Fisher said.

"Go away. Go back to your masters, whoever they are. To be honest, I don't care. I'm long retired. I don't even know who the director is anymore. Or, more accurately, I don't want to know. Who trained you? Muppets."

Fisher eyed him levelly. Here was the old warrior, twenty years past his prime. But like old warriors, he had one more dragon to slay. If he could be convinced of it. "That may be the case," he said. "But I can tell you something. New information was recently entered into the system—information about your son."

There was a long silence. The sea turned and broke. Somewhere in the village, a cat knocked over a bucket and yowled. On a distant road, tyres rolled.

"Go on," Tallis said eventually.

Fisher cleared his throat. The gun barrels moved until they were barely inches from his eyes. "Days ago, a prisoner in . . . prison . . ."

"Doing well so far, son," Tallis said. "A prisoner in a prison. I assume there will be more revelations."

"A prisoner," Fisher went on, "was under interrogation. He was a hitman. Organised crime."

"Where?"

"A Northumbrian team. He killed your son. He killed him with a tent peg."

The shotgun wavered slightly. Two black eyes swaying like a cobra. The heat of the stove was now becoming uncomfortable. Tallis again told Fisher to go on.

"He said he killed him on the orders of three people. A gallery director, Mr. Carver, whom we believe you killed. His body was found in Leith harbour, full of holes."

"Hmm."

"And two others—an heiress named Farquharson, who we believe had committed tax fraud. We believe your son had uncovered this in his role as an art expert for the UK government. There was a painting involved."

"*The Goldenacre*," Tallis said, nodding. "I'm aware of it. And who else?"

"A man named Reece Proctor."

"Who is he?"

"Lower the gun."

Tallis dropped the gun to Fisher's chest.

"An interesting man," Fisher said. "A one-way mirror. He's the money man for the Newcastle crime mob. Has been for several years. He launders the money from drugs, human trafficking, online fraud, illegal waste dumping, taxi firms . . . They're into everything, so he has his hands full. But he is very good at it."

"What did my son have to do with this?"

"Proctor made some kind of deal with the Farquharsons. Might have been to do with land, might have been something else. We don't know. Special Branch couldn't make head nor tail of it."

"I'm surprised."

"But we do know there was quite a complicated financial deal involving the painting, which your son

206 • PHILIP MILLER

disrupted—unintentionally, possibly even accidentally. I have a document which explains what we know . . . It's quite a story. I have it in the caravan."

"Tell me more . . ."

"Proctor's straight name is Robert Cotton."

"Right."

"And, as Cotton, he's been clean as a whistle. Upstanding member of the international finance community. Tangentially involved in politics. Set up a policy think tank called Dovetail. It's had some influence."

"Busy boy. And?"

"Cotton and Farquharson and a whole circle of their friends will be at Stag Hall this weekend to celebrate a significant business deal. And there's more."

"Pray tell."

Fisher's eyes were trained on the gun. "According to the killer, Cotton had what was left of your son's body removed from a lake in the Borders and buried beside the M6, near Tebay. That's where he is now. Not in Scotland. He's in a hole beside a road."

Tallis blinked minutely.

"Chopped up and buried like a fucking dog in a bin," Fisher said.

The gun did not move.

Fisher looked momentarily to the window, out to the darkness, and his mind turned inwards.

When he was a child, an angry, neglected and disruptive child, his foster parents had an orchard, and in that orchard, there were crab apple trees. They were low-hanging and easy to climb. He would climb one in particular. He knew where to put his feet as he climbed, where to stretch and grip his hands, where to duck as he crested its height to avoid scraping his head. He knew it so well he could climb it with his eyes closed. And he knew when he could stand tall at the top and survey the house, and the houses beyond, and their gardens, and the long-grassed field behind, which led to scrubland and deserted roads, and, further, the headland of a chalk cliff, which rose above the sullen sea like a great stained tooth. In that cliff there were smugglers' caves. And from his tree, he could see all this, and no one could touch him—only the tree, holding him like a giant might hold a prince. In those great hands, he could feel the warmth of the sun, and the fresh pitiless rain, and the cold of the winter, and see the wet lies of spring, when all seemed green but was doomed to wither and die.

One day he returned from his hideous school, battered and bruised as usual, to find that his foster father had cut down all the apple trees. Their sawn corpses were piled on a flatbed truck belching diesel fumes. It was never explained why the trees were cut down, but he heard the grown-ups talking in front of the TV one night about how much better the reception was, now that the trees were gone.

And Fisher, waiting for the old man to speak, was lost in that memory of trees, of his own beloved tree—its gnarled branches and its sharp, inedible apples, green and smooth like fat little frogs—when the butt of the shotgun struck him hard in the head and he fell to the kitchen floor and slipped into an agony of darkness.

PART III
THE AMBER WOMAN

23

"I can't actually believe it," Shona said.

It was late morning, and she was sitting opposite Adam Rokeby in the café of the Scottish National Gallery. High windows looked over the enclosed valley that held Princes Street Gardens and the main railway line into Waverley Station. No trains moved along the black tracks. The jagged Scott Monument stood like an abandoned temple beneath the Old Town's skyline of tenement, tower and spire.

Shona had a copy of the *Edinburgh Post* in front of her. On page twelve, beneath an advertorial for a golf course, was a short news story:

> *Police Scotland are investigating the death of a man in West Register Street yesterday.*
>
> *Hector Stricken, 49, a civil servant, was struck by a large black vehicle, which exited the street and proceeded to drive across St. Andrew Square towards Queen Street.*
>
> *Stricken, a former journalist of this paper, is survived by his partner, Sandy, a nurse, and their young son.*
>
> *The street remains closed to traffic.*
>
> *Police are appealing for witnesses to the incident . . .*

Shona stopped reading. Adam stirred his coffee. She had not met Adam before. She had heard Hector mention him, but she never paid too much attention to what Hector did outside work. His social life had always seemed tedious to her: interminable folk festivals, climbing Munros, hiking and tents. She assumed Adam had been a legal contact for Hector, a source of stories, of tip-offs, affirmations or denials. Now he sat before her, darkly handsome and trim and sorrowful.

"I hope he died instantly—that there was no suffering," Adam murmured.

"There's not much description of the car," Shona said, staring at the inky type.

"Nope," he said. "The security cameras should have caught it."

She visualised grainy CCTV images of Hector being struck and killed and realised she felt like crying. She bit her lip. There had been too much crying recently. Too much sorrow. And her head, although healing, still hurt.

"Poor Hec," she said at last.

"Do you know his partner?" Adam asked. "Sandy?"

Shona shook her head. She had never met her, didn't even know what she looked like. Until his email arrived, Hector hadn't called or messaged her for weeks, maybe months. They had known each other for years, and for a spell had sat across from each other at the reporters' desk at the *Edinburgh Post*. Back then, they had met often outside work. For coffees, for drinks. He was fond of her, she knew. But she had pushed all that away. She had never had the time and certainly not the inclination for that kind of relationship. He had been a good friend. That was the worst of it—now a good friend was gone. A lost companion. Like all the others.

"I texted Sandy. She said she was at the hospital," he said quietly. "With the . . . body . . . She called me back after a while, but she was distraught. She doesn't know what to do. Her folks are on their way from Quebec, which is a blessing. I'll see her later today."

Outside, birds were gathering. Fluttering shapes against the melting snow. Framed by the window, none of it seemed to be real. It could have been a projection on a screen. The world was black and grey and white. Colour had been bled away.

Adam was speaking: ". . . with the baby . . . and a funeral . . . I can't begin to imagine—"

"He emailed me," Shona said, feeling a catch in her throat.

"Oh, yes?" Adam said. His large brown eyes were watery, tinged pink at their corners.

"He mentioned this *thing*," she said, lowering her voice. "It was a tip-off. I was going to meet him."

Beside Adam was a work bag. Adam reached into it and brought out some paper, a security pass on a lanyard. He put the pass on the table. In the picture Hector was smiling—a new man in a new job.

Adam leaned into Shona, his face close to hers. He spoke in a deep, earnest voice. His accent was elusive. He could be from Glasgow or Edinburgh, Dumfries or Inverness. "Was this thing called Grendel?"

Shona's heart caught on a snag. "How do you know?"

Adam laid out his thoughts. Hector had stumbled across something odd at his work, something extremely sensitive. A project called Grendel. He explained how they had been drunk and each had taken home the wrong bag. Now he had Hector's belongings. There was no way of accessing the government laptop—it required three separate passwords—but he had this office pass and a printed document.

"Show me the paper?" Shona said.

"It's barely anything," he said. "It's an agenda note for a meeting." He passed it over to her.

CARS/OUWO/CRASH MEETING

Attending: Legal Dept (CARS), Chief Exec, Bruce Cowie (SpAd), Comms (?)

Agenda

1. *OUWO/ECHR/CARS outline (if necessary)*

2. *GRENDEL confirmations (SpAds). Summary memo: with SpAds.*

3. *Bird table.*

4. *AOB.*

"What the hell is OUWO?" she said. "O.U.W.O."

"Sounds like an owl," he said vaguely.

"Shut up," she said.

"Well, it's an acronym," he ventured.

"No shit. I thought you lawyers were meant to be smart?"

"Oh, no. We just have good memories."

"Like most liars."

"Funny. Who knows what it stands for?"

"*Organisation Underground . . .*" Shona shook her head. Guessing was futile.

"*Operational something*, I am going to surmise," he said. He looked around the café. A thin man in a grey suit sat nearby, reading from a tablet. Adam caught a waiter's attention and indicated that he wanted to pay the bill.

"What are you doing?" she said.

"I want to move. Who knows who's listening in here," he said. "Who knows who's watching."

Shona was about to call him paranoid but stopped herself. Proctor, or Cotton, was dead. An assassin had chased her across England. And now Hector was dead. Maybe they had killed him too. She could not quite believe it, even though she knew it possible. Hector only had this thin meeting agenda; he was not a man who knew too much—he hardly knew anything.

Adam pulled on an expensive, tailored coat. Shona pulled on her ratty woollen hat and jacket with a tear under its left armpit and gripped her stick. They left the café. Adam suggested they walk down to Stockbridge, a pretty, bourgeois quarter, full of high-end charity shops, bespoke tailoring, candle emporiums and pâtisseries, down by the Water of Leith. They could get another drink there. Shona agreed.

They set off across Princes Street, which felt empty, navigating the piles of dirty snow and slushy pavements. They did not speak for a while, walking side by side as they picked their way downhill through the New Town.

"What's the stick for?" Adam said at last.

"To walk with," she said.

"Sorry, I didn't make myself clear. I meant why do you need it?"

"So I can beat irritating lawyers to death," Shona said.

He shrugged.

"I got shot by a gangster in Venezuela," she lied. "Lost a leg."

He looked at her and chuckled. "Okay, fine. I won't ask."

"Neither should you," she said. "It's rude."

She looked down at his highly polished black shoes and his maroon socks. His clothing was annoyingly pristine, his honey-coloured skin similarly flawless.

"I know a bit about Grendel," she said quietly, her breath steaming before her.

He seemed startled. "Oh?"

She hesitated for a moment. "It's not a person or a thing. It's a list of companies that have agreed to something. I got the list from a contact in London."

"How curious," he said. "A list?"

"Yes. But the list doesn't say what these people are doing, or why they are on the list at all. What they have agreed to. It's quite a long list, mind."

"Grendel as a plural," he said, musing. "They sound like some kind of stakeholder group. Something tied to this OUWO. People and businesses with a shared interest."

"So Hector attended a meeting about this?"

"Yes." Adam nodded and readjusted his cashmere scarf. The air was getting colder, sharper. The leafless trees in a private garden cast a spray of shadows on Adam's shoulders. Shona watched him move against the backdrop of the elegant buildings. He walked with an easy motion, his back straight.

"He mentioned this Grendel when we met," he said.

"And now . . ." She opened her palms.

"Exactly," he said. "But we cannot, we should not, draw a link between that and his death. We must not assume a link between the two. That way madness lies. We don't live in a gangster state. Let the police investigation run its course."

She stopped. "I think we already are, though—aren't we?"

Adam halted. He turned his head slightly to her. "I can see why Hector liked you," he said.

She screwed up her face and huffed. "I can't," she said. "Did Hector ever mention someone called Moriah?"

"Maria?"

"Moriah as in—"

"What—*Lord of the Rings*? Wasn't that the castle where all those little squirrels lived?" he said, with a quick grin.

"What? No. No. As in . . . It's a reference to something biblical . . . or so I believe."

"No, he never mentioned it. Why?"

"Never mind."

They were walking down the steep hill to Stockbridge.

The stone buildings about them changed from the impersonal, poised elegance of the New Town to a more jumbled Scottish vernacular, with cobbles, pitched roofs, older stonework and a kind of scrambled neighbourliness. They passed a block of grey modernist flats and crossed an old bridge that spanned the fast-flowing Water of Leith. Bubbles and foam tumbled down its tree-lined course.

They passed charity shops and tiny cafés until they reached an old basement pub on a corner, with an entrance down a bowed flight of stone stairs, which they wordlessly agreed to enter.

Inside, a blood-orange fire spat and crackled. Adam ordered a glass of red wine and, without asking, bought Shona a Jack Daniel's and Coke. The ceiling was comfortably low, the seats recessed and dark. It felt cosy, warm and amenable. The weight of the city was above their heads.

"Hector once said this was your drink," Adam said as he put the liquor down on the table.

"It is," she said. She opened her mouth to say something and then closed it again.

"You okay?" he said gently.

"I knew him for so long . . ." she said, and then could not think of more to say. She thought of Proctor. His nervous bonhomie at the awards ceremony. His gaping bloody face at the white house. She shivered.

"He was a good man." Adam raised his glass. "Here's to Hector. And to Sandy and his baby."

Shona raised her glass and drank. She thought of the many times she had been rude to Hector. Downright obnoxious. It was too late now. Everything was too late. Adam nodded at her, as if acknowledging her thoughts, and they drank companionably for a while, in silence. The firelight reflected in tiny flames across glass, brass and shiny optics; the logs shifted and sparked. In another corner, two men in suits drank silently.

"I have an idea," she said.

"Go on," he said. "I'm always open to an idea. All kinds." Adam smiled at Shona. His eyes were alight with intention and capability. She liked him. She tried to ignore it.

"I need to see this memo," she said. "The one mentioned in Hector's agenda note."

He opened his hands. "But how? These papers are officially sensitive or even officially secret. No civil servant would give it to you."

"I know," she said. "And a Freedom of Information request is pointless. They take weeks, and then all you get back is a pile of evasive shite and pre-prepared reasons for avoiding releasing stuff. There's a million ways for government agencies to get around handing out anything useful in an FOI. Believe me, I've asked for all kinds of things over the years. So . . . I have an idea, but it's not exactly legal."

"Try me," Adam said.

"You have to remember," she said, putting a finger on the table, "I'm only after a story here. An exclusive—that's what I'm interested in. I'm not the cops. It's not about right and wrong. That's for other people to decide. I'm a hack."

"Okay. I understand. I want to find out about Grendel, too. I am a man of the law, after all, and curious—"

"Yeah, whatever," she said, waving a hand. "Right. Here's the idea. First, you return Hector's laptop and files to his work. In his bag. They'll be happy and relieved. They'll think their security risk is over."

Adam took off his jacket and arranged it neatly over the back of his chair. He was relaxed now, engaged.

"But I'll keep his security pass," she said.

"Interesting. Why?"

"Well . . ." Shona looked into the fire, as if for reassurance, but there was none there. "I find a way to get inside his office, using his card, and get the paper. Get the memo."

He suppressed a grin. It annoyed her.

"Well, good luck with that," Adam said. "You won't get past the front desk. You don't know Hector's login, and—I hate to state the obvious—you don't look anything like him . . . I mean, how can you possibly—"

"Did you look closely at his pass?" she said, raising her eyebrows.

"No, why would I?" Adam reached into Hector's bag, pulled out the lanyard again and slapped it on the table. "What about it?"

Shona turned it over. A small square of yellow paper was wedged between the card and its holder. She pulled it out and unfolded it. On the Post-it note was written a series of numbers and letters in Hector's left-handed scrawl.

"Stupid sod," Adam said, shaking his head. "His passwords?"

Shona took a final swig of her drink. "What else would they be?"

T,

And so I have another man's blood on my hands again. But I am inured now. Have been for many years.

I was in Ireland when you last called me. In my exile. I never answered any calls. My time was medical, delineated by doctors and therapists. And in between sessions with the doctors, I would swim—drive to lonely beaches and swim. There was one day I swam out too far into the Atlantic. The current was strong. It was so cold, and I was so weak, I was surprised by my own weakness. I was an old man overcome, in the waves, drifting out further and further. A sea of hands was pulling me out and down. But I caught sight of the shore and my pitiful pile of clothes, the grassy dune and the bent trees on the shore. And I determined, again, to win—to beat the waves, beat the sea, beat the current. Where does that come from, that anger? That fury? The spite to win?

I made it back. And I lay naked on the beach in the rain as the sea retreated, and I was surprised. Because I thought of you, as a baby. I remembered a family photograph—your mother resplendent in her maternal bed, her hair down, you in her arms—and could only think of loss, of sorrow, of all the days I had wasted. Your beautiful mother.

I wept then, on that grand long Irish beach, in the rain, naked under the green sky, beside the black sea. I had buried it all. I had buried my love so that I could hate. Hate for a living. Under duress of grief, of loss, I allowed that hate to melt away. A kind of love had returned. But too late, my boy. Far too late.

24

It was the worst hour of the night, and Shona could not sleep.

She had passed the evening with minor domestic chores, petting the cat distractedly, listening to music and looking over the Grendel list again. She searched online for twenty or thirty names before she tired. She then realised she did not need to do this tedious task. Someone else at the Buried Lede could do it. So she had called Ranald, who was back in Shetland, and they had spoken for a while about Hector and about what could have happened to him.

"Capacity and Resilience?" Ranald said. "What the hell is that?"

"It's a new quango. Hector jumped there before he could be sacked from the papers. He had some comms job . . ."

They had talked on. But she had not told Ranald everything about Proctor and what had happened with Loxley. She could not think of that: it would complicate everything. Ranald would be frightened, over-cautious, perhaps even put her investigations on hold. She could not bear that. So she told half-truths and approximations. Not for the first time, she elided the facts. But it was necessary. Sometimes, she knew, you had to lie to get to the truth.

"So Loxley broke into this device that Proctor gave you and found a list of companies and individuals who are calling themselves Grendel?"

"Yes . . . by my reckoning they're mainly UK-based or international, but there are some Scottish firms, too. Agriculture. Power. Human Resources."

"This was the day after Proctor's body was found in that fire in London."

"He could hardly give me it afterwards," she said firmly. Maybe too firmly. She saw Proctor's fixed dead eyes. The hole in his head, the ragged edges of it. The nameless assassin's black hair, his hard eyes like shards of flint.

"This could be brilliant," Ranald said, exhaling heavily. "This is really excellent. Listen—can you photograph the list and send it to me? I'll get my little gremlins to run through the entire list, do a proper audit on who these bastards are and what they're doing."

"Can we see how many of them have contributed to political party funds? Fundraisers? Sponsorship, that kind of thing?"

"Sure. And this government paper? How can we get it? You have any sources there?"

"I used to," she said, staring out of the kitchen window. "Not anymore."

"Oh, Jesus, of course. Sorry."

"It's fine. I have another idea. But you may not want to know about it."

"If I know about it, can I be implicated?"

"Aye."

"Don't tell me, then. But, look, we already have a dead guy in a burning house, a list of companies doing something with the government and a curious code word. The beginnings of something very interesting, Shona."

"Yeah, I always say it could be the big one. But this really could be the big one."

"Here—your contact, the one for the Brexit story?"

"Moriah."

"Moriah. Have we heard from them? You have found Grendel, after all."

"We haven't. We have found a list of names. We don't know what it really means. What they have agreed to."

Ranald, somewhere in his wind-blasted home in Shetland, whistled. "Of course. Someone somewhere doesn't want anyone to know what it means. Which means it's a plan. And it's secret. And what is a plan that only some people are part of?"

"A conspiracy."

"Exactly! Keep digging. Send me the list and I'll get the gremlins on it straightaway."

But now it was 3 A.M., the Devil's Hour, and she could not sleep. She lay in bed in jogging bottoms, an old T-shirt and a tangle of bed sheets. A slash of white light from the streetlamp outside cut through a gap in the curtains. Mac-Diarmid, oblivious and silk-soft, snored in a loose coil at the foot of the bed.

Shona's sojourn in England seemed like some kind of hallucination, some kind of horrendous dream. Her eyes flicked about her room—this was real. Her bedside table. Her drying rack. Her chest of drawers. Her badly framed pictures. Her ragged dressing gown hanging like game on the back of her door. These were real.

Her father's absence: that was real. Not an assassin with a hammer. Not a rotting ruin in a forgotten orchard in the mist. Not a fugitive family escaping the end of the world. And Hector, now dead. Was that real? What if he wasn't dead? But he was. Mowed down by a car in an Edinburgh backstreet. His head crushed. His ribcage splintered. His life ended. That was real.

She swung her legs out of bed and moved through the dim hallway. It seemed as if she were floating. The microwave in the kitchen blinked digital time. In the living room, furniture loomed in bulky shadows. She flicked on the television, which illuminated the room in too-bright flashes of white and blue.

A face she knew shimmered in blue lustre. There, on the muted screen, on a twenty-four-hour news channel, was Vali Grammaticus. She was sitting in a high-backed chair, a black curtain draped behind her. She was wearing a dark blue dress, and her hair was piled on her head, clasped in silver. She looked regal, an empress.

Shona turned up the sound.

"We have to remember *everyone*. And although I am grateful and honoured to be making *The Names of the Lost* for the Civic Gallery, I am very aware that it will be in situ for only a year. After that, it will be taken down and packed away. Out of sight, out of mind."

"Could it not be exhibited elsewhere? Housed somewhere permanently? Has that been discussed?" a news reporter asked.

"I hope so. It's a very good idea, but not one that has been mentioned to me or the gallery. Funding, resources, are key. But there is something more important to consider: our national amnesia."

"Amnesia?"

"Of the COVID dead. They are hardly mentioned. We do not talk about them. Where are they discussed, where is their loss marked? Tens of thousands of people dead. And yet the nation moved on. Yes, there are some memorials, but not enough. And too much silence. Politicians turned the page. There has been more public discussion about the economy, about people working from home, than there ever has about the loss of life. The terrible loss of life. More than two hundred and twenty thousand people in the UK. That is the entire population of Hull. Aberdeen. All gone."

"We remember the war dead with stone memorials. They're in every town and village," the reporter said.

"Indeed," Vali said. "And this was a war, too—against a virus. Fought valiantly by doctors and nurses, by volunteers and scientists. But, as in all wars, it was ordinary people who suffered before the government knew what it was doing. There were thousands of needless deaths. *Thousands upon thousands.* The elderly moved out of hospitals, to their deaths. Nurses and doctors with no protection. And the national government, it seemed, always fundamentally against lock-downs. Against protections. Against, in some way, the idea that this was indeed a deadly virus, a generational event. I will leave discussion of the corruption, the grift, the fraud, to better-informed people than me. But, on a human level, on a civic level, on a societal level, we surely have to remember the dead. And it is left to me, an artist, to make some kind of marker in time, to mark these people, these victims. This was real. This was a pandemic. Why is it suddenly *unreal?*"

The setting shifted to the darkened main hall of the Civic Gallery, hung with clusters of tiny lights that twinkled and burned. Between them, small blinking drones drifted, controlled by Vali's assistants. Vali was pointing up at the lights and talking to a young woman with an iPad, who was taking notes.

Then Vali was in her office, looking through her ring binders, fingers flicking through the files of the dead.

"The complexities, the subtleties, of one single life," she said. "Each of us is a central star in a constellation of inter-locking lives, so our task in representing this is about editing, about abridgement. You see? How much information do we include, how much do we omit? How are they connected? Where do the connections end? Every person, every single person, even if they think they are alone, is connected to everyone else—by family, by friendship, by work, by shared interests. Look at the details of this man, for instance—this poor man . . ."

She pulled a page from a file and looked straight into the camera. "Hugh Donald Sandison, of Edinburgh. Aged eighty-one. Survived by a daughter. He was a retired journalist. A widower. He had heart disease. He caught COVID in the first wave and died, very quickly, in hospital. Who was he? Who was Hugh? Well, he loved to garden in his allotment. He loved to read, do crosswords, and he liked to walk around his city. And here, apart from his surviving daughter, is another connection: his companion. Bernadette Comfort, who was ill, but survived. A former nun, she left the orders in 2017—"

"What the actual . . ." Shona murmured.

Vali looked away from the camera and down to the ground. "One person. One death. Multiple tragedies. And yet if we mapped out his relationships, his connections, the lines of love and care, of friendship and family, we could draw a web of love and loss to fill an entire room . . ."

Shona looked around the room to check it was still there. She shook her head, to see if she was hallucinating. The news report moved on, but the footage would be repeated through the night, filling the lonely hours.

Shona stared at the muted news channel for a while, and MacDiarmid, stretching her back legs like a flexing ballerina, joined her. The news ran through its roll call of woe. Hurricanes and floods—wooden houses submerged in torrential rain, a forest inundated. Ice shelves collapsing in Antarctica in an atomic blush of blue and blinding white. A patrol ship pulling the bodies of dead children from the Mediterranean. A city crushed to rubble. Bodies white with ash dragged from the ruins. Slaughtered children wrapped in white sheets. She reached for the remote control and turned the television off. The room blinked back into the deep of night.

She would be a civil servant in the morning, she realised. She stood up, suddenly as awake as if it was daytime; she needed to find her suit and a shirt to iron. Tomorrow, she would be lying. She would, she hoped, be stealing. But, she thought, who would notice?

2 5

Sandy was asleep, under sedation, and two of her friends were in the flat.

Adele cleaned the bathroom, while Carla shushed the nameless baby in the crook of her arm.

Adam had come with flowers, some basic supplies in a plastic bag and an open offer of assistance. Sandy's friends, both teachers, were polite and self-assured. They told him Sandy needed to rest and was not to be disturbed. Her parents would be here in the morning.

Adele, clipped, efficient, made coffee. She told Adam how she had been at the hospital with Sandy when Hector's body was identified. He had died instantly, the doctor said. His life had ended with a single, sudden full stop. He likely knew nothing about his death.

"It must have been terrible," Adam said.

"As bad as you can imagine," Adele agreed.

Sandy had been distraught. Insensible. A policewoman had told Adele that she would be in touch if anything came to light. A cordon had been set up on the site of the incident, and they were looking for traces of the car and assessing CCTV footage.

Carla brushed a hand over the baby's smooth head. He was asleep, wrapped in a fleece blanket, a tiny hand to a cheek, eyes closed like two wrinkled shells. His tiny chest moved in and out, and somewhere in the folds his toes wiggled. Although the friends had been kind, it was clear to Adam that they wanted him to leave. Hector had been his friend—he was now gone. It was Sandy and the baby who needed their help and support. The world had changed, and with it, its demands and duties. Carla's phone buzzed and she quietly took the call.

Adam turned away and moved to the window. Outside, heedless Edinburgh continued with its business. Workers trudged to their duties. Deliveries sped by on bikes. Suits disappeared into glass cubes. A gritter noisily decanted pink salt onto the roads. A tram slid smoothly down Leith Walk. Schedules and timetables were being kept. Hector's death had not altered the world outside this apartment.

Carla finished her call. She looked to the baby, who was as fast asleep as any human had ever been, lost in an ocean of deep and oblivious slumber.

"Would you mind leaving, Mr. Rokeby?" she whispered. "Sandy won't be awake for a while."

Adele came through from the kitchen, with a spray of white flowers in a vase. She put them on the low table.

"I will," Adam said. "And thank you. Does the baby have a name yet? Hector said—"

"Sandy is calling him Hector now," Carla said. "Little Hec." She looked with sudden, fierce love at the baby. "I'm going to put him down now."

"There was one thing," Carla said quietly as she showed Adam to the door.

"Anything," he said.

"Before we got to the hospital, Sandy said his friends should be told. There was one—she said she was called Shona? Do you know her? A journalist. Sandy specifically asked for her to be told."

"Consider it done," Adam said, arranging his scarf. "I think I know how to get hold of her."

He left the warm flat and stepped into the cold stairway. His polished black shoes tapped on the worn steps like a hammer on a row of nails. He pulled on his black leather gloves.

He reached Leith Walk. A truck, massive and white, rumbled past him. He resolved to buy a bottle of red wine from a local delicatessen. He was worried and unnerved.

He walked past a red postbox, circled with a skirt of dirty snow. His heart began to pulse.

He thought of his visit to a post office earlier in the day. How nervous he had been, ensuring his neat parcel would be delivered the next morning to *Chief Executive, Capacity and Resilience (Scotland), Alacrity House, Edinburgh.* How anxious he had been, preparing the box of parts, making sure the electronic alarm would sound at 8:45 A.M. exactly, double and triple checking it was set and ready to go.

Ready to reveal itself as Shona arrived, at the home of Grendel, pretending to be someone else.

The young man is still unconscious. It has been a while. Perhaps he has suffered a bleed on the brain. He may be dying. I have neither the energy nor the desire to end his story and dispose of the body. Those days are long past. And it is so much harder to do, these days.

Not for the first time since my retirement, I am torn. Torn to pieces. I could come and find you. But I know the moors of Cumberland. You may be near Shap or Tebay, but that is still too much land to survey. Only your killer would know the exact location of your grave, and I cannot contact him.

So I have decided: I will leave you there. There are worse places to have your final rest. The mountains, the clean air, the ragged woods, the memories of misty Elmet. Dreams of ancient Rheged. And maybe there, up on the high grounds, you can view a beautiful valley or hear the run of a river. Maybe foxes and badgers will live about you. Rabbits, deer. Maybe they will sense your presence, know that there lies a wonderful man. A good man.

And in the long run, the very long run, you will be bones. And, if this fallen, broken race of ours survives what is to come, someone—some future archaeologist—will find you and gently, with wonder, lay out your bones and clean away the earth and dust of ages, and ponder your life and what things you had seen and done. Question how you died, and why. Most of all, why you were buried in this way and in this place. And they will never know, and could never know, and instead they will concoct theories and create narratives and weave stories about this bone man, lying alone, with a wound in his skull, in this lonely place. But all their science, their expertise, their reconstructions and conjecture won't be able to even glimpse what a fine man you were, how graceful in your movements, how handsome you were, what a wonderful father you were, what a dutiful, loving and perceptive father you were, and how much a better man than your own father you were.

All I have known, in the end, in this attempt to summarise in this unpublished testimony, is that I dedicated my mind, my energies, my capacity, my considerable thought and expertise— in their entirety—to the perpetuation of a state that cares not a jot for its people, for its land, for its future. That cares only for the perpetuation of itself. I could not see this. I was amidst it. I was in it. I <u>was</u> it. And now, without my son, without my wife and my life, at four in the morning in a village by the sea: what is there? No evidence of my works. No signs of my life. No <u>substance</u>.

An unconscious spy tied to a chair in my kitchen, his head a little dented: this is what I have. More bodies to deal with. As always, the <u>inconvenience</u> of the earthly remains.

What else do I have?

Revenge. It is nearly nothing. It is worse than nothing. But at least it is mine.

2 6

Shona was worried about her stick.

Walking was hard and awkward and, ultimately, painful without it, but with it, she would stand out. She would be remembered. "She had a stick," she imagined a future witness saying. The plan was for her not to be noticed at all.

The pregnant clouds made up her mind. Shona moved to her father's room. In the corner was his umbrella, plain, dark green, with a smooth wooden handle. She would use that.

She sat on the bed, which gave beneath her with its habitual creak. On the bedside table was a framed photograph. It had been one of his favourites. When he was a journalist, he had placed it on his desk in the *Herald*'s office, where it had absorbed the sunlight and cigarette smoke over the years, tinted and faded. He'd had it framed more than once; its original frame had once been drunkenly broken, but for the last decade of his life, it had sat here in its ivory frame.

The picture had been in her house for so long, sometimes she had not really seen it. The landscape was a long strand of beach, ochre and brown, with a smatter of gleaming rock pools, stretching out into the waves. And there in the foreground, in her final year alive, was Shona's mother, Elizabeth, sitting on the sand with her legs crossed, her plain shift dress rumpled high across her thighs, holding a hand to her face, her head tilted to the sun. Smiling. She had thick dark hair and a white brimmed hat. A silk scarf. Beauty and quiet glamour.

At her feet was a little girl, chubby legs on the sand, tiny toes splayed, wide-eyed with a lopsided grin. In her hand was a half-eaten ice cream cone. This was Shona, aged five, on the beach at Elie. The sun was past its height. The shadow of her father was cast over the sand, over the mother and child. Above them all, a fading watercolour sky.

Shona stared at the picture until it disappeared, and she was on the beach, holding the images of her father, of her mother, on that endless beach, the waves turning over themselves, the sky like the sea, the sea like the sky. Water captured like mercury in the rock pools, sun gleaming on the drapes of bladderwrack, and free white birds wheeled over the harbour, as the fish glittered on the quay like freckles of living silver . . .

. . . and then she was back. Back in her father's cold single bedroom, her father gone and dead, reduced to ash in an urn, and all his love and memories reduced to grey dust, and her alone, alone in the world. Ned, a traitor. Hector killed by a drunk driver, or something much worse, and now she was about to break the law for yet another story. A story. Some words on the page. A byline. Three words that meant more to her than they should, more than most things, and some days, more than anything—*By Shona Sandison.*

It wasn't much. It was barely anything. But it was hers. And she had another story to get. No one else would get it. No one could get it. And this story, whatever Grendel was, whoever Moriah was, had been bought in blood, death and terror. It had to be worth it.

She pulled herself together and stood up. She checked her appearance in the wardrobe mirror. Smart suit. Ironed shirt. Hair brushed and tied back. Some jewellery. Dark lipstick. Some reading glasses she had never used. She looked like someone else. She looked like she imagined a civil servant might look, on a good day. Composed, dedicated and sober.

MacDiarmid, mewling, rubbed against her ankle.

"Here goes nothing," Shona said, crouching to stroke her. "Stand by to bail me out, fatso."

Then Shona left the flat and caught the bus into the centre of the city.

It was 8:30 A.M.

The stone and steel of Alacrity House reared above her, its towering wings casting deep shadows on the road.

Workers were moving steadily into the entrance, a vast space five storeys high, and she followed them, mouth dry, heart pumping like a ripped artery. Between the entrance hall and the main building was a sheer glass wall. At either end were two security doors, set in rotating frames. Three uniformed security guards sat behind a large desk.

She had placed Hector's photocard upside down in the lanyard, to obscure his face. Pretending to check her phone, she watched as an employee went up to the security door on the right, tapped his card, typed in some numbers and pushed the door, which opened. He walked through to the main corridor, straight to a coffee shop around which workers were gathering, yawning and murmuring.

Her plan, such as it was, depended on both the swiftness of time and the sober deliberations of bureaucracy that the repercussions of Hector's sudden death had not yet been fully acted on by his work's security operations. That, as yet, his entrance card had not been cancelled. From what she knew of the slow grind of government, there was a good chance that button had not yet been pressed.

"Four-four-one-nine-seven-one," she muttered to herself. Hector's security number. Her side began to throb. It often did when she was stressed. She felt beads of sweat gathering on the nape of her neck, but she quickly realised no one was looking at her. The guards were chatting amongst themselves, and people were bustling to and fro, in and out of the doors.

She strode across the hall.

"Maria?" a cheery female voice said.

A woman came close. She was beaming.

"Maria," she said, smiling. "How are you this morning?"

Shona startled. "Hi," she said, affecting a Northern English accent, looking at the floor. It was marble, or fake marble. Swirls of grey in a hard sea of pearlescent white.

The woman stared into her face with a sudden look of disappointment. "Oh, so sorry," she said. "I thought you were Maria! My bad. It must be a Monday." She laughed, raised a hand in apology and went through the security door. The spinning glass rippled with light.

Four-four-one-nine-seven-one, Shona repeated in her head, gripping the umbrella.

As she approached the door, an image of Hector, crumpled against a wall, dead in the snow, flashed into her mind.

She tapped the black magnetic strip beside the revolving door. She could hear the security guards talking to each other.

Hibs were robbed . . . bloody offside . . . and Hearts next week . . . not sure I'll be going, mind . . . I don't think I can take much more . . .

The black strip made a beeping noise, and ten numerals on an adjacent touchpad suddenly glowed blue.

. . . I mean, it's been thirty years, man and boy . . .

She typed in the numbers, and no alarms sounded. No music played. The black strip beeped again, and the rotating doors shuddered. She reached forward and stepped through. She was in. Her hunch had been right. Hector was dead, but the card was live.

She was standing in a wide corridor which ran from east to west. The smell of fresh coffee bloomed from the café opposite her. On the wall facing her, in large brass letters, hung the words CAPACITY AND RESILIENCE. Two wide staircases rose to the upper floors. Civil servants drifted up and down, lanyards bumping on their chests; voices echoed in other corridors. Three lifts faced Shona.

The Grendel memo was with Dyce's political advisors. She would have to find their office. She had an idea of how she would do so, but wasn't sure it would work. She needed to find a place to hide, first. She looked at her phone: it was nearly time.

It would be soon.

She pushed through double doors which opened automatically into a stairwell. One staircase descended to a lower ground floor. She decided to head there. She felt a surge of panic, and she had to stop for a moment. She counted to ten. People were passing her on the stairs like the souls ascending and descending Jacob's ladder. But everyone was preoccupied, and no one was paying any attention to her.

Shona carried on down. The basement level was busy. There were offices off one long corridor, and it looked very different from the ground floor. Beneath her feet was blue linoleum. A line of harsh electric lights ran like tracers overhead. Banks of pipes and tubes, hundreds of wires, tightly wrapped, lined the ceiling.

She found a toilet marked as unisex and ducked inside. She locked the door and leaned against it. There was no loo. That was through another door. As she moved through it, a light came on, flickering, and she then closed that door and locked it. She was double-sealed in a simple space: a toilet, a mirror, a sink, a bin. She put down the loo seat and sat and waited.

In this bright, enclosed, hygienic box, with smooth sanitised surfaces, with plumbing and electricity, her mind drifted to Loxley's savage rotting mansion, and his urgent questions: Could she hunt, could she distill rain, could she forage and survive? Here, the electric light buzzed, and the tap would give her water, and someone had put soft towels in a dispenser. Civilisation held. For now.

She took out her phone. It suddenly buzzed, and its movement was so sudden, she dropped it. It clattered on the floor.

"Fuck's sake," she said, and the swearing seemed to calm her. She picked it up. She had received an email. But not in her normal inbox; in her encrypted email account.

FROM MORIAH. 5TH FLOOR. ROOM 5W2. NOW.

And, at that moment, like all the animals screaming in an abattoir, howling alarms went off in every single corridor and every single room of Alacrity House.

27

Adam's plan had worked.

They were clearing out the building. The package, full of batteries, two alarm clocks, a heap of mobile phone charger wires and ball bearings, all held together with masking tape, had reached the post room, and as it had, its alarm had sounded with bleeps and buzzes.

Following protocol, the staff in the post room handled the vibrating, bleating parcel, felt the bulk of its mysterious contents, and had immediately called security. Security had, in turn, ordered everyone out, and the police and the bomb squad were on their way. The parcel had been placed carefully into a secure room, behind blast doors.

Shona could hear multitudes of feet passing outside. Everyone was leaving.

Over the tannoy came a recorded message, a soft female voice purring instructions: people were to leave in an orderly fashion by the nearest exit. To leave all their belongings behind. To not exit by a window.

The lifts would be stopped. She would have to get to the fifth floor on foot. And she would be going up while everyone else was going down. She stood up and looked in the mirror. Her hair was still neatly in place. Her face looked normal, just a little flushed. Neither innocent nor guilty.

Who had access to the fifth floor?

She left the toilet. People in suits thronged the corridors. Workers in hi-vis bibs were waving their arms, directing the human traffic. There was no panic. There was a murmuring rumble of talk, and some anxious laughter.

She joined the crowd walking up to the ground floor. She was beside a young man in a tight suit holding a stack of photocopied papers. He had a distracted air, as if he might be planning a holiday.

Shona touched his hard shoulder. "Hey, my friend's on the fifth floor, in a meeting with . . ."

He smiled at her. "Oh, right? With the SpAds? I guess they'll be coming down the side stairs to the car park."

"She's left her mobile in our office, so I thought—"

"Och, she'll be fine. Can't believe we're doing this again. It'll be like last time, right? Everyone out, fire marshals take a head count and everyone straight back in again."

"I wonder if Maria knows . . ."

"Oh, aye, she'll know. The SpAds'll be cleared out, too," he said, grinning. "But they'll go kicking and screaming."

"Ryan, isn't it?" she said, fishing for his real name.

"Eh, Jordan!" he said, surprised. "I'm in External Affairs. Who's Ryan?"

"I'm sorry—he looks just like you," she said. She wondered if he knew Hector. Jordan shrugged and disappeared into the crowd, which had reached the ground floor.

Everyone was flowing towards the main doors. Some, clear-eyed, saw the mass of bodies near the doors and turned to exit by the side doors, east and west.

The alarms suddenly stopped. Some people whooped, but the recorded voice still insisted that people leave the building immediately.

From behind her, Shona heard raised voices. A stream of police in black flowed into the building and quickly headed for the stairs. She heard the squawk of radios, the rap of boots on marble.

When she reached the side door, there were, as Jordan had said, more stairs climbing up the side of the building.

There were no stewards, no one was minding the flow of exiting staff, and so she quickly moved up them. Someone walked past her.

"Forgot my phone," she muttered, but she did not know if they heard or cared.

She climbed upwards as quickly as she could, leaning heavily on the umbrella. A stitch bit with sudden venom into her side as she emerged on the fourth floor.

She paused for breath on the landing. She held her side. Through a thin window she could see down onto the street, where hundreds of staff were gathered. Some were on their phones, chatting excitedly, some were peeling away to go for coffee. One man had his laptop out and was typing, leaning on a rubbish bin. Two police vans with luminous green and yellow stripes stood in the middle of the road, lights flashing.

Suddenly, a heavy armoured truck drove up and abruptly parked. Men in bulky protective suits rolled out, their heads helmeted in black, peering through thick visors. Two men in black carried a large box hung with caterpillar tracks from the van.

Bomb squad, Shona thought. She darted away from the window and pressed on to the fifth floor. She heard footsteps thumping below. She peeked down the tight coil of the stairs. Police were moving up, their dark heads bobbing.

She moved as quickly as she could through two sets of doors and entered a silent corridor. It was different from the rest of the building: dark with wood panelling and polished doors with brass plates. There were framed paintings and a deep-red carpet underfoot. The smell of fresh flowers. The empty corridor ran the length of the building, disappearing into a distant horizon.

Shona looked to the door on her right. The brass plate read 5W5.

She walked quickly down the corridor, her feet sinking into the plush carpet. The muffled sound of footsteps rapping on the staircase was behind her. Loud voices boomed, and communication devices crackled. Somewhere, suddenly, there was a dull percussive noise. A resonating thump.

The door from the stairs was opening. She could hear its swish and creak. There, to her left, was the room: 5W2. She pulled on the door, but it was fast. Her hands were slick with sweat.

"No," she moaned.

She pushed harder, it opened, and she almost fell into the room, her heart pattering like a trapped bird in her chest.

As she did, a man swept past her and put a hand on her back, then firmly pushed her into the room. Shona stumbled over an office chair, then regained her balance. Her eyes focused. She was in a chaotic office. There were rows of used cups, stacks of folders and books, a series of charts pinned to the walls, and four banks of televisions silently showing images of war: a destroyed city, plumes of billowing smoke and the corpses of children being pulled from rubble.

The man was saying something gruff to someone on the other side of the door. He stood in the doorway, blocking Shona from view. She moved further into the office.

The man closed the door firmly and turned to her. He had a neat silver beard, spectacles and a small blue tattoo on his neck. He looked at Shona fiercely. "Is this your fucking doing?" he said. "This pantomime?"

"I . . ." she mumbled. She did not know what to say. She did not know what to do. She gripped the umbrella handle.

"Relax, Shona. I know who you are," he said.

"Well, that's great, because I don't have a clue who *you* are."

"Did you ring a fire alarm or something? Call the police?"

"No," she said truthfully.

"Come with me," he said. "Quick." He moved past her, deeper into the office. Shona hesitated. "Come on!" he hissed over his shoulder.

She followed him through a heavy wooden door, which took them into a small private office. It was dark, oppressive, with blinds drawn. A laptop was open on a rosewood table. In a stone art deco fireplace, instead of a fire, there was a hydrant. The man shut the door firmly behind them.

"Sit down. We have three minutes max," he said. His eyes were piercing. A raptor's look.

From outside came the wail of a police siren, and then it suddenly stopped.

"Are you Moriah?" she said quietly.

He removed his wire-framed glasses and rubbed his eyes. "This is what you need," he said, in a softer tone. He pulled an unlabelled blue folder from beneath the laptop and passed it across to her. "That's all you need to write the story."

She took it. It had no weight to it.

"It's a two-page summary memo. He's going to make a final decision on it in the next week or two and pass it on to ministers down south. They'll rubber-stamp it. Get it in print before then. It's short and not so sweet. It won't tax your reading skills. But it's enough for you to go on. Enough for you to piece it all together."

"Who are you?"

"I am very worried, and, to be honest, right now? I am alarmed the bomb squad are here. They've got a robot rolling around down there. What the actual fuck?"

Shona tucked the folder in her shoulder bag. A tiny bloom of joy spiked in her mind. She had the story. She had something. A fragment of undisclosed truth. No other journalist did—it was hers.

"Who are you?" she asked again.

"Cowie's the name," he said, closing the laptop. "And, no, you don't need to know why I am doing this."

"It might help?"

He shook his head. "Listen to me," he said. "You need to take that and run with it, okay? I can't do any more than I have already. I gave you the Brexit stuff, and now I've given you this. Hopefully, it'll bring some of the scaffolding down."

"What do you do here?"

He scraped a hand through his thinning hair and put his glasses on. He walked to the window and gazed at the outside world through a bent blind depressed by a single finger.

"I was a true believer, Shona. I was in the vanguard. I'd swallowed it all hook, line and sinker. Then they switched, started building something else. These bastards . . . My party, this country—we're fucked. We've more than lost our way; we've forgotten we had a way."

He took his finger from the blind and turned to Shona. "And now look at me. Pretending to be Saint Paul. Trying to make amends. Seeking a form of repentance. Too late. You'll see when you read that—you'll see."

"But what are you talking about?"

"You'll see. Just bloody read it." His bottom lip was shaking. "Jesus wept."

"Are you all right?"

He laughed a short, harsh laugh. "No, I'm far from all right. You did a good job with that Brexit stuff. But I thought you would," he said. A tear ran down his cheek; he didn't rub it away. "You're good. Ah, shit. I wish I was."

There was a loud rap at the door, and Shona jumped.

"I said five minutes!" Cowie barked.

"Sorry, sir! That's them letting everyone back in now," a stiff voice said through the door.

"Thanks," Cowie replied.

"Controlled explosion, Mr. Cowie. False alarm," the voice said. "You can inform the chief exec everything's fine. We'll let the security room know that—"

"Fine! I already told you he's at his golf club," Cowie yelled, his face becoming blotched with pink. "But I'll let him know. Thank you, officer."

Heavy footsteps plodded away.

Cowie turned to Shona again, his voice dropping in tone and volume. "Okay, you need to leave," he said, "before everyone in the office comes back. They can't see you here. And the comms crew definitely can't see you—one of them will clock you. Won't they? It seems they're all ex-hacks."

She looked at him levelly. "What happened to Hector?"

"Who?"

"My friend, Hector. Hector Stricken," she said, her voice becoming firmer. "He worked in CARS. He was killed in a hit-and-run half a mile from here."

"Look," he said.

"Look what?"

"Even if I knew, I wouldn't tell you. I am done. You won't hear from me again. I can't do this any longer." He stood up, rubbed his eyes. "It's bigger than me. Bigger than bloody Capacity and Resilience Scotland, that's for sure. They're listening to everyone."

"Bugging?"

He shook his head impatiently. "You need to leave."

"How do you know Vali Grammaticus?"

"You need to leave by this other door," he said, pointing to a plain white door in the opposite wall. "Head straight for the lift. Now."

"Why Moriah?" she said lightly as she moved to the door.

"You wouldn't believe me."

"Try me. I'm curious."

"I found God," he said, half-smiling. "Or some kind of god." He stopped as he put a hand to the door. "I met Vali at AA while I was in London. She never approved of my line of work . . . And she was right. But she saw a repentant sinner. She tried to help me." He stopped, his forehead against the door. "They're meeting Saturday," he whispered. "Grendel. At this place in Fife. Stag Hall. If not all of them, then nearly all. Okay?"

Shona put her hand to the door handle. "Why do this? Why not just resign if you hate them so much?"

His face crumpled. "How could I help anyone, then? They think they've found a way, legally, to do what they want to do. But maybe you can help. Now fuck off. Write your story. I'll pick up the pieces. Divert and distract and distort. I'm more useful to the world as a traitor. And when it comes to judgement, maybe the scales can be righted, just a bit."

He became still, like an animal evading a predator in the high grass.

"Hey," she whispered. "How did you know I was here? In this building? To send me the directions?"

"Oh, I knew you'd show up," he said. "Also, I saw you in the lobby, sticking out like a sore thumb."

"These people—I think they tried to kill me," Shona said. "I . . ."

He palmed away another tear. "Shona, this is bigger than me, or us, or Dyce. Do you understand? They have a plan, and they cannot have anyone disrupting it."

"Bigger?"

"Goodbye, Shona. Do your worst."

Shona walked unnoticed through the corridors of Alacrity House.

At the security doors, she pressed in Hector's code with

shaking fingers. It worked again. Soon, she was out of the building, out of the warmth and bustle, and into the cold and the quiet.

Police cars were still parked in the road, but their lights were no longer turning, and the sky was turning dark as clouds moved slowly over the city from the west.

She looked back as she walked away. On the fifth floor, she thought she could see Cowie's face at the window. He stepped back and passed from view.

Soon, as if someone had cast a spell, Shona was climbing on board the number 21 bus home. She tottered to the back. The windows dripped with condensation; everyone was bundled in winter coats, staring at their phones, cocooned in earphones, blocking out reality. The only sound was the rhythmic grind of the engine. It felt warm, human and communal, a world away from hard stone and marble, glass and plastic.

Shona extracted the Grendel memo from its folder and read the first few sentences.

"Holy shit," she said.

She shoved the folder to the bottom of her bag and gripped her father's umbrella with trembling hands.

It started to rain.

2 8

Shona had stopped shaking.

She hastened home, the rain spitting into the dirty snow, the world a sink of spiteful grey and cold. She passed the corner shop, the takeaway chicken place and the nail bar and ducked into the stairwell of her apartment block. As she climbed upwards, she sensed something was awry. A change in the air, a gust of wind. Somewhere, a door was open.

She saw it before she reached her landing—the door of her flat was askew. The lock was smashed, splinters cracked around the keyhole. She slowly moved towards her door, then pushed it open with the tip of the umbrella. It moved with a screech. The hallway was full of clothes, of papers, of upturned books tented on the floor.

"Oh, God," she moaned to herself.

She edged into her bedroom. It had been turned upside down. Her clothes were scattered. The mattress flipped. The bedding bunched and twisted on the floor. In the living room, every drawer and cupboard had been emptied. DVDs and tapes had been flung about, the TV tipped over. Everything had been ransacked.

With a lurch in the pit of her stomach, she stepped into her father's room. It, too, had been turned into a mess of upturned furniture and scattered belongings. His neatly folded clothes had been thrown on the floor. His other belongings were scattered about the room. She stepped into the mess and moved to the dresser, now empty of its drawers.

The urn of ashes was missing, removed from its resting place on the desk.

She slumped down on the bed frame and swore. Something brushed against her ankle: MacDiarmid crawled out from under the bed and made a squeaking noise.

Shona picked her up and checked her over, but she was unharmed. The cat wriggled and fought her embrace, and Shona let her go. MacDiarmid landed on the floor, then elongated herself like a furry spring and poked at something beneath the bed. Shona slid in misery off the bed and onto the floor. The cat's paw was open, and its claws were out. It was tapping at the urn, which had rolled under the bed. Shona pulled it out. It was unbroken, the lid stuck fast.

She breathed out heavily. "Hey, Dad," she said softly.

The cat walked away at pace, its head bobbing, as if pleased with herself.

Shona called a locksmith and an old friend of her father called Tam, whose son, also Tam, knew how to fix things. She did not call the police. Nothing of value had been taken, and her passport was upside down on her bed.

They had been looking for the information on Grendel. But that had been in her bag, with her all day, beside her laptop. She wondered if they would be back. She wondered if they would be back for her. She looked outside. The usual parked cars were there—nothing unusual. She considered calling the police. Maybe they knew she would. But she had the story now—she could not let that be derailed or delayed by their involvement. That moment would come, but not now. Not yet.

It was late by the time the locksmith had been and gone, and the younger Tam had done something loud and expensive to the door so that it closed again. She tidied, as much as she could. But she knew she would have to spend some nights away.

After a call to Ranald, which went unanswered, she called

Viv, who did not hesitate to invite her over. Her friend lived in a redeveloped area of North Leith, not far from the docks, in a new apartment block built on the land where the old fort had once stood. In the winter night they looked like drawings of ideal flats from an architectural competition, rather than real homes. But the door was real when Shona knocked on it, with a rucksack on her back, a satchel over her shoulder and MacDiarmid in a cat carrier, protesting fiercely.

"You didn't say you were bringing that ratbag with you," Viv said, sleek in a silk dressing gown, her long hair up, exhaling vapour that smelled of virtual strawberries.

"I could hardly leave her there," Shona said, bustling into the light, out of the cold. "Someone might steal her."

"That's very unlikely," Viv said. She ushered Shona, after a hug, to her spare room.

Cross-legged on a single bed in the box room, Shona stared at the Grendel memo. A single bed lamp illuminated the tiny temporary workspace. Rain battered the window in waves.

Downstairs, a mildly drunk Viv, recently divorced from a limp rag of a man called Wayne, was burning sausages in a pan.

Earlier, in the kitchen, they had talked warmly. It had been a while since they had seen each other. Viv was from the North of England and spoke plainly. On the wall was a blown-up photograph of her long-dead brother, which Shona had framed for her. Viv was full of sympathy and advice. It was good to see her.

Now, Shona's phone buzzed. It was a text from Adam.

No news? I assume it worked.

Sorry. Busy day. Yes, it worked. I know what OUWO is now.

Her phone buzzed again—Adam was calling. She answered.

"So, Jane Bond," he said, his voice mischievous, "what is it?"

"Where are you? Are you by yourself?"

"I'm at home in my study," he said. "My wee dog is walked and sleeping, and I have an Old-Fashioned on the go. Apart from that, I'm alone."

"How very old-fashioned of you."

"I'm a classic kind of fellow, don't you know. So what is it? OUWO?"

"You sitting down?"

"Always, if I can help it."

"OUWO stands for Obligatory Unpaid Work Order."

"Go on . . ."

Shona settled back on the bed with the memo in her hand. The paper curled, like a creature, like something reptilian and poisonous. It was as thin as skin and had the weight of the ocean.

"They are going to trial a new obligatory, or mandatory, unpaid work system in Scotland," she said. "Like they trial-ran the poll tax in Scotland in the 1980s. If it works, they'll roll it out across the UK."

"Christ," he said.

She took a breath and started reading.

Obligatory unpaid work orders (OUWO) will be designated and applied via this Special Regulation to subjects in five categories: 1) those who have not sought work for six months; 2) those on disability benefit for longer than eighteen months; 3) those who have not been in employment for twelve months; 4) those who have claimed and received asylum; and 5) those found to have entered the UK illegally.

OUWOs, legally underpinned and administered

by Capacity and Resilience (Scotland), will legally require those affected to work in five general areas: agriculture, social care, manufacturing, food production and construction. The General Regional National Distribution Link network (GRNDL) will co-ordinate OUWO workers, state or public designation, private sector stakeholder governance and public sector sponsorship. GRNDL will be established as a separate, non-charitable body with UKG representation on board and operate as a business under—

"Stop," Adam said. "Obligatory—unpaid—work?"

"Yep," Shona said. "The legal advice is all there. It is feasible, as long as we are detached completely from Europe. And the world."

"Make slavery legal again? Slaves? Is this what we're doing here?"

"Unpaid and obligatory. Isn't that slavery?" Shona said. "There's more."

"What? I'm struggling to believe this. Can it be true?"

"Avoidance of an order to work will be a criminal offence. So will leaving the country to avoid one."

"I never would have thought this . . . this would be remotely achievable."

"They think they can. They have found some legislative path. They're using Capacity and Resilience to make it happen. I think that's its sole purpose, why it was set up. And there's a lot of money to be made from a free workforce, isn't there? Billions. That's how empires were built. This paper estimates it will apply to tens of thousands of people in Scotland alone."

There was silence for a while.

"Adam?"

"Yes? Sorry, I think I'm in shock. Maybe I shouldn't be. I need to phone some friends immediately. This can be blocked in the courts. There is clear law on this. Since the Second World War. This must be—"

"Hold your horses," Shona said abruptly.

"What? We have to—"

"You need to wait until I get the story published."

"I'm not sure we have time, Shona. This is more—"

"It will go to print this weekend. Look, it's only a day or two. I don't want my story screwed up. Your wee crusade can wait forty-eight hours."

"But . . ."

Shona flinched as the fire alarm in Viv's kitchen began to scream.

"Sorry!" Viv yelled up the stairs.

"Shona? You all right?" Adam said.

"Yes, I'm fine. My dufus friend can't cook. Thanks for your help today, for all your help."

"It's fine. I've finally found a practical use for my 'Build a Fake Bomb' Scouts badge."

Shona found herself smiling.

"I need to phone my editor. I need to write this. So, please, hold off on your phone calls. Just until it's in the public domain."

"Okay. You have until Monday. Then I'm getting organised," Adam said.

Shona sucked her teeth. Then she asked, "Do you think Hector knew about this?"

She heard the clink of ice in a glass. "No," Adam said quietly. "I've thought about it."

"Do you think he knew too much?" she said.

"I can see what you're getting at. But, no, I don't think so.

I think he would have told me. Or you. He had stumbled into Grendel, but I don't believe he knew what it was."

"But he knew it existed."

"Don't be paranoid, Shona," he said. He sounded reproving; it irritated her. She bit her lip.

"I might have good reason to be."

They were both silent for a while. Shona wondered where Adam lived.

"I spoke to the police today," he said. "I'm handling the legal side of things for Sandy. They're working on the basis that his death was just a terrible accident. They have pulled some footage of the car on St. Andrew Square, going the wrong way on the tram tracks. It didn't have a registration plate. They think it was likely to be some coked-up idiot in an urban tank. There's a lot of them around."

"Really?" she said quietly. She wondered how much to tell him. But the truth of her recent days could wait. Maybe forever.

"And the funeral's next week," he went on. "A church service. It's what his parents want. You'll be there?"

"I'll be there."

"Good. Listen, Shona, you know this is more than just a news story, don't you? That there is much more at stake?"

She ignored the question and the sentiment behind it. "I used to call Hec about stories, you know. Just to talk things over. The whys and the wherefores. He was a good journalist. He knew his way around a story. I could do with his advice now. I need it."

"He was a great friend," Adam said. "And he could keep a secret. He had some of his own. Like the man said, everyone lives a public life, a private life and a secret life. Sometimes, the three have concerns that do not touch each other. I think in Hector's case, his secret life, his secret love, was something he would not even discuss with himself."

Shona flinched. "Thanks, Adam." She jotted down the time, place and date of the funeral and hung up.

She immediately called Ranald.

"Shona!" he shouted immediately. He sounded high.

"Ranald," she said, "I have the scoop on Grendel. You were right: this really is the big one."

"Tell me more."

She outlined what she had been given by Moriah: the OUWO memo and the forthcoming meeting in Fife. She told him about the break-in and reassured him she was fine. He did not seem convinced. She could hear his germinating concern, but she said instantly that she would rather concentrate on the story. He said, with what sounded like relief, "Okay, scoop." He asked how she got the memo, and she told him it was best if he did not know.

"Fine by me. So can you write it all up?" he said. "How can I help?"

"I need to get to a place called Stag Hall, with a photographer, this weekend. It's near Anstruther. Can we do that? Can you arrange a snapper and a ride? We need to get this story out as soon as possible."

"Tell me how you're going to write this," he said, taking a drag of a cigarette. "I have some ideas of how to sell this already."

29

Fisher woke from his dreamless state to spiking pain and an immediate surge of vomit, which splattered in an acidic slurry onto the kitchen floor. He tipped over, into it, helpless. His hands were now bound by plastic cable ties.

Rough hands pulled him upright and wiped his slick, swollen face with a tea towel. Fisher could not see from his right eye, which was swollen and sealed with blood. But through his woozy left eye he saw a washer-dryer, a freezer, a large fan in a square window and, above him, damp clothes hanging innocently from a drying rack. He'd been moved to another room.

Tallis stood over him and wiped his face some more. There was a desultory dab of Fisher's shirt, which was strung with blood, snot and vomit. "I'll get you some clean clothes," Tallis said, his voice rasping, as if he had been shouting or screaming. He took out a short sharp knife and cut the cable ties.

Fisher opened his mouth. He could feel broken teeth and pulpy gums. He spat out a shard of tooth.

Tallis bent down to look him in the eye.

Fisher tried to speak, but only a thin soup of blood and saliva dribbled from his numb red mouth.

"If you survive, you can go," Tallis said. "Back to your incompetent bosses. Let them know I cannot be easily tempted or swayed by such crude invitations—such insultingly clumsy provocations." He sighed and knelt on the floor beside the washing machine. His socks were woollen and had holes in the toes. "I assume, now, that your presence is evidence that there are factions within the state. One side wants something and the other wants to stop them?"

Fisher nodded. His head screamed.

Tallis rubbed his face and seemed momentarily distracted. "It was always the way," he said. "Nothing is straightforward. There have always been factions, cliques, contradictory endeavours. Those at the top think those at the bottom are an undifferentiated mass. That is, of course, not true. Those at the bottom think the top is a monolith. That is also not true."

Fisher opened his mouth to speak but could not. His broken nose was pulsing, and his cheekbone was fractured.

"Spit it out, green man," Tallis said.

"Son," Fisher said eventually. A fresh spray of blood spattered on the stone floor.

"Thank you. Well, I have something serious to ponder," Tallis said, wiping a dot of blood from his finger.

Fisher was sinking back into darkness. His good eye was closing.

"I may be back," Tallis said. "Your car has been driven to an abandoned farm near St. Monans. Your mobile is in the sea. No one knows you have failed. How lucky for you. Not many people can say that."

The old man slowly got to his feet.

Fisher slid into a crimson oblivion.

30

"So the top line is . . ." Ranald was shouting. He was excited, his mind racing. He had called her back, anxious for an update.

Shona was pacing outside Viv's apartment. The sky was clear again, after hours of lashing rain, and the cobbles shone. Almost all the snow had reduced to strips of grey on paths and lines of silver gilt on the slate roofs. It was the afternoon, and she had slept well on good wine and charred food.

"What? You don't know what the top line is?"

"*Government Plan to Force Unpaid Work? Unpaid Work Plan to Be Trialled in Scotland . . .*" he trailed off.

"No, Ranald. It has to be: *Plan to Enforce Slavery in Scotland.*"

"Yes! We can sell that. I've got a call with a national broadsheet in two ticks, but you're right. We could think bigger—we could sell it first to an international paper and let it bounce back here. Let them all scurry to follow up. *New York Times* might take it," he said, and then made a whooshing noise. "*Conspiracy to Introduce Slavery Revealed: Shadowy Quango Plans Obligatory Work Orders . . .*"

He was shouting again. Shona and Ranald exchanged potential headlines for a few minutes at increasing volumes until both ran out of energy.

"What a story," he said, breathless, as if he had just been for a run. "I'm doing a lot of this work off-grid, but you'll have to take care, Shona, I mean it. You've been broken into, and this story—it's the kind of thing people kill for. Seriously."

Shona nodded, wordless, and stared at her feet. She knew that was true. "Are you telling me you're scared?"

Ranald laughed. "Am I fuck! These bastards are done for. We have the proof."

"I agree, though I think we have to be very careful."

"Wow. This does not sound like the Shona Sandison I know and love. You're not even as sweary as you used to be."

Shona suddenly wanted a stiff drink with an alarming urgency. "Whatever. I think I might make myself scarce after we've sold this. Once it's broken, I need a break myself."

Ranald, pounding a pebbly beach, whistled. "Sure. Of course . . . So who knows, right now, that we have it?"

"Moriah," she said.

"Okay, well, they won't leak."

"Loxley."

"Nah, safe as houses. He's gone, anyway—totally disappeared. Can't get hold of him."

"Maybe parts of Grendel."

"Which parts?"

"The parts that killed Proctor? Cotton. Or whatever he was really called."

"And what about your friend Hector?" he said softly.

"He was just a low-level comms officer. Who in power gives a fuck about them?" she said, trying to convince herself.

"Well, okay. What about this lawyer you mentioned? This pal of Hector's."

"Adam? Nah. He's totally on our side," she said.

"Well, I'll have to trust you on that. There's one thing bugging me, though."

"Fire away," she said, moving towards the door. It was cold, and she was tired.

"Why would Proctor—Cotton—want to tell you about Grendel in the first place? He was on the list as a stakeholder, wasn't he? What was there to gain for him? He'd be exposed. His company would be exposed."

Shona looked out over the street, its cobblestones, its ordinariness. She looked up and down the street, which ran from Ferry Road to the sea. But there were no parked cars; there was no one watching her.

"He said something at the awards do," she said. "Something about conflicting interests. And . . . oh, man!"

"What?"

"Well, he sent me to a sex shop. A really freakin' dodgy place in Soho. That's how I got the data. I went there, and he told me to ask for bondage. The woman there seemed to know what was going on. She handed over the device when I said the word."

"Now that is weird."

"Yes—but *bondage*. It's another word for slavery, isn't it? He knew what Grendel was all about. Maybe he just flat-out disagreed with it. Who wouldn't?"

"Yeah, but his company are part of it. Dovetail is on the list. He founded the think tank. He was up to his nuts in it."

"I don't know. Maybe he just changed his mind, realised how wrong it was. He said he wanted to talk to me about monsters, and he paid for it. Ultimately—"

"It doesn't matter," Ranald agreed. "We have the information now. Anyway, if he was talking about conflicting interests, what did he mean? Political interests?"

"I can only assume so," Shona said. "Unless his think tank was actually in *favour* of human trafficking."

"What do you mean?"

"Well, if modern slavery is legalised, there's less money to be made from illegal slavery, right? It's like legalising cocaine—cuts the legs from under the crime gangs."

Ranald laughed. "Jesus, Shona."

Shona could see Viv at her window, holding up a cup of hot tea. The cat appeared, bemused, alongside her.

"Did you hear that?" Ranald suddenly said.

"What?"

"A beeping on the line?"

"No."

"I heard it earlier, too, when I was talking to my wife about the shopping."

"Maybe you're being bugged, Ranald," she said, half-joking. "MI5 want to know what you're having for tea."

"Ach, you can't easily bug a mobile phone—right?" he said.

"I'm sure they can do whatever they want to," she said. Her skin began to crawl. She looked to Viv. Shona had moved quickly, maybe thoughtlessly, to her friend's house. She knew she would have to move again soon. She was putting her friend in danger.

"Anyway. This is a new phone. So I doubt it. The snapper will be with you in the morning," Ranald said. "Don't hang about. It should take just over an hour to get there, so let's say about eight for pickup. We just need to catch them when they arrive. Snaps of guilty faces. Handshaking. Red-faced bastards. Then we can get it all done and dusted for the Sunday."

"The secret cabal plotting to enslave Scotland," she said.

"The conspiracy to . . ." he said.

"Exactly," she said. "Who's the photographer? I can't drive—as you know."

"I'll text you," he said. "In the meantime, spend today writing up what you know and send it over."

"Fine, boss," she said, and closed the call.

She hurried back inside and got to work, the cat curled on her lap, as the computer keys tapped like rain on a windowpane.

31

Many miles from Scotland, in Uzès, Inspector Benedict Reculver was making himself comfortable on a padded seat at La Fontaine café and asking for the menu and a glass of red wine. He was wearing an expensive new cashmere coat, a recent purchase from Paris, and a soft tartan scarf. His hat was pulled hard over his large head, but he still felt the cold. He needed to buy gloves. His boxer's hands were, he noticed, the colour of ham this morning. Even the south of France could be chilly. The market square was quiet, walled by high apartments, with cafés and shops nestling under medieval arches.

He was perturbed. His first evening in his elegant rental apartment on the Avenue Jean-Jaurès had been thoroughly ruined by the report from his colleague Menteith on the discovery of a certain Thomas Tallis. The corpse had now been located and raised from its temporary grave in a field near the M6.

A forensic pathologist was examining the body, but had temporarily confirmed its identity through dental records. The skull had a large puncture, and the body had previously been immersed in water for some time. The postmortem was ongoing.

It had, therefore, been a working evening. The father of the dead man, Sir Raymond T. Tallis, was now fully, and belatedly, retired from his role in the security services and had recently moved to an undisclosed location. Force colleagues had contacted the wife of the younger Tallis, a professional pianist now living in Paris with their son.

Upsetting his evening routine further, Reculver had then

264 • PHILIP MILLER

been called personally by the chief constable, roaring down
the line from what sounded like the deck of a windblown
ferry. The CC had told him that, given the sensitivity and
former status of the elder Tallis, he should be informed of
the discovery of his son by "a high-heid yin." Despite his
current leave of absence, Reculver had been assigned the job.
A private landline number had been passed along, with the
instructions for it to be forgotten afterwards.

Reculver had then settled himself at the marble-topped
table in the dining room, naked apart from a silk robe, and
lit a cigarette before raising the telephone.

It had been a cold, formal conversation. On the other end
of the line, in contrast to Reculver's soft baritone, had been
the dry, clipped voice of Tallis. He had answered the phone
with a voice emerging as if from a depth, faint and distant
at first, and then sharper. He had quietly acknowledged the
information, then asked where the examination was taking
place. Reculver had told him Carlisle, to which Tallis had
made an assenting noise. His final question had been whether
his son had died from the head wound or from the water.
Reculver had told him that it could not, at this stage, be
known. There had been silence on the line for a moment
and then a brief thank-you from Tallis, who ended the call.

A cold case was now warm, and Reculver was thinking of
Shona Sandison.

Shona, he suspected, had colluded with Tallis for a news
story that may have led to his death several years ago. She
had reported on the disappearance of Tallis, but then the
story had dropped out of view. He wondered whether she
still cared. It was, after all, many stories ago. Many tons of
newsprint, many trees of paper and many pages on the web
had been published since then.

The wine arrived at his table, and it was excellent. Reculver sighed. He had wine, he had cash in his wallet—and months of his sabbatical to go—but he was agitated. Worse—he was agitated about being agitated. His new friend Luc would be joining him that evening, and he did not want the evening to be clouded by an unconsummated duty, even if it was not a formal obligation.

"Lord Jesus Christ, Shona Sandison," he said, running a finger around the rim of his glass. The menu arrived, and it looked sumptuous. He wondered if he could order everything on it, in part or in full. He patted his soft belly and sighed; maybe not. He thanked the waiter, who had wheeled over a gas heater, which suddenly came to life with a blue purr of licking flame.

He reached for one of his mobile phones from a silken pocket inside his coat. Shona's number was listed under *Pencil.*

"What is it?" she answered, as usual.

"My dearest Shona, how lovely to hear your dulcet tones so early in the morning."

"Reculver," she said. "It's not that early, and I'm working. What's up? Where are you?"

"I am in France. The exact location is between me and my delicious wine here. This is a quick call, and I won't interrupt your misery a moment longer than is needed."

"Fine—don't," she said. "Fire away. I'm listening."

"You will remember the man Thomas Tallis, the art curator you knew briefly? His body has been found."

The sound of typing continued. There was a soft exhalation of breath.

"Oh, my," she said. "I didn't think he was alive. I guess no one did. Poor guy. I thought he had maybe wandered off drunk or got lost somewhere. Was it in that lake at Denholm House?"

"No. He was in a large refuse bin, buried beside a motorway in the North of England. But his body had been moved. It had been submerged for quite some time. So he may well have been in the Farquharsons' lake. But it's hard to know right now. Given you worked closely with him, I thought you might like to know."

"It wasn't close, and we weren't close," she said. "But thanks. That sounds dodgy as anything. He was a melancholy man. He's had a melancholy end."

Her typing appeared to have ceased.

"Well, that's the end to that sad story," he said. "A sorrowful story."

"Yeah," she said. "Is that all? I'm onto something. Enjoying your holiday?"

"Yes. I shall shortly start to eat and not finish eating until the evening. What are you working on, my dear?"

"I can't tell you, as you well know. And even if I did, you wouldn't believe it."

"Bad people doing bad things for bad reasons?"

"As always, Reculver," she said, "as always. Now give me peace. I'll call you when all this is over—if it is ever over."

"Dearest Shona, please don't," he chuckled. "I intend to enjoy the rest of my time here. À bientôt."

A basket of fresh bread arrived on his table, and Reculver, exhaling with a mild oath, took a sip of his wine. It was rich and deep, a very good wine, and he felt the tension in his shoulders and chest release, a fraction, if only at some subatomic level.

As Reculver drank wine and the marketplace fountain gushed water, far from Uzès, in cold Scotland, an old man with a gun made up his mind. A story that murderous forces did not want the world to see had begun to be written.

My son—

I leave this page open, and this diary in plain view, but after tonight I suspect it will all be destroyed, hidden, lost forever.

What can a warrior say before he enters hell? Even if it is a hell of his own devising? I will say little of what I intend to do; I will leave others to judge.

I had endeavoured to leave a life behind, to leave another time behind, but it seems the past is never past, and is still alive in the present. I cannot erase it.

Thomas, you have now been risen from the earth, ruined, and now you shall be put to rest. It is arranged. Your wife knows, and your son knows. Maybe they shall have a ceremony for you somewhere, perhaps somewhere you loved, and songs can be sung and poems read, and all the empty gestures of our arid lives can be performed. And yet you are still gone and you are still dead and you are gone and I could not save you because I was only interested in myself and my work, the value of which is nothing, and the weight of which is nothing, and is only, in fact, worth what I leave on this world: just a series of marks, a series of stains, a series of burnt traces, a scratch on a window on a skyscraper. I tried to find you. But St. Augustine had it right, did he not? How could I find you if I did not know you?

A last dragon coils in the cave, bent around its treasure. The dragon waits in the hall of stags.

I shall go and face the dragon. I shall see it through. I loved you, my son. It is my sin to have never told you or made it known. I have never paid for it. I shall now pay in full, for both of us.

"Fate has swept us all away / and sent my whole brave highborn clan to their final doom."

Now, I must follow them, and follow you.

3 2

Shona had written up her story and filed it in the early hours, and the first draft had been read by Ranald.

OMFG, he had texted within minutes.

Now, Shona was waiting for the photographer to arrive. Her sleep had been deep, so deep that she did not believe morning when it came, but she felt fresh and awake. The bump on her head was smaller, its scab dry and numb and invisible under her hair. She stood at the bedroom window, eating a cold pancake, looking out onto the wet street, seeing the last of the melting snow hug the walls like a memory.

The previous day, Shona had not only worked long and hard on the story; she had also looked into the details of her destination, Stag Hall. There had long been a Stag Hall near St. James, a fishing village in the East Neuk of Fife. There had been archaeological digs there in the 1980s, which had unearthed ancient remains: votive offerings and scatterings of Roman money. The site had lain in ruin for a time but had been bought in the 1990s by a flush media tycoon who had sought to redevelop it, construct a new road and expand its private grounds. On his death at sea, however, it had been sold to a finance company, and it then passed through several hands. It was now owned and run as a business, its current owners being Kenning Solutions. She checked: Kenning was on the Grendel list.

That morning, Ranald had called her, jubilant. A UK Sunday newspaper was "all in." The front page and four pages inside had been knocked out, ready for her copy. Her story, once checked by the paper's lawyers, would be the splash.

A tight editorial circle had already met with Ranald in an online huddle. The political editor would be calling Shona, as he had a full-page opinion piece to write—they were pulling the stops out. Her stomach had turned with a fierce thrill. The exaltation, the bump of an exclusive about to be broken still brought her a wordless high. On the hard carapace of this world, she would be making a dent.

Ranald had just confirmed that he'd booked the freelancer who would accompany her to Stag Hall and back—an experienced old hand called Tony Spink—and Shona was texting Viv to let her know when a car horn sounded outside. He was early.

Shona immediately began to gather her belongings. She threw a notepad, some pens, her laptop and a tape recorder into her satchel and did a final scan of the room. There, by Viv's bedside lamp, was the urn containing the remains of her father.

St. James was not far from Elie. She could ask the snapper to drop her there on the way back. She could stay somewhere for the night, walk down to the sea and let him go. She placed the urn carefully in her bag. Hugh Sandison would help her file one more story.

The car horn sounded again. She flicked a look outside. A large silver car was waiting. She grabbed her stick and locked the door behind her. Her departure felt final.

The man in the driver's seat waved. He had short hair, a neat moustache and a nose that had been broken some time ago.

She moved to the open passenger window. "Hiya. You Tony Spink?"

"That's me," he said, smiling. A thumbs-up. "You must be Shona Sandison?"

"The one and only," she said. She pulled open the heavy

door, but on the passenger seat was a large holdall. "I'll go in the back," she said. "No bother."

"Cheers," he said. "Hop in."

She entered the car and settled into the back seat, stick between her legs, bag at her feet, and the car drove off. Tony Spink was lean, dressed in dark greens and browns, with heavy boots. He looked relaxed, professional. She was in safe hands. Her mind drifted to the angular face of Terry, a photographer with whom she had worked with only once. They had not kept in touch. *Maybe after this job is over*, she told herself, *I'll give Terry a call. At least a text, to see what she's up to.*

Tony drove steadily along Ferry Road, the long main artery of North Edinburgh that would take them to a new bridge, the Queensferry Crossing. Then they would skirt the ancient capital of Dunfermline, pass Kirkcaldy, Methil and Leven before reaching the East Neuk of Fife, a snout of land edged by fishing villages that jutted like a dog's head into the North Sea.

"So," she said, "St. James—about an hour and a half away?"

"If that," he said, with an unplaceable Scottish accent. "Let's see how we go. The road was busy on the way here— rugby traffic, I think."

She glanced around the back of the car. In her long experience, photographers' cars resembled skips on wheels, with seats covered in camera bags, crushed coffee cups, sandwich wrappers, receipts, spare boots, umbrellas and waterproofs. This car was immaculate, antiseptic.

"Tidy car," she said.

"It's a rental. My car's in the garage," he said. "So Stag Hall? What d'you reckon we'll be facing there?"

"I've no idea who'll be there or what the setup will be like. I couldn't find any images online at all. Probably a private gate? Hopefully not electronic. Let's play it by ear. It's a conference, so we can just wait and front them up as they arrive. If Sir Charles Dyce is there, even better. I'll try to get him on the record. Worst-case scenario is we make enquiries and try to get a comment. That's all we need for the piece."

"Right. So what do you need from me?" Tony asked as the motorway purred beneath them.

"Just some pics as I speak to them. Headshots. Anything you can. They're not going to be posing, trust me."

"No. I very much doubt that. They'll be rushing in."

"You might need to get your old paparazzi pants on."

"It's been a while." He smiled. "Will there be security? That might be a problem."

"Potentially. But if there is, we just report on it. Get some pics from a safe distance?"

"Grand."

"So how long have you known Ranald?"

"Oh, we go way back. When is this for?"

Shona sighed. "Did he not say? God's sake," she tutted. "Tomorrow. For a Sunday."

"Easy to turn it around," he said. "No bother." He momentarily stroked his moustache. "So this is a group of politicians?"

"Nah. More like business people. Money people."

"Up to no good?"

"Definitely up to no good."

He turned the radio on, and a spike of pop music leapt from the speakers. Shona groaned. The music sounded to her like an energy drink. But she said nothing.

Shona could see the tall silver struts of the bridges up ahead, and beyond, the far hills. They soon passed over the bridge, its three towers like giant maypoles with taut steel cables in the place of whipping ribbons. As they crested its span, Shona looked out at the Firth of Forth. It was gunmetal grey, flecked with eyebrows of white wave. Boats bobbed, tiny toys sliding on the tilting planes.

The car hummed, the music shrieked and boomed and Tony drove steadily north. As they reached the other side of the water, Shona's phone buzzed. Tony flicked her a look in the mirror.

It was a message from Ned. Her stomach turned over. She remembered the shadowlands of Fleet Lanshome.

She opened it.

PLEASE READ THIS! DO NOT GET INTO ANY CAR.

Shona looked at Tony. His eyes were on the road. Beside him, on the passenger seat, was the large black holdall. Not a camera bag.

"Problem?" he said suddenly when he realised Shona was staring at him.

"No, no," she said. "Just a message from my old man."

"Your old man?"

"Aye, he's a worrier." She looked out of the window at the undulating Fife fields and took a deep breath.

She looked at Ned's message again. Her heart convulsed. She texted back: *Why?*

"So who have you worked for, Tony?" she said. "*Scotsman, Herald, Record?*"

"All the big ones," he said. They were moving fast now; industrial estates and the edges of towns were skimming past beyond hedgerows and trees. There was still snow on the high ground and lingering in miserable little islands in forecourts and supermarket car parks.

"Ever done stuff for the *Glasgow Mercury*?" she said. "I did a news shift for them last week. Funny lot."

"Oh, yeah." He grinned. "Some real characters there."

Shona's heart rate spiked. The *Glasgow Mercury* had closed in 2017.

This man was not a photographer. Ned had warned her for a reason. The car doors were locked. The man did not have a map on the car screen, or a map on a phone.

"Not long now," she said shakily as they drove past the neat houses of Lower Largo.

He looked at his watch. "Not long."

Her phone buzzed again. Ned.

JUST DO NOT. PLEASE.

They had entered another landscape. They were heading into deeper countryside, the sea distant now, off to their right, along a narrow road flanked by low hills and fields. The sky was darkening.

"I'm just going to call Ranald," she said. "Check in. Let him know we're on the way."

The car slammed to a halt. A sudden flurry of crows rose into the slate sky. Shona lurched forward.

The driver reached back. He grabbed her phone, ripped it from her hand, and in one swift movement, opened his window and threw it out.

The window closed. The engine snapped and roared, and he drove on.

Shona's heart felt as if it was racing as quickly as the car as it sped up, too fast, on the lonely road. They passed a sign: St. James was only a few miles away.

Shona closed her eyes in shock. She felt herself plummeting. Her mind swirled. Images flickered through a rapid carousel of memories. She saw her father's cold face on a hospital pillow. His lips blue, his eyes closed. She saw a bearded man, eyes like dead stars, bleeding with wounds, coming for her with a long nail in his hand. She saw Hector on a surging ferry, laughing at one of her lame jokes, beer foam in his beard and his anorak hood tangled about his neck.

And a memory of her father, again. But this time, he was alive: smiling, healthy, telling her he loved her. Holding her close. His beard prickly on her cheek, earth on his hands from the allotment, stirring his metal mug, being there, alive, in this world. Telling her that she was loved.

They passed a junction for Anstruther. The car barrelled into a land of flat, edgeless fields. They were near St. James and Stag Hall, but they would not arrive there.

The driver's face was impassive, a grey slab.

"You don't have to kill me," she said quietly. He did not move or acknowledge her. "You don't have to kill me. You don't have to do anything for those bastards."

He looked into the driver's mirror and said nothing.

"What's your real name?" she said. "Jack? Tom? Kevin? Gary? Ross? You don't look like a Ross. I bet you're a Craig. You look like a Cr—"

"Shut the fuck up," he said, his voice like a bullet.

The car took a sudden turn, moving off the road and onto a single track, heading towards a thorny spinney.

Beyond the trees, she could see a blasted cavern in a chisel-cut cliff, an acre of rutted mud heaped with scraggy rock and sand. A yellow truck, parked and unmanned. A quarry, a rupture in the earth.

"You need to take a good look at yourself," she said, her voice rising.

"Shut the fuck up," he said again.

"I'm going to call you Craig," she said, leaning forward.

"Shut it."

"All these bastards, Craig," she said, her heart thumping wildly now, "that you work for—you know what they're wanting to do? Bring back slavery? Fuck up the poor and the weak and the homeless? And you're on their side? Really?"

The car shuddered on the rough road. It clattered over a metal bridge and slewed onto a muddy path.

"You're not like them, Craig," she said. "They use people like you. What are you—ex-army? Ex-forces? I bet you are. They've used you up and they'll spit you out."

The car sped on.

"They don't give a toss about you, you know. They'll get rid of you after you've got rid of me. If not now, then later. Use you and then dispose of you, Craig."

"I said shut the fuck up, bitch," the man said, his voice flat now, his eyes black, heavy hands clamped to the wheel.

"They'll look for me and find you, Craig. But people will look for me. That's the difference. There are people who care for me. There are people who love me. Who'll look for you, soldier?"

She looked down at her shaking hands. There, ahead, in the quarry, in the mud and desecrated land, was her end. There would be a wounding blow to the head, and then she'd be dropped down a shaft. Down into a hole in the earth.

Then the world suddenly shook and shuddered. A man in a long coat stepped out suddenly from the roadside. His hood was up. All Shona could see was a dark, featureless face. Tousled hair. He tipped, and fell, and vanished. There was a loud thump. The driver hit the brakes and swore.

The car rocked and came to a sudden halt. The driver seemed momentarily dazed. Shona reached into her bag, grabbed a pen and unlocked her seat belt.

Fuck it, she almost said.

She whipped her hand from the bag and lunged forward. She rammed the pen as hard as she could, aiming for the driver's neck. But he had turned his head. The pen plunged straight into his open eye, hit hard flesh and sank.

The man grunted. Something hot and wet jetted from his eye socket. His moustache was suddenly thick with sticky liquid. He brought a great slow hand around to Shona, but she was already past it, lurching from the back seat, reaching across the holdall and slamming the passenger-door lock. The lock released, and she clambered over, dragging her bag, kicking as she went. The man clawed at his burst eye, scrabbling for the red, red pen embedded there, but Shona could not see him. She was out and down, splayed on the muddy road.

She heard a cry, a kind of shriek, and she did not know if it had come from the halted car or beneath it. Maybe it had come from herself. She was face down in filthy mud and gravel, she panted and moaned, then she found some untapped strength and saw the woods were ahead of her.

She staggered into them, tumbling and scrambling and fighting her way through trees and branches and weeds, her bag catching on scrags and rocks, her stick left behind, her mind white with fear of being hunted, being chased, until she was suddenly at a break in a stone wall, and the main road was right there, and on the road was a man riding a grey horse.

He looked at her, his black velvet hat shifting as he did, and he then slid down from the horse, which whinnied and stamped, its hooves cracking on the tarmac.

The rider walked slowly to her, his head tilted in concern, and Shona collapsed into him, and the stranger, a kind stranger, held her. As he spoke to her, she looked back over his shoulder, into the dark of the tangled woods, but no one was there.

33

Rain was falling, spitting on the high tower of Stag Hall, washing away the last of the fugitive snow and ice.

The old man had emerged from the tree line, then crossed the perimeter fence and moved quickly towards the outbuildings, crouched and loping like a night fiend, the rifle broken over his elbow. He was now in a hiding place behind a generator shed, covered by the fanning branches of a fir tree. In the shadows, he watched as the guests arrived down the long gravel drive. He could hear light music playing inside the house. Grendel was gathering: chief executives, financial directors, advisors, consultants.

Tallis would wait until the pagan night fell under the full weight of darkness. All the old gods were dead. Soon these new gods would be ripped from their false pedestals. In fire and blood, death and damnation, he would finish this. Bodies would lie in piles. Heaven would swallow the smoke.

He reached into his pockets for his cartridges. They slipped and clinked in his wet fingers. He had enough.

• • •

In London, at his kitchen table after supper, a domestic scramble of empty plates and glasses before him, Ned Silver stared at his phone.

There had been no reply from Shona.

His wife was upstairs. They had snapped at each other earlier—something to do with filling the dishwasher—and she was grimly undressing for the night. His daughter was in her room, headphones on, ignoring the adults who had dragged her into the world.

Ned was someone else to them; they saw the presentation and the performance. The rest was theatre. His heart was elsewhere.

He moved quickly, and in silent, utter desperation, reached for his coat. He felt nauseous. Without a word, he left the flat and walked in the dark, step after step, stone after stone, street after street, to the river's edge.

Everything that had been worth something in this fallen world had been destroyed. Yet, even now, there was beauty. The city glimmered. Electric light rippled and broke on the waves. Lanterns swayed and glowed on a row of barges. An old ship's chain, older than the boats, older than Ned and everyone he knew, ran from the wall, through mud, to the deep flowing river.

Ned pressed his head to the stone parapet. Somewhere else in the world, somewhere far from here, was the woman he had betrayed. A woman he had loved, even if she could not return in full the devotion she had once inspired.

Now, somewhere, she was in pain. Or something much worse. Nothing offered consolation. An impenetrable black wall was before him. He had cleaved to power—for money, for status, for reassurance in an unsure world—and thus become part of it. He could no longer be extricated from it. He had been weak and had cast his lot. Now, he was part of the problem, part of the intractable, immeasurable forces carving the world into their image. And now, the only way to end the game was to leave it.

The Thames ran heavy and deep beneath him. The city lights twisted and fractured on the water which flowed to the deep, unremembering sea. He threw his phone in, first.

• • •

The old man's house was in darkness. The pelting rain had roused him from oblivion.

Fisher knew he was beyond saving. He thought now, as his heart slowed, of his earliest day here: the fields of white, the transfigured land. A brief moment of beautiful erasure.

He crawled closer to the window. He could see the winter night, the majesty of the night sky in all its hostile distance, its constellations, its cruel stars. He wanted to be in his tree. He wanted to grip his own branch again, to survey the slow turning beauty of all the galaxies.

His eye closed for the last time.

• • •

Ranald Zawadzki was fidgeting in his swivel chair at home, humming to himself as he edited Shona's copy. It was not quite complete.

The Shetland wind whined outside the thick glass. He had locked all the doors, and the windows were shut tight. By the roaring wood-burning stove, his dogs slept soundly, and in the kitchen his wife was baking and chattering on a video call to her mother. There was warmth and sweetness in the air. He wanted to finish his work and press *send*. The backbench at the newspaper were growing anxious; they'd called three times already.

He checked the time: 7:34 p.m. He had to send the final copy. It was half an hour late. But then again, deadlines, he had long believed, were merely guidelines. Like a tea bag, he often told people, he was best when he was in hot water. But he needed to speak to Shona. Where was she?

He scanned the piece again.

Shona had listed the key issues in bullet points:

REVEALED: SHOCK PLOT TO "LEGALISE SLAVERY"
World Exclusive by Shona Sandison

- *Secret plan to leave European Convention on Human Rights and initiate Obligatory Unpaid Work Orders (OUWO)*

- *Long-term unemployed, disabled, migrants and asylum seekers to be forced to work for nothing*

- *Cabal forms sinister "Grendel" group and agrees plot to back modern-day slavery*

- *Scotland to be guinea pig for trial by Capacity and Resilience (Scotland) agency using post-Brexit laws and loopholes*

- *Mysterious London death of financier Robert Cotton linked to conspiracy*

Shona's copy was tight and pacey. She had government documents as sources. It was tight as a drum. But there were no reaction quotes from the chief executive. None from any members of the Grendel group. Ranald would have to make a call soon, himself.

Meanwhile, other members of his team had been sourcing reaction quotes from the opposition parties, from human rights organisations. All had been firmly told of the embargo that lay like a heavy hand on the story. It would break in the morning.

He had tried to call Shona several times throughout the day, but her phone was switched off. He needed to know what had happened at Stag Hall. He did not know what she had got. Had Dyce spoken to her? Who else had she spoken to? And he wanted some images to accompany the text.

His phone buzzed. It was Tony Spink, the photographer.

"Tony! Thank God!" Ranald shouted. One of the dogs stirred by the fire. "What did you get? And where are the pics? Is Shona with you? Can you put her on? I need a word."

"Aye, well, sorry about today. My fault," Tony said. "I tried to call her, but I got a last-minute call from the *Post* to cover the Celtic game, so once I got the car sorted, I had to do that. Sorry, Ranald. Another time."

Ranald was bewildered. "What are you on about?"

"I left you a voicemail," Tony said hesitantly. "What do you mean?"

"What the hell are you on about?"

"Calm down, man! I left you a message before I went out. I'm only back in now."

"Shit, man, I never listen to those." Ranald screwed up a Post-it note and threw it across the room. "So you weren't at Stag Hall with Shona?"

"No. I just told you. I was at the match."

"Oh, fuck," Ranald said. He felt hot. And then scared.

"The whole day was a fiasco from the off," Tony continued, oblivious. "Woke up to find my bloody tyres slashed. Had to get the motor sorted—"

"Tony, Tony, Tony—"

"I tried to call your girl Sheila, too, but no joy—"

"*Shona.* For fuck's sake, Tony." Ranald was standing up now. "So you just left her hanging? You were her ride, Tony! She can't drive. Doesn't have a car. And I can't get hold of her."

"Well, I'm sorry, but I can't afford to turn down a Celtic game. I mean, your rates, Ranald, they're no—"

"Fuck the fuck off, Tony," Ranald said. He slammed down his phone. Then he picked it up and threw it.

The fire leapt in the grate, and the dogs started barking.

"What's up, love?" Magdalena called from the kitchen.

Ranald walked across the room, picked up the phone and redialled Shona's number. It went straight to voicemail.

He looked out into the night. The wind was shrieking, the sea thundering, and the darkness was gathering like all the shadows of the past congregating as one.

• • •

The baby was finally down. Adam had cooed him to sleep after a messy feed with a bottle of baby formula and settled him in a soft cot on the floor. His absurdly pretty face was soft and pink; a tiny, curled hand rested by his fluttering eye. Adam looked down at Hector, son of Hector. What lay ahead for him? Never knowing his father. A lifetime of silent yearning. A space, echoing. In the next room, exhausted from crying, Sandy was tossing and turning, her future splintered. Her aged parents, shattered, exhausted, murmured in the kitchen.

Adam's daytime had been busy, making confidential calls, thinking of the right legal minds, slowly putting quiet wheels in motion to build an opposition to Grendel, to the planned abominations. People of good intention would gather. He had tried to call Shona, but his calls had gone unanswered.

He looked down at the baby again. He spoke to him. *If not for Hector, your father, who would know? Who would ever know? What a clever daddy.*

Adam, suddenly deep in sorrow, looked from the sleeping baby to the sleepless dark. Outside, all the light was man-made. Dim candles in the ocean of the night. Winter would be long. Spring, as the baby slept, as his mother wept, seemed beyond a dream. Nothing more than a promise.

• • •

Hecate, bundled in a duffel coat and woolly hat, her tiny hands in mittens, clung to her father. Black mountains had passed by, and now the open sea rolled to a bare horizon. Loxley was standing beside the captain's cabin, one hand on a metal rail, the other on his daughter's shoulder. His bare hand was still swollen and sore, as was his face. There were grazes on his knuckles. His right eye was puffy, a deep purple and black, where the assassin had struck him.

Now, the long-haired killer was underground, slowly reducing to bones in the grounds of a rotting mansion, and they were skimming across the sea to their new home.

Below deck, Hecate's brother and sister were minding the stores, her brother's mind full of the warnings his father had given him about the new pistol in his care: keep the safety catch on, never play with it and never, *ever*, point it at your sisters.

As the waves churned, her father looked down at his last mobile phone, and his thumb hovered. But he decided not to send a message. What did it matter now?

The rushing air was icy and slaked with salt. The sky was a deep, swirling mercury. Loxley gripped his daughter as the boat bucked and rolled on its journey.

Europe had been left behind. At the edge of the world, a bare new country of black sand and hard lava rose under a slow sunrise.

34

Shona had been lucky: there was a room at the Harbour Inn. Elie lay outside, its beach slumbering in the night. She could hear the sea caressing the shore.

Clean and comfortable, the room was calm. She had showered and washed her clothes. Her mobile was lost, her laptop closed. She was wrapped in a towel robe, a large whisky warming her.

She looked at her hands—they were livid with cuts and bruises. The man on the horse had wanted to call the police, but she had talked him out of it. A taxi had arrived instead. The kind-eyed horseman had clopped away. Shona had not asked his name.

Downstairs, people were drinking and eating. Families and lovers were huddled around the inn's fire. She reached for the remote control and turned on the television.

She found a news channel. The screen was all flashing light. The beam of a helicopter illuminated a scene: a flower of flames bursting from a broken roof; smoke and fire in a confusion of darkness. A glowing building in a field of night.

What the hell?

The caption blared:

MAJOR INCIDENT IN SCOTLAND . . . ARMED POLICE SURROUND BUILDINGS NEAR ST JAMES IN FIFE . . . PRIME MINISTER CALLS COBRA . . . WITNESSES HEARD GUNSHOTS . . . STAG HALL CONFERENCE CENTRE ABLAZE . . .

286 • PHILIP MILLER

Shona stared, uncomprehending, for a time. A news reporter was gabbling about gunfire, about a figure moving through the flames. She muted the TV.

She opened her laptop and emailed Ranald; she said there would be nothing more from her, but that she was safe. She was all right. She had not even reached Stag Hall. They could speak in the morning.

> . . . WITNESSSES SPEAK OF ARMED MAN IN GROUNDS . . . SEVERAL BODIES SEEN OUTSIDE . . . FIRST MINISTER OF SCOTLAND: "CLEARLY A TERRIBLE TRAGEDY IS UNFOLDING"

The email whooshed away. Almost immediately, Ranald called via the laptop. She rejected the call. She lay back on the bed, wedged a pillow under her sore side and booted up the call system. After making sure the video function was switched off, she called Benedict Reculver.

The call beeped and blooped for a while before it was answered.

"Shona," he answered huskily. "Light of my life. A call at this time of night?"

On the television, a blazing roof sagged and collapsed. Fierce sparks rose. Blue lights swirled.

> GOVERNMENT CONFIRM MASS FATALITIES AT STAG HALL INCIDENT

"Oh, man," she said. "No, no, no."

"Shona?"

"Reculver . . . I'm sorry," she said. "I just needed to talk."

"We are talking."

"I need your advice."

"Well, I'm astonished."

"I'm a bit of a mess," she said shakily. "I've had the worst time of my life."

"Well, that is a high bar," he said warmly. "Let us discuss what I can do for you. But, first, let me extricate myself." There was the sound of whispers, of sheets being moved and of bare feet padding across a wooden floor.

"Why are you calling from a laptop?" he rumbled.

"I've lost my phone. And I'm not sure I ever want to use one again."

"Tell me more," he said. "But, first, just to set the scene, I am naked, sitting in a very fine, if a little threadbare, Louis XIV chair, and the fire is still warm in the grate. I have half a bottle of brandy, a sliver of Pont-l'Évêque, a pliant lover slumbering in silk sheets and the whole night before me. Now, go on, child."

Shona couldn't help but smile. "Too much information, but I am very happy for you," she said. She lay back on the soft bed and took a deep breath. "So . . . I met this man in London, then he was killed. But I ran away. No. Maybe let's start today. Today, a man was going to kill *me*. Then I blinded him. I didn't mean to hit his eye . . . But they have these terrible plans. *Terrible*. And my head still hurts from falling . . . but, Jesus . . . maybe I start . . . I've filed the copy anyway. It's all going to be printed. You can read it. There was this family in an old ruin, too . . ."

"Shona Sandison," Reculver said firmly.

"What? I'm just trying to bloody explain . . ."

"Start at the beginning. There is no need to rush. I'm all yours. But not literally. That would be obscene, and to be quite honest, ridiculous."

Shona laughed, and, in a burst of surprise and panic,

began to cry. Her mind was a raw jumble of new trauma and old wounds. It was too painful to articulate. She wept as she lay there. Tears poured down her face.

He waited for her.

Once her sobbing had eased, she turned off the television, and Reculver and Shona talked long into the night—of all that had happened and all she had not yet told. Eventually, he invited her to France, and she agreed.

She also agreed to call the police. But she would leave that to the morning when her story would be published. After the call ended, with Reculver quite drunk and slurring his words, she washed her face, dried her hair with care and dressed.

Then she walked through the warm and noisy bar, taking a walking stick from a bucket near the door as she went, and stepped out into the night.

The sea breeze tingled her flesh. Her eyes watered. The rain had been and gone, and shredded clouds were drifting across the Wolf Moon.

She held her father, gripped the urn to her chest.

Men had tried to destroy her. But they had failed. *Let them destroy each other,* she thought, as she walked slowly down to the broad sands. *Let all the men destroy the world as it is.* She alone could not stop them. Something else, something new, would grow from their ruin.

As her feet sank into the wet sand, the borrowed stick left little dots beside each footstep.

The men Shona had loved were gone. Her father. Hector. Ned. All gone, in one way or another.

Now, she would leave what remained of her father here, on this beach, where the winter moon hung over the constant sea and the rocks flung black shadows over the beach of Elie. In the distance, the sea swelled, rose and broke. White foam flashed in the darkness like teeth.

What does a single life contain? she thought. Growth and, with it, pain. Perception and, with it, knowledge. And time, inevitably passing, and, with it, change.

The tide continued, the only noise she could hear. It murmured in its rhythmic rise and fall. The tide changed the sea, and the sea changed the beach. *The world,* Shona thought, *is renewed in this way. New in each new moment.*

Maybe, she thought, she could also be renewed. As she walked on the soft sand in the dark, she wondered if all the experiences of life could be held and weighed and measured. If they had to be carried, or if they could simply be discarded. She had long been burdened with sorrow, anger and grief. She had been carrying them for a while. But why? If she could let them fall, find a way to let them go, she could move on through her time on this troubled world less encumbered, less heavy—free.

You do not have to carry them, a voice told her as she paced. *They can be put down. You do not need them.*

After a time, Shona sat down, the stick beside her, the urn on her lap. Her head was aching, her limbs were aching, but she felt somehow lighter, and the rising wind murmured about her. She wondered if, one day, the fragile fingers of hope and love and patience could slowly spin tender new flesh on her fragile and damaged heart.

She put her father beside her and stared at the advancing waves. And she did not move. She waited.

Shona waited until the long night ended, at last, and light began to fall again on this beloved and wounded earth.

ACKNOWLEDGMENTS

I would like to thank my friends and early readers: Simon Stuart, Allan Donald, Rosie Ellison and Callum Smith. I owe so much to my patient and excellent editor Alison Rae, as well as the unwavering support, skill and enthusiasm of Taz Urnov. Thank you, again, to Robbie Guillory for wise counsel. And, finally, to Hope, for everything.